Warlord Metal

Warlord Metal

D. Jordan Redhawk

Fortitude Press, Inc.
Austin • Texas

Published by Fortitude Press, Inc., Austin, Texas. For further information about this or other titles, please contact Fortitude Press, Inc., P.O. Box 41, Melbourne, FL 32902, or visit our website at www.fortitudepress.com.

ISBN: 0-9718150-2-X

First Edition, April 2002
Printed in the United States of America

Edited by Cindy Cresap
Book and cover design by Ryan Daly
Web design by Mya Smith

Author's Note

So here it is - the final printed version of a trial by fire. I won't get into all the little details of its inspiration or culmination. Suffice it to say, it's been a long, rough road and I hope you enjoy the ride.

A couple of things need to be mentioned before you continue to the first page, however. There are some pretty tough scenes ahead and the entire novel is an emotional roller coaster. Unsafe sex, cheating, drug addiction, alcoholism, child abuse, overt sadistic sexual practices — this isn't a tale for the romantic. It takes a long, hard look at the life of a very messed up young woman and her road to ... redemption? Love? Self?

Regarding the overt sexual practices, the situation described in this book isn't the norm for those individuals who enjoy that kind of play. It's not a dissertation on how wrong the S&M lifestyle is. I know several people who are very much into the "darker side," and I've found them to be wonderful, loving and kind. The situation described in this book is a plot device, nothing more.

Don't think of it as standard or use it as an excuse to turn up your nose. That's not what it's for.

Enough said. Relax, get a drink and settle down. Welcome to the world of rock and roll.

D. Jordan Redhawk
June 29, 2001

Dedication

To my wife, **Anna Trinity Redhawk**. All that I do, I give to you.

In loving memory of our daughter, **Robin Dee Burbach** (June 10, 1979 - September 19, 1994,) may you find the peace you couldn't find in this life.

To the youth shelter **Outside In** of Portland, Oregon. They work diligently to give food, shelter and health care to kids on the streets, an almost insurmountable task.

Many, many people need thanking but foremost is **Susan Mullarky** who validated the mental health of a troubled teen. Her psychoanalysis of each chapter as it was posted online was quite helpful.

Thanks to the people at **Fortitude Press**. They're some of the hardest working people in the industry.

To **Coffee People** on the corner of Park and Salmon, Portland, Oregon. Most of this story was written there during the winter of '98. Velvet Hammers kept me warm as I scribbled away.

Thanks to **all of you** who read the original story online and wrote me. It was a hard thing to read, let alone write, and your responses made slogging through the whole thing worth it. I am pleased to announce that a portion of the profits of this book will go to charity.

Part I: Fifteen

I hear the flames of Armageddon
roaring hungrily in the dark.

TORRIN C. SMITH, "ARMAGEDDON"

Sonny's Journal – September 23, 1998

I had a dream about Mom and Dad last night. Tom and I were kids again, and we were out on a Sunday drive. The road was getting smaller and smaller and smaller until there wasn't enough room for the car. Rather than turn back, we got out of the car and continued. Pretty soon, we're walking on this teeny little ledge over a huge cliff. And then Mom lost her balance and fell. Dad tried to catch her and went, too. I was so scared. I couldn't look down, just leaned back against the cliff behind me. I don't know what Tom was doing. Then I saw Mom and Dad again. They were floating in front of me – they had wings like those stupid cartoons, you know? They smiled at me and waved and then kept on going up.

I woke up pretty scared. I almost got up to go check on them before I remembered that they were dead. So I watched some of the Christmas videos instead. Fell asleep on the couch. Weird, huh?

Day after tomorrow is the audition. Tom said I could come and watch. It's too bad about Chris having to leave the band. He's a pretty good guitarist. Oh, well. Maybe they'll find an even better one!

"So, can I take that Women's Lit class this winter?" Sonny asked.

Tom Middlestead steered the beat-up Honda through traffic. "I dunno, Sonny," he began only to be cut off.

"I can pay for it! That's no problem," the brunette insisted. "I've still got the money from babysitting last year. Since I'm a resident, the cost per credit is cheaper."

The man grimaced and shook his head. "Money's not the issue, Sis. The trust fund will cover your education."

Sonny's brow furrowed. "Then what is it?"

Her brother shrugged. "I just think you're pushing yourself too hard, that's all. You're barely a sophomore in high school, and you're already taking college level classes." He stopped at an intersection and looked at her with eyes that were a darker shade of blue. "I don't want to see you burn out."

Deflated, the teenager looked out the windshield. "Green

light," she muttered.

Reluctantly, Middlestead returned his attention to the road and continued driving. He hated telling his little sister no on anything, much less a decent education. *But damn it! When she isn't writing, she's reading. When she isn't reading, she's writing. That can't be a good thing.* Watching her out of the corner of his eye, he could almost see the gears working. *You might as well just say yes,* he told himself. *She'll talk you into it anyway.*

Sighing, he drove on in silence.

As they pulled into the parking lot, the girl spoke up. "Hey! I didn't know Rita was gonna be here!"

Middlestead parked the car and glanced at the woman in question. "She must have come with Chris. I wanted him to look over the new meat." He shut off the ignition and unfastened his seat belt.

"Cool!" Sonny exclaimed, unbuckling her restraint. "We can sit at the bar and heckle you guys." She tossed an impish grin at her brother and bailed before he could grab her.

"Now wait a minute!" the man growled, making the expected lunge. He grinned at his sister's giggle and waggled a warning finger at her. She slammed the door with a grin, jogging off to meet the pregnant woman at the bar entrance.

Middlestead locked her door and exited the Honda, securing it behind him. *Not that anybody'd want this hunk of junk ...*

A young blond man, tall and thin with closely cropped hair, had joined Sonny and another girl. The pregnant redheaded girl he was wrapped around was laughing as she ran her fingers through the stubble.

"What the hell happened to your *hair,* man?" Middlestead demanded, reaching out to grasp his friend's hand. He nodded a greeting at Rita.

Grinning ruefully, the man scratched the buzz cut. "Well, figured they were gonna cut it all off in a couple of weeks anyway." He shrugged. "Might as well get used to the look."

"Yeah, well, we need our toilet cleaned at home. Can I use you?" the dark man quipped.

Sonny swatted her brother on the arm. "Stop that!" Turning to the couple, she continued with a smile, "Never mind Mr. I-Have-No-Fashion-Sense. You look great, Chris."

"Thanks, Sonny."

"And *I* like it," Rita said, a warning eyebrow lifted at Middlestead.

Raising his hands in surrender, Middlestead took a step backward. "Far be it for me to insult a mother-to-be!"

Sonny brushed by her brother, rolling her eyes and pushing him with her shoulder as she passed. She opened the door to the bar, emitting a yelp as she entered. Pale blue eyes glared over her shoulder as she rubbed her rear. "Payback's a bitch, Tom," she warned. "You have to sleep sometime."

Middlestead looked innocently back until she entered the establishment. When her back was turned, he grinned and held the door for the couple.

The bar was closed and quiet. A handful of people lounged near a small stage in the back. Most of the chairs were up on the tables, and an older man was sweeping the floor. He looked up when he heard the door, his face lighting. The broom was promptly set aside as he stepped forward, arms wide. "Sonny! How are you?"

"I'm great, Lamont. How's business?" She gave the bar owner a hug.

"Not bad, not bad," he responded. "These guys bring in some steady customers on the weekends. Even if they don't know how to play," he concluded with a conspiratorial whisper and wink.

"I heard that, old man," Middlestead growled as he came in. "Are Lando and Max here yet?"

"Yeah." A work-worn thumb shot backwards. "They're dumping the recycling from last night. You got some people waiting for you by the stage, too." He dismissed the men, attention falling on the pregnant woman. "Rita! You're looking wonderful!" Taking the two females in tow, Lamont escorted them toward the bar. "Can I get you beautiful ladies something to drink?"

Middlestead stared after the trio. With a sarcastic grin he said, "I'm fine, Lamont, how are you? Certainly, Lamont, I'd *love* something to drink."

Chris chuckled and slapped him on the back. "Let's go check out my replacement."

Seven people were lounging around the stage area, all carrying guitars. Most wore the standard heavy metal leather jackets, though one was in a button-up shirt and tie. It was a toss-up on which was weirder, the preppy or the punk rocker kid in the corner with red and green hair. Climbing onto the stage, Chris began checking over his instrument, and Middlestead rummaged around behind the drum set, pulling out a clipboard.

He handed it to the first person within reach. "Hi, I'm Tom Middlestead, drummer for Warlord. I want you to go ahead and write your names down and a number where we can reach you. If you have any references, jot them down, too. This is Chris," he said, indicating the guitarist. "He's the one we're needing a replacement for. Max Hampton and Lando Atkins, our bassist and other guitarist, will be here shortly and we can get underway."

Eventually, the other band mates arrived. The second guitarist was tall and well muscled with a strong jaw, long brown hair and a wicked grin. Hampton was short and stocky, his chin sporting a stylish goatee. Both settled down into chairs at the base of the stage with the drummer. Chris stayed onstage under the lights.

One by one, applicants were called to the stage. They were required to first play samples of different musical styles to show aptitude with metal, funk and blues. Next was a jam session with the guitarist on the stage. Chris would play a few bars from one of Warlord's songs, and the applicants were required to pick it up and go with the flow. Finally, if any had songs of their own, they were encouraged to play a couple of tunes.

It was a fairly quick weeding process. One man bowed out even before his name was called, citing a doctor's appointment and maybe next time? The preppie went soon after. The third on the list appeared competent and had definite potential. He was asked to stick around for a while longer. Numbers four and five were good, but not good enough. One didn't compose, and the other wasn't able to pick up the band's tunes. Next came the punk rocker.

Sonny sat at the bar, keeping time on the brass footrest beneath her shoe. She'd decided that it was going to be either the third or the last one who got the job. She could tell by the tilt of her brother's head that number three interested him. Chris appeared to be impressed with him, too. The brunette was merely giving the last applicant the benefit of the doubt, since she hadn't heard him yet.

As the kid with red and green hair climbed under the spotlights, she frowned. She'd dismissed the man because of his style of dress. Warlord wasn't a punk band; its roots were in hard rock and blues. Squinting, she scanned the slight form. Dark eyebrows rose in amazement, and she interrupted her friend's chatter. "That's a *girl*!"

"What?" Rita turned and looked up on the stage. "No way!"

"Yes, it is! The hips are too wide. See?" The teenager watched, fascinated.

Middlestead glanced back to the clipboard. "Torrin Smith?" he repeated. Looking back at the young woman onstage, he raised an eyebrow.

"Yeah, that's me," a decidedly feminine voice burred. Her hair was shoulder length with the colored striping messily parted in the middle and long bangs hanging into gray eyes. Near the scalp, a reddish-gold hue was testament to the dye job growing out. The apparition was clothed in baggy black trousers and a black, sleeveless Bloodworks T-shirt, the combat boots dyed a rich green. She hefted a beat-up guitar, plugging it into the system.

The drummer glanced at his companions. Atkins shrugged and leered at him. The bassist scratched at his goatee. Chris, on stage with the newcomer, wasn't paying any attention, keeping an eye on the woman. Middlestead cleared his throat and looked at her. "You *are* eighteen, aren't you?" he asked, concerned. The band didn't need an underage member getting into trouble at the bars they played.

Bristling, the woman glared daggers at him. "Yeah. Need to see my ID?"

He pursed his lips, deciding to let it drop. *Hell, it's not like it's gonna be an issue.* "No, no problem. Let's go ahead and get started." He gestured for the punker to begin. *She can probably only play punk and ska anyway.*

Sonny's eyes were riveted to the stage. It wasn't often she saw a woman play in the rock genre, though it was getting more popular in recent years. Usually, the women played pop, not metal.

After a moment of almost spiritual silence, the woman broke into the strains of a popular heavy metal ballad from the sixties. A few moments then the music melted into an old blues number. From there, it floated on to another sixties metal tune, followed by progressive rock and thrash. She spent three to five minutes on each song, moving effortlessly between them. Her eyes closed under the spotlight, she seemed far away.

When the music faded, Sonny found herself standing behind her brother. "Wow," she said. "She's better than the third guy."

Chris appeared impressed. He nodded grudgingly at the woman and began clapping. She inhaled deeply, opening her eyes as the people in the room also began to applaud.

Middlestead shook himself from his reverie. He heard his sister and agreed wholeheartedly, but they weren't finished yet. "Well, okay, Torrin. That's great," he finally said, as the applause died down. "Are you familiar with any of our songs?"

The Christmas-colored hair shook as she busied herself with her guitar. "Nope. Just what I've heard today."

The drummer nodded at Chris.

"You know the drill then," the blond onstage began. "I play a set, you join in." At her nod, he began.

As strains of music filled the air, Sonny felt something against the back of her legs. She looked up to see the owner, Lamont Atkins, smiling at her and holding a chair for her to sit. Grinning her thanks, she settled down to watch the proceedings. Rita joined her, but the high school student was oblivious, all her attention with the stranger onstage.

Chris began a familiar song, one of the more difficult sets the band played. He hadn't used it with the other applicants, and Sonny felt a stab of anger that he might be setting this woman up for failure. Her anger dissipated, however, as Torrin took up the gauntlet and ran with it, her own instrument providing harmony and counterpoint to his. There was very little flubbing as she played, interweaving the tune with her own and improvising along the way.

In front of Sonny, the other band members sat in silence. Finally, Hampton left off scratching at his beard to lean over and mutter, "Her," to the drummer.

Middlestead glanced over in surprise. "Let's just wait until we see if she can compose, alright?" he asked in a whisper.

The bassist shrugged nonchalantly and resumed fingering his beard.

With the second part of the audition complete, Atkins finally spoke up. "Not fucking bad, girlfriend," he commended.

Gray eyes narrowed in suspicion, searching for sarcasm.

Finding none, the determined set of her jaw relaxed a bit. A slight blush pinked her skin. "Thanks," she mumbled.

"You write your own tunes?" Chris asked.

"Yeah, I've written a couple."

Middlestead piped up, "Okay. Let's hear one."

The woman hesitated. "I'm not a good singer," she warned.

"Doesn't matter," the drummer said. "We'd only use you as back up vocals anyway. Lando and Max do most of the leads."

The punk nodded, brushing bangs from her eyes. With a few adjustments to the equipment, she began. It was a simple melody: deep, slow and smooth. Unable to help himself, Chris listened for a few moments and began an accompaniment.

She's right, Sonny thought. *She's not a good singer. At least not metal.* The woman was able to hold a tune, but her voice was unusually high-pitched for the music she was playing. The lyrics were what caught her attention.

I'm slithering through the
Darkness of my soul,
Crawling through the ooze
Of my perverted sensibilities.
I yearn for deviation,
Want to feel just this once.
Not this smothering warmth that
Surrounds me, sickens me, seduces me in...

The woman's guitar and voice became rougher, gaining an edge that grated on the nerves.

This darkness.
Is this all there is?
Darkness.

Torrin broke into a guitar solo, her instrument mourning the loss of light and love, Chris following her lead as he played backup. Sonny noticed movement on one side and glanced over to see the second guitarist's fingers twitching as he followed along. She grinned as the woman on stage began to sing again, her voice smooth once more but no less intense.

Watch the metamorphosis,
Distorting who I am
Weakening, hardening.
How long can I remain here,
Living with this suffocation?
I reach out blindly
And pull you in.

Then it was over and quiet filled the room. Silence reigned as everyone stared at the young woman dumbly. She began disconnecting her guitar from the equipment.

It's like she's a completely different person when she plays, Sonny observed. *Everything just stays bottled up inside and then she explodes.* Finally, the dark girl stood and began clapping, breaking everyone's reverie. "That was great! Do you have any more?"

Torrin peered through the spotlights to locate the unfamiliar voice. "Yeah, I've got some."

"She's the one," Atkins murmured to the drummer. The bassist on the other side of Middlestead nodded in agreement. On stage, Chris was looking pointedly at the rest of his band mates.

Middlestead glanced at his companions. "Alright then, Torrin. Can you stay a bit longer?"

The punk nodded curtly, red and green hair flopping, before stepping down from the stage and resuming her seat.

For courtesy's sake, the final applicant was given a shot, though he was not nearly as talented. After several minutes of discussion, all the applicants were herded to the door. Torrin Smith, newest member of Warlord, remained seated in the corner, a black stocking cap on her head and the leather jacket she had donned gleaming in the light from the stage.

Sonny's Journal — September 25, 1998

Well, Warlord has a new guitarist. And it's a girl! *Actually, she's a 'woman.' She doesn't look much older than me, though!*

I got to see Rita today. She's only four months along, but she's definitely showing! Chris should be out of basic training and AIT before the baby's born. He ships out in two weeks. All the paperwork is signed. Rita's hoping he gets a stateside post first. Otherwise, she won't be able to fly to wherever he gets posted until after the baby's born, and she really wants him to be there for it.

I think I might have talked Tom into letting me take that college course this winter. I guess he's worried that I'll go bananas and freak out or something from all the 'stress' of schoolwork. All I had to do was remind him of his obsession when he was fifteen. Rock and roll ... And now *look at him! His own band, regular gigs, making enough money to live on even if they haven't hit the big time yet.*

I just want to be a journalist. Nothing exciting. Well, maybe exciting. It'd be pretty cool to be a consultant somewhere like Europe or something – that would be so fantastic. Or maybe working a crime beat in L.A. or New York. Have my name right up there with Dan Rather and Walter Cronkite. Yeah, I could dig that!

Oh! And Shelly called tonight. The party she was talking about's gonna be next Friday night. She said that Jay would definitely *be there, even if he is a jerk. It's gonna be a little scary, though. There's supposed to be a lot of seniors going, too. Hope us poor lower classmen don't get razzed too much while we're there.*

"... The look on his face! It was priceless!" the blonde girl gushed, snickering. "I *told* you he was a jerk."

"Yeah, yeah. I know." Sonny dug her hands deeper into her jacket against the chill air and continued walking.

It was after eleven p.m. in downtown Portland. The two girls were walking along the SW 5th Street transit mall, heading for the bus that would take them home. Despite the crisp weather, there were quite a few denizens in the downtown area, people awaiting buses, hanging out or just moving from one place to another.

The party was a major mistake. Quite a bit of alcohol was flowing, as was often the case with a heavy senior population in attendance. Sonny was no stranger to beer and limited herself to one. She was, of course, a minor. And a girl. And a lower classman at that. Her level headedness turned out to be a major asset. She had been lusting after a boy ever since she'd seen him on the track team, and he was there. Jay showed quite a bit interest in her even though he was popular and could have any girl he wanted. Sonny could hardly believe her luck.

Eventually, the couple had made it out to the back deck. They were as alone as they were going to get, what with a hundred teenagers crammed into a three-bedroom townhouse and adjacent yards. He made a pass; Sonny caught it. Tentative kisses soon escalated toward a more heated exchange. It was oh-so-romantic.

Until the young man attached one hand rather blatantly to her breast, his lips on her throat and moving slowly southward. She demurred. There were people present, and she wasn't about to do this without getting to know him better. He pushed the issue, insistent, not letting up.

Unfortunately, Sonny got scared. Following close on the adrenaline rush of fear was anger. There was a scuffle, an angry shout followed by a grunt of pain as a knee came in contact with a sensitive area. Sonny stomped away, blushing in anger and embarrassment as she pushed past her wide-eyed girlfriend. Jay yelled after her, and his friends hooted at his inability to score.

Jay the Jerk, Sonny thought over and over like a mantra. She was still pretty pissed off, especially when Shelly had told her that she'd seen a couple of his friends exchanging money. She was more furious with herself than anybody, however. *God, you're an idiot. You* knew *he was an asshole.* She shook her head.

"Did you see Stephanie ...?" asked the blonde.

"What ...? No, I didn't. What about her?"

Her friend leaned forward, dark eyes sparkling with glee. "She's wearing Todd Victorian's letter jacket! Isn't that *cool*?"

Sonny nodded, disinterested and continued walking. Her friend chattered along beside her, oblivious to the silence.

The bus stop appeared devoid of other people, though there was an odd looking heap on one bench. *Somebody's clothes?* Sonny thought as they neared. She distracted herself by wondering who would leave a jacket and extra clothing at a bus stop on a night as cold as this. The girls were steps away before she realized that it was a person.

Pale blue eyes narrowed, she watched the body as they entered the bus shelter. Her friend's sudden silence and sharp intake of breath indicated her awareness of the apparent bum.

"Sonny!" she whispered, brown eyes wide. "There's a corpse over there!"

The teenager shook her head. "No. They're still breathing, see?"

Hips and shoulders on the bench, the transient's legs stuck outward as if the person had fallen sideways after sitting down. Dark trousers, ragged at the hem, combat boots and a black shirt of some sort were evident. The leather jacket was pulled halfway up to cover the head and shoulders more fully. As the girls watched, the legs stretched out a bit, green boots digging their toes into the cement in a reflex action.

Sonny frowned. Something was familiar here. *Where have I seen boots like those?* Shelly was still chattering, albeit in a whisper now, verbally curious about who the bum was, where he came from, how he got here and in this state.

The blonde interrupted her whispered monologue with a gasp and a squeak as the other teenager moved forward to squat by the unconscious figure. "What are you *doing*?!"

"I think I know her," Sonny explained with a glance over her shoulder.

"Her? *That's* a her?"

Nodding absently, she returned her attention to the person on the bench. "Torrin? Is that you?"

Another stretch of the legs was the only response.

Sonny tentatively reached out and grasped the shoulder, giving it a shake. "Torrin? Wake up." Encouraged by a feminine-sounding rumble, she pulled the jacket back a bit and saw red and green hair.

Her girlfriend stood out of arm's reach, nervously moving from one foot to the other. She watched the brunette try to wake the transient, eventually getting her to sit up on the bench. "Eeeww, Sonny," she exclaimed with a grimace. "She's puked all over herself!"

Sonny kept Torrin propped up with one hand on her shoulder. An odor of stale cigarettes, alcohol and vomit floated off her. There was vomit on the T-shirt — *Same one she wore at the audition last week* crossed her mind — and on the leather jacket. Most of it had run down the side of the bench and into a puddle, though. *Whatever she's on, she's gone.* The woman before her slumped in a boneless heap, mumbling under her breath and unable to open her eyes.

Sighing in consternation, Sonny glanced around, her eyes lighting on the monitor of schedules. *Bus'll be here any minute.* She wasn't going to be able to muscle Torrin onto the bus and then off and the four blocks from the stop to her house. The band was playing tonight and wouldn't be done for hours yet, so she couldn't call for a ride. *Now what?*

Her eyes lit on the pay phone on the wall of the shelter. After some quick calculations, she looked at her anxious friend. "How much money have you got?"

"What?" The blonde frowned at her. "What are you gonna do?

Give it to *her*? She'll just find another bottle." Dark eyes looked the seated form over with distaste. "Providing she wakes up before the liquor store closes."

Sonny rolled her eyes and shook her head. "No, silly! If we can afford a taxi between the two of us, I want to get one."

The girl stared at her for a full thirty seconds before shaking her head suspiciously. "What are you up to, Sonny?" she growled.

"Look, we can't leave her here. And I can't get her home by myself on the bus. With a taxi we can get her right to my driveway." She heaved a sigh. "You know I'm good for it, Shelly. I'll pay you back on Monday when I can get to the bank. I've got plenty in my savings, just not with me here."

"You're taking her to your *house*?" the blonde demanded disbelievingly.

Sonny felt a niggling doubt in the back of her mind. Crushing it, she raised her chin and glared at her friend. "Yeah, what's wrong with that?"

"What's wrong with that? You don't know this chick from Adam, girlfriend, *that's* what's wrong with that! For all you know, she'll go apeshit and stab you and Tom tonight in your sleep!"

The dark head shook. "No, she won't. She's the new guitarist for Tom's band. She's just tied one on and needs a place to sleep it off." Sonny looked at the semi-conscious form she was holding up. "She won't hurt me," she said softly, knowing it was so.

Shelly argued with her friend until the bus came and went without them. She sighed explosively, digging into her pockets. "Oh, alright! Here's five bucks!" Slapping it into Sonny's outstretched hand, she snorted. "I'm *not* sitting next to her! If she pukes again, it's gonna be in *your* lap!"

"Thanks, Shelly," the taller teenager said with a relieved grin.

Pain. The world was pain. A dull ache from head to toe. All nerve endings extremely sensitive, screaming at the slightest provocation. Faint rose colors testified to the daylight behind closed eyes. Even hair follicles complained at the abuse of living. The mouth was filled with sand, the throat with glass.

Torrin groaned and rolled over, the sheets scraping angrily across her skin. *Sheets ...? Did Lucifer change my sheets?* She lay there, eyes closed against the shards of sunlight that would stab her when she opened them, frowning at the feel of cool linens against her, the softness of a pillow and mattress beneath. The faint smell of coffee wafted past, interfering with the stronger and more familiar aroma of vomit.

What the hell happened last night? Scenes slowly flashed across her inner vision – partying inside the Orestes, then outside the Orestes, scoring some dope and feeling no pain. There was a woman – brunette, long, shapely legs in a tight leather miniskirt. *Made me wet just watching her walk. Wasn't there an angry boyfriend, too?* Bloodshot gray eyes opened a crack, and she peered at what was within her vision.

A standard white wall met her gaze, before it a white vanity with gold trim and a large mirror. On either side of the mirror were posters – one of the band KISS and the other of Aerosmith. Reflected within, a white bookcase on the opposite wall was full of books and stuffed animals. The top of the vanity was cluttered with bottles of perfume and other personal items.

Torrin's frown deepened. This was definitely not her room, and as the cobwebs inched away, she remembered that she was no longer staying with her father. *Did I score?* She hadn't imagined that the brunette's bedroom would appear quite like this. Her nose itched and she sneezed explosively, groaning loudly at the pain in her head. "Ow, shit!" she muttered, her voice cracking as she curled into a ball and put her arms over her throbbing head.

She lay in a fetal position for a long time, drowsing despite her discomfort. With her sensitive hearing, she could detect someone rummaging around in a kitchen somewhere, the sound of a toilet flushing, a shower running, the soft ticking of a nearby clock that was driving her to distraction. Eventually, the shower shut off, and soon there were voices, male and female. *The angry boyfriend ...?*

Deciding it was better for her to be up, if not necessarily about, when he found she was there, Torrin forced herself to move from the bed. Narrowly missing the white trashcan of vomit, she caught a whiff of the scent and her stomach roiled dangerously. She stood still, eyes closed and breathing deeply through her nose. Gaining control, she looked blearily around.

All she wore were her black silk boxers. *Did I score?* She shook her head, her aches and pains making it too difficult to tell. Finding a neatly folded pile of black clothing on the opposite corner of the bed, she picked up the shirt and shook it out, nose twitching at the smell of laundry detergent. *Whoa! I'm surprised that shirt made it through a washer without falling apart.* She nudged through the pile and found her trousers as well as a fresh pair of socks and flannel boxers.

"Shit, I'm gonna have to pass out here more often," she observed with a raised eyebrow. Gray eyes glanced around the obviously feminine room. "Wherever the hell 'here' is." Torrin quickly donned the clean clothing. Finding her boots by the dresser, she located her belt, cigarettes and lighter, wallet and change on the corner. Out of habit, she checked the wallet and found a five-dollar bill still there. "Huh ... Well, she ain't a thief," she muttered to herself.

A low voice from the door responded. "No, I'm not."

Torrin stiffened, eyes narrowed. Glancing slowly over her shoulder, she saw an ebony-haired girl. *Aw, shit! Don't tell me I fucked a* kid *last night!* She growled at herself, not showing any of her inner turmoil. *Yeah, but ain't that just like you?* Lucifer's voice asked, a familiar stabbing comment. To the girl she said, "Thanks for washing my clothes." She returned to picking her items up from the dresser and putting them in her pockets.

The adolescent shrugged. "No problem." Setting a coffee cup on the dresser, Sonny walked past and flounced down on the bed, leaning against the headboard. "How are you feeling?"

Torrin shrugged. "As well as I can, under the circumstances." She bent down and picked up her boots. Glancing around the room, she walked over and settled down on the small bench for the vanity, not willing to get onto the bed. *Well, put another notch on your belt, Horny Torry,* the voice said. *Looks like you got a virgin this time.* The guitarist growled, viciously stomping her foot into a boot. Bending over to tie it, she ignored the strain on her rebellious stomach.

Sonny watched curiously. "Your jacket's downstairs," she commented.

"Thanks."

"You don't remember me, do you?"

Bloodshot gray eyes peered up at her. "What do you mean?" *Jesus! Was I that fucked up last night? That even* she'd *notice?!*

"Well, we never were formally introduced, and I think the

lights at the bar last weekend kinda messed up your vision." She smiled at the obvious look of confusion. "I'm Sonny Middlestead. My brother's the drummer for Warlord ...?" As comprehension filtered through the woman's face, Sonny shrugged and continued, "You're lucky I found you at the bus stop. It was near freezing last night."

Torrin frowned, trying to make the connections in her foggy mind. She sat upright and winced, grabbing at her head.

"You want some aspirin or something?" Sonny asked, sitting up in concern.

"Yeah, if you've got it," the punk muttered darkly.

"'Kay. Be right back." She padded out of the room.

Watching her go, lips pursed, the woman considered. *Bus stop?* She didn't remember any bus stop. *Wait a minute.* A feeling of exhaustion, a hard bench and lights overhead. *That musta been it. So maybe I didn't score with her. Good thing if her brother's Tom Middlestead!*

Sonny came back into the room, handing her visitor a glass of water and some pills. Thanking her woodenly, Torrin gulped them down, not bothering with water.

"Ick!" the brunette exclaimed. "How can you *do* that? Makes me want to drink this water in sympathy!"

Torrin blinked and shrugged. "I dunno. Water's not always handy." Another thought slowly made its way through her mind. "What about your parents? Do they know I'm here?"

Something flickered across Sonny's face before she answered. "No, I live with Tom. Our parents died in an accident a couple of years ago."

"Oh." Uncomfortable, the woman finished tying her boots and gingerly rose. "Guess I should be going now. My jacket's downstairs, you said ...?"

Sonny quickly stepped forward to intercept. "Uh, well, yeah, it is. Um ..." She blushed. "Can I ask you something though?"

Seeing the faint flush and the icy color of those eyes up close, Torrin paused. *Damn, I wish she were older.* "Yeah ...?"

"Well, I don't wanna pry or anything." Sonny's redness deepened as she prepared to do just that. "Are you homeless or anything?" At the blank look she received, she blurted, "I only ask because you're wearing the same clothes you wore last week. And, if you don't have any place to stay, we've got a spare room, right over the garage. I've already talked to Tom about it." She paused, swallowing nervously. "I mean that's if you *want*. It's no big deal or anything. It's a mess over there, and it'll need some cleaning up ..."

Torrin's eyes narrowed and flashed suspiciously. She stepped forward, invading the teenager's space, only stopping when she was a fraction of an inch from her. Gray eyes bored into frightened blue. "Why are you doing this?" she demanded harshly.

Sonny had difficulty thinking. Those eyes demanded an answer, the woman's breath soft against her face. She swallowed convulsively as she rallied her thoughts. "I just ... I just thought you needed a place to crash," she whispered. "And you're a Warlord now. Warlords stick together." Her heart pounding in her chest, she wondered what this strange woman was going to do.

Warlords stick together. A puzzled look crossed Torrin's face. She stepped back a bit, giving the girl breathing room, amused at the obvious slump of relief. *You're a Warlord now. Wouldn't do for the new guitarist to be rolled in an alleyway or something. Kinda defeats the purpose, doncha think?* She studied the pale eyes across from her in speculation. Coming to a decision, she said with a faint smirk, "So, what's this room over the garage look like ...?"

Sonny's Journal – October 3, 1998

Whew! Well, I'm still alive, though I had my doubts earlier this afternoon! That Torrin is a real pistol, as my dad would say. Between Tom and I, we were able to talk her into staying in the room over the garage. She insisted on paying rent and all, but it's not much – she'll be making plenty to cover it with the band. And it'll be nice to have another female here to back me up against my bratty brother!

Seriously, though, I was a little scared there for a minute. Thought for sure she was gonna take me out! And all I did was offer her a place to stay! Wow! Must be what happens when you spend too much time on the streets. I don't think she's had much in the way of family life. I kind of wonder how long she's been out there. (Excuse me while I shudder.)

Well, last night's party was an absolute bust. I've forever ruined any chances of dating for the rest of my life. I kneed Jay in the nuts because he was getting too pushy. He might be a jerk, but he's still a cute one. Don't think I'll have to worry about the senior prom in a couple of years. Hell, I don't think I need to worry about the Christmas Dance this *year! *sigh* My social life is ruined!*

Why are boys such jackasses?

Warlord Metal

Lucifer lives in my
soul.
TORRIN C. SMITH, "CHILDHOOD"

Part II: Sweet Sixteen

My humanity shattered,
Determination battered.
I'm exhausted and obsolete.
TORRIN C. SMITH, "ADDING UP"

Sonny poured coffee. The house was quiet, as neither band member in residence had awakened yet. *This is my favorite time of day,* the teenager decided with a grin. *All quiet, nobody around ... Nice.* It was seventy-five degrees and predicted to hit ninety-eight. In anticipation, Sonny wore a pair of tan shorts and a white tank.

With a fresh pot of coffee brewing, she picked up her cup and padded barefoot into the dining room, resuming her seat at the table. The daily paper spread out around her, she picked up the local section and began reading. Sonny didn't hear anything until the soft tapping at the patio door gained her attention. Looking up, she saw a stranger smiling uncertainly at her.

"Um ... hi. Torrin said there's a shower somewhere ...?" Barefoot and clutching a handbag, the woman was the epitome of a groupie – tight shorts, a stretchy midriff shirt that left nothing to the imagination, long platinum hair and heavy club makeup. Her hair was mussed, her makeup smeared, and there was a very evident hickey on her neck.

Another one? That makes twelve now! With practiced nonchalance, Sonny answered, "Yeah, come on in." When the woman entered, she said, "Right through there, around the corner. It's the door under the stairs." She surreptitiously watched the woman pass, comparing her to the others she'd seen over the last ten months.

It didn't appear that the guitarist had any sort of color preference in hair or eyes. All her women were drop dead gorgeous, promiscuous and tall. *That would put Torrin at about level with ...* Sonny blushed at the imagined sight. "Well, I guess she's a breast woman, then," she muttered, rattling her paper and trying to get back to the article she had been reading. Despite herself, her mind wandered to when she had figured out why all these women were hanging out in Torrin's room.

The band had played a Halloween gig at the Starlight the previous evening. It was a private party with three other bands, so despite being underage, Sonny was able to attend. The other bands were pretty good, but in her opinion, Warlord was better. *It's not like I'm biased or anything!* She giggled to herself over breakfast the following morning.

As usual, the early hours were hers alone. Eventually, her brother woke and descended to the dining room for something to eat. It was late October, cold and wet. The house was warm, and the siblings sat at the table chatting over coffee and cereal. A strange woman wearing little more than a leather jacket appeared at the patio door and interrupted their discussion. Middlestead let her in and directed her to the bathroom.

Sonny frowned in thought. "Ya know, that's the second time Torrin's had somebody sleep over. You think that girl's homeless, too?"

Fighting the urge to inhale his coffee, Middlestead sputtered. "Um ... no, I don't think she's homeless," he said, eyeing his sister carefully.

"Really? Then why'd she stay the night?" Sonny asked, confused. "I thought slumber parties were for kids, and I can't see Torrin at one of those."

Her brother's face turned a deep pink, and his eyes darted around as he tried to think of a tactful way to explain the situation. Unable to come up with one, he finally said, "Well, look, you know about the birds and the bees, right?"

Puzzled, Sonny rolled her eyes. "Yeah, I know. I had that talk with Mom and then there was Sex Ed at school." She chuckled at her brother's obvious discomfort. "But what's that got to do with anything?"

The man looked at her, *willing* her to make the connections.

Pursing her lips, she fumbled with the puzzle pieces. *Torrin, strange women, sleepovers, birds and bees ...* Pale eyes widened as she stared at her brother. "No way!" she whispered.

"*Yes*, way," her brother responded with an evil grin – smug, embarrassed and relieved all at the same time.

"You mean she ..." Sonny waved vaguely in the direction of the garage.

"... Gets laid more often than the rest of the band put

together?" he finished. "Yeah." A thought crossed his mind. "Well, maybe not. Lando scores about as often as she does. Last week she and Lando had a little ... thing going."

Astonished, Sonny sat back in her chair with such force it rocked. "Torrin and *Lando*?" she demanded incredulously.

Middlestead waved his cereal spoon at her, shaking his head. "No, no, no. That's *not* what I meant. They spent the night at his apartment with a couple of chicks and … uh … shared."

Unwanted thoughts and images filled Sonny's vision. Blushing furiously, she glanced up at her brother's chuckle. "Not a word!" she hissed, pointing a finger at him.

Dark blue eyes widened in feigned innocence. He pointed at himself with a questioning eyebrow before dragging his fingers across his lips.

Sonny shook her head and ruffled the newspaper again. Most women didn't get beyond the initial visit, though some made it to two. Two had slept with the guitarist three times – not necessarily in a row. No one made it past the third visit. *Three strikes, yer out.*

Occasionally at rehearsals a familiar face would show up on the arm of Lando Atkins, the band's other insatiable guitarist. Sonny had been intrigued by the absolute disinterest Torrin displayed toward her prior bedmates. *It's like they don't even exist!* The looks of longing shot at the rainbow-haired rocker left Sonny intrigued. *Exactly how good is she?*

Shrugging off her thoughts, she returned to the article as the downstairs shower came on. Minutes ticked past. Eventually the shower shut off, and Sonny moved onto another article. The sound of a boot scraping concrete drew the brunette's attention outside.

Torrin sat on a bench, smoke from her cigarette sending wispy tendrils skywards. She was dressed in baggy black shorts and a gray sports bra, elbows propped on her knees and staring into the distance. On her left upper arm was a tattoo – gleaming silver claws slashing a black hole with red eyes glaring from within. It seemed as if a beast was trying to rip its way out of her soul. Her boots were still green, but her hair was the shade of a bird's egg, off white and speckled with baby blue.

Sonny had not seen the woman with a head of normal hair. She knew Torrin was a redhead because of the rich hue that grew out close to the scalp and had complimented her on the color, dropped hints and finally almost begged Torrin to let it grow out. Heedless, every six weeks or so the smaller woman would get a trim and dye her head some god-awful color. Last time it had been brilliant red, like a clown.

These occasional moments were what the adolescent enjoyed, when she was able to see Torrin without the tough posturing, when the woman was off in her own little world and unguarded. *She's got a nice profile*, Sonny mused. *But always so serious. Almost sad.* She watched the woman toss her cigarette into a nearby coffee can and rise in a fluid, full body stretch, admiring the way the rocker was built. Sonny's eyes looked into gray fire. *Uh oh! Busted!* Her heart pounded, and she felt the heat rise to her cheeks.

Torrin's mask dropped firmly into place. A slight, knowing smile crossed her face, and she raised an eyebrow in mute challenge. As expected, Sonny blushed darker and ducked behind her newspaper. Chuckling, the woman combed fingers through her hair. After a final glance around, allowing the girl inside to compose herself, the guitarist entered the house. "Morning."

"Morning," Sonny mumbled from behind the Metro section, embarrassed at having been caught staring.

A grin flickered across Torrin's face as she went into the kitchen and prepared a cup of coffee. Rummaging around in the refrigerator, she found a bowl of grapes, putting them on the breakfast bar. Coffee in hand, she leaned against the end of the bar and drank, watching the rattling newspaper. "Anything interesting going on in the world?" she drawled.

Pale blue eyes peered over the top of the paper, looking for any sarcasm. Finding none, Sonny said, "Some. There was another shooting in North Portland last night. The police say it's gang related."

Egg-colored hair nodded solemnly. A grape was eaten.

Encouraged by the lack of a snide response, the teenager continued. "And they're trying to find funding to re-open Outside In. That's a youth services organization that concentrates on runaways," she explained.

Gray eyes flashed before becoming mild once more. "I know what it is" was the bored response.

"Oh." Sonny shrugged. "Well, that's about it today," she

finished lamely.

Torrin sighed, an insistent stab of conscience attacking her. *Shit, give the kid a break, Torry! She's never been anything but kind to you, and you know you don't deserve it!* She popped another grape into her mouth. "Save the crossword, okay? Maybe we can work on it after rehearsal today."

The resulting smile lit up the room. "Sure! That'd be cool!" She dropped the section she'd been reading and began searching through the rest of the paper.

For about the billionth time, Torrin mourned the circumstances of the girl's birth. *The kid's a hot little number, I'll give her that!* she thought idly as she watched. *Long legs, beautiful curves ... And those eyes! Mmm, mmm, mmm, Torry. Way too bad she's straight!* She sipped her coffee and another little voice – Lucifer's – spoke up. *Maybe she just hasn't met the right woman, huh?* Unbidden images and feelings coursed through her – the sight of that long, dark hair fanning across her abdomen, those lips caressing her, the low voice thick with need as it begged for release, the feel of warm nipples stiffening into peaks under her palms.

This last sensation caused Torrin's hands to actually twitch, spilling hot coffee on her belly and shorts. "Fuck!" she shouted, setting the cup on the counter with an angry thump.

Sonny was up and across the room in an instant, grabbing up a hand towel. She blotted the shorter woman's stomach, studying the red mark closely. "I don't think it was hot enough to burn too much," she said as she worked.

"I'm fine," Torrin said gruffly, batting her hands away. "Just pissed." *That and wanting to fuck your brains out!* When Sonny didn't back off, the guitarist snatched the towel from her and stepped back. "I'm *fine,*" she insisted, swallowing the desire to take her right there against the kitchen counter.

A confused look of hurt crossed Sonny's face, Torrin's anger and intense eyes causing a flutter in her belly, and she dropped her eyes. "*Sorry,*" she mumbled, getting ticked off as well. "Just trying to help."

Score another one for Horny Torry! The woman stood still with eyes closed as she fought to gain some sense of control over her temper and libido. She sighed deeply, shaking her head. "I know. Didn't mean to snap," she offered after a deep, steadying breath. "I was more startled than anything." *Ah, the lie is so easy, isn't it?*

Sonny peered at her, slightly mollified. "You sure you're okay?" she pressed.

With a lopsided grin, Torrin winked at her. "I'm okay, *mother.*"

Blushing, Sonny ducked her head with a smile. "I'll remember that next time you don't eat your vegetables," she joked, moving back to the dining room table.

"Hey, what's going on?" a new voice asked.

The two turned to see the blonde woman standing in the kitchen, her hair in a messy bun and her makeup freshly applied.

Torrin had planned to call a cab and send her away. Another flash of dark hair, whispering moans and silky wetness brought a halt to that. Turning on all her charm, she smiled warmly and stepped forward into the other woman's arms. "Just tried to scald my stomach, that's all," she said.

"Oh, no!" the woman said, concerned. Long fingernails painted fire engine red gently traced the discolored area on Torrin's abdomen. "Are you okay?"

Leaning closer, the guitarist whispered in her ear, "Feeling horrible. Wanna kiss it and make it better?" She nuzzled the ear, raking her teeth across the lobe. A sharp intake of breath gave her the answer.

Not pleased with the interruption, Sonny scowled at the intimate flirting going on and resumed her seat. *Get a grip, girl!* she scolded herself. She smiled weakly at the guitarist as the couple went out the patio door.

Sitting in the quiet house, her mind and emotions a turmoil, the youth stared off into space, unable to make heads or tails of what she was experiencing. She shook her head and forcibly brought herself back to the present. "Crossword," she muttered. "Where's the crossword?"

Sonny's Journal — August 16, 1999

Torrin almost blew up this morning. Boy, she has a hair-trigger temper! She spilled some coffee on herself and really got pissed. I think she was madder at herself for being so klutzy, though. I know I would have been.

It's still morning. Tom's up and roaming around. Number Twelve and Torrin are probably going at it as I write. Jeez! And I thought Lando was a hound dog when it came to women! I do have to admit, though, I am curious – I mean, I learned all the normal stuff from Sex Ed at school. But how to women do it? Is it like ... mutual masturbation?

I also wonder what Torrin's not getting. Why else would she go through girls like underwear? I think she needs to fall in love with somebody. It's not the sex she's looking for; it's the intimacy. I hope she finds it someday. She's a nice person underneath all that 'I'm a Bitch' 'tude she's got going.

Rehearsal's this afternoon, and then we're going out to dinner for my birthday. I'm sixteen now. Doesn't feel much different from yesterday, really. Oh, well. I think I'll go get my license and drive Tom's insurance rate up! Ha ha ha!

As the Honda pulled up to the dilapidated warehouse, it sputtered and died.

"Damn it!" Middlestead growled, hurriedly stomping on the clutch to keep the vehicle's forward momentum. Fortunately, he had been pulling into a parking spot and simply coasted into position.

"What happened?" his sister asked, studying the dials on the dashboard. *Maybe I* don't *want to learn how to drive this thing.*

"Dunno," the man grumbled. He fumbled with the brake, securely parking the car. A few tries on the ignition only resulted in a growling noise. "Shit."

Sonny sighed. "Well, it's no big deal. We can always bus it for tonight," she suggested.

Middlestead sat back in a huff, glaring at the steering wheel. "Yeah, I guess." Not willing to let it go, he leaned forward and grabbed the key. "You go on inside. Tell 'em I'll be there in a sec."

"Okay," the teenager agreed, releasing her seatbelt. She climbed out of the Honda and slammed the door behind her, hearing the motor struggle laboriously. As she opened the warehouse door, the car roared to life. She turned to grin over her shoulder, taking a step into the warehouse without looking. Her brother grinned and winked at her, and she waved before turning back.

"Surprise!"

Startled, Sonny jumped, eyes wide as she stared at the sight before her. A group of smiling people surrounded a table – one side held a sheet cake ablaze with candles, the other a small mound of gifts. Balloons were tied at the four corners, and a banner hanging overhead proclaimed, 'Happy birthday, Sonny!' She blinked back tears as Lando and Torrin began the birthday song, metal style, and her brother came up behind her.

"Happy birthday, Sis," he said with a grin, draping an arm over her shoulder.

Playfully, the brunette slapped his shoulder. "You set this up!" He nodded smugly and she hugged him, whispering, "Thanks."

Middlestead returned the hug. "It's not much," he said. "But Mom and Dad would've killed me if I didn't do something special for your Sweet Sixteenth."

Sonny squeezed him tightly. "You did great."

The song came to a crashing finish as the two guitarists tried to outdo each other on the grand finale. Their singing done, the rest of the partygoers stared blankly at them, waiting for the accompaniment to stop. When there was no end in sight, Hampton strode up and disconnected the power supply.

Silence rang through the warehouse.

"Thank you," a small redhead with a fussy baby said.

"Rita!" Sonny exclaimed. She released her brother and ran over to the woman, a tall blond man in an Army dress uniform nearby.

Torrin sat on the edge of the rehearsal stage, playing her guitar. *It hasn't been too bad, as birthday parties go.* Most of the faces were familiar – band members, the usual hangers-on that attended regular rehearsals, a couple of groupies that Atkins had invited and the married couple with the kid. It had been interesting to see Chris Fleming again. He and the band had jammed a bit – at least until his daughter started to cry, and he called a halt to appease her tender ears.

Focusing on the music, Torrin found chords that played with the tune. She loved music. When she played her guitar, she was millions of miles away. No one could touch her here. *Not even Lucifer.*

Satisfied with the song, Torrin played it through two more times, committing it to memory. Self taught, she found that music could protect her from the worst of the pain. When things were really bad, she would go into her head and hear music. The tunes were intriguing new guitar riffs that dominated her thoughts. They wouldn't go away until Torrin wrote them down.

Song firmly embedded in her mind, she lit up a cigarette. Smoking, she held the guitar in a loose grip, her unconditional lover.

Wish I could at least have a beer, she sighed. The thought of birthday cake and beer together caused her to frown. *Okay ... Maybe some blow then ...* Another sigh and she took a swig of soda, scratching an itch under the wool knit cap and watching the Birthday Girl play with Rita's baby.

Atkins wandered over and plopped down beside her. "Man, I'm stuffed!" He groaned.

Torrin smirked. "Where're your girlfriends?"

The tall man lay back on his elbows. He waved vaguely. "Powdering their noses or something."

"Probably 'or something'."

"Ya know, you're right," he said, sitting up. He brushed long brown hair back from his face and looked at the woman intently. "What is it that women *do* in a bathroom that takes hours anyway?" he asked.

With a skeptical stare, Torrin said, "And you think *I'd* know?"

Atkins rolled hazel eyes. "That's not what I meant, Torrin." He shook his head. "Yer a girl! You can get into the women's bathroom. I can't." His eyes became distant and the corners of his mouth quirked up a bit. "Well, maybe 'can't' isn't the right word."

"And what *is* the right word?" the woman asked with a coolly raised eyebrow.

He chuckled but ignored the question. "Okay. You go in there all the time when the babes are 'powdering their noses.' What the hell does it mean though?"

Torrin leaned back and considered. "Well," she drawled, "it's been my experience that they're doing one of three things. First ..." and she held up a finger, "... doing upkeep on their makeup, just like they said. Second..." Another finger, "they're discussing how best to jump your bones." She stifled a chuckle at Atkins' smug look. "Or third, they're trying to figure out a way to ditch you without being too bitchy about it."

The guitarist's face screwed up in concentration as he seriously thought about her last statement. He apparently came to some sort of loggerheads with himself from the look on his face.

Unable to help herself, Torrin chuckled, leaning over to smack him on the arm. "It's probably the first one, dude," she said. "Makeup's a pain in the ass to keep up."

"Oh." He tried to hide his relief. "Hey, if you're not doing anything tonight ..." he offered, wiggling his eyebrows with a leer. "We had a blast last month with the twins. I know Rachel has been eyeballing you this afternoon."

In her mind's eye, Torrin saw the two women who accompanied Atkins to the party. A blonde and a brunette, both leggy and busty and just what the doctor ordered. A memory of smiling pale eyes blotted out the vision. She heaved a sigh, reluctantly shaking her head. "Naw. Not tonight. I promised the Birthday Girl a little one on one with a crossword puzzle."

Atkins nodded and both of them turned their attentions to the teenager who was now talking with Lamont Atkins, the bar owner and Lando's father.

"Damn! You know, I've known that brat since she was ten?" he asked idly. "She's growing up mighty fine."

"I'll say," Torrin agreed. She felt eyes on her and leveled a cool gaze in return.

"You *know* she's off limits," the man said, his voice a trifle flat.

"Well, duh, Lando," she responded. "Jailbait's nice to look at and nice to dream about, but shit! Like I wanna get tossed outta my room, my band *and* have statutory rape charges pending!" She shook her head, rolling her eyes. "Get a fucking clue ..."

Lando chuckled sheepishly. "Well, you know. We're all kinda protective of her."

You should be, the woman thought. *You've got a wolf in the fold, and you don't even know it.* She could hear the voice inside, howling and laughing, but merely nodded in agreement. Looking back over the party, she said, "Looks like your girls are back."

Atkins saw them as well and rose. As he stepped away, he looked over his shoulder with a lopsided grin. "Crossword ain't gonna take all night, ya know. I'll leave the door unlocked."

Torrin watched him saunter into the women's waiting arms.

Sonny stifled a yawn and leaned against the doorframe, arms laden with presents. Nearby, her brother was collecting the remains of the cake in preparation of leaving.

The party had gone on for some time, a never-ending flow of

well-wishers floating through. As some left, others arrived to take their place. There were twenty or so people in the warehouse at any given time. *Tom did a fantastic job. Mom and Dad would have been proud of him.* A pang ran through her, wishing her father had been there. *He always said he wanted to have my first Sweet Sixteen dance.*

Distracting herself, she thought of the baby. *Tanya was adorable with that red fuzz on her head and her daddy's nose. Now that was a total surprise. I'm amazed Chris was able to get leave so soon after enlisting.* And all the different visitors – there'd even been a distant cousin showing up who she hadn't seen in years. Sonny sighed contentedly. *This has got to be the best birthday ever.* Her thoughts were interrupted by a voice.

"You're looking kinda tired," Torrin commented with a raised eyebrow.

"Yeah. I am a bit. Can't wait to get home. It's amazing how tired a person gets when having so much fun," the dark girl said with a smile.

Gray eyes sparkled. "So, you're not up to a crossword puzzle then?" The guitarist scratched at the wool cap she was wearing, expecting the girl to disagree with her.

Sonny froze before remembering what their plans had been. "Oh, no!" she exclaimed. "I totally forgot! I'm so sorry!"

Torrin felt a flash of anger. *What the fuck? Why'd I even bother?* She looked away and shrugged with nonchalance, gaining some composure. "No biggie," she drawled. "It's been a long day. Maybe tomorrow." *It's just a fucking crossword puzzle, Torry. Don't get all bent outta shape.*

The adolescent flinched away from those fiery gray eyes before they looked away. As the woman turned to leave, Sonny juggled her armload and reached out to stop her. Muscles stiffened, but when the guitarist turned back, she was grinning. *Is she mad or not?* "If you want, we can still do it," she offered tentatively.

Turning further around, Torrin pulled her shoulder away from the girl's touch. *What's your problem, Torry? She's just a kid! Jesus!* "Naw, it's cool. Lando invited me over to his place tonight anyway. If I'm lucky, I can catch a ride before they leave."

"Oh." Sonny looked down and chewed her lower lip, feeling sad and angry for some strange reason. She peered from beneath her dark bangs. "Tomorrow then?"

Torrin's forced grin became a more natural smile. "Yeah. Tomorrow's good." There was an awkward silence. "Well, happy birthday, squirt," the woman finally said.

"Thanks." Another pause. "I'll see you tomorrow then ..." she said, a statement that wasn't quite a question.

The guitarist moved away. "Yeah. I'll be there," she tossed over her shoulder. She got a couple more steps away before slapping her forehead. "I forgot to give you your present!" she said with a grin, returning to the girl.

"Oh, no, Torrin. You don't need to –" Sonny broke off, speechless.

Torrin whipped off the knit hat she had been wearing. Long, red-gold hair tumbled down to her shoulders. She smiled at the girl's response.

"Wow!" Sonny finally breathed.

Gray eyes sparked and caught fire. "This *is* what you wanted, isn't it?"

Mouth suddenly dry, Sonny tripped over her tongue. "Um ... yeah. Yeah! It's just. ... Wow."

"Glad you like it." Torrin ran hands through her hair.

"Oh, yeah. I do! Are you ...? Are you going to keep it this way now?" She held her breath in anticipation.

Torrin studied her. "Maybe," she finally conceded. A glance over her shoulder and she said, "There's Lando! Gotta go!"

Sonny watched the lights play in the red tresses. "Wow," she whispered.

Sonny's Journal – September 10, 1999

Well, the first week of school is officially over. Thank God! I can't believe I actually missed this torture during the summer!! Might as well just tattoo a huge "S" on my forehead – "SUCKER!"

Tonight's the first school dance of the year. Pete Bailey asked me to go with him. He plays center on the basketball team. I'm looking forward to it.

Torrin just walked by (I'm in the living room.) She's still got her natural hair. Well, not exactly natural – she had to dye it back to what it should be. I'm surprised she hasn't had it redone in purple or lime green or something ...

"Oh, yeah, baby. That's it," Torrin crooned, eyes closed. She sat in a chair in her room, a naked woman kneeling between her legs, nibbling at her breasts. "Harder," she said, feeling teeth brush the jewelry on one nipple.

The dark-haired beauty complied, biting down. Torrin growled, holding the woman in a firm grasp, tugging ungently. There was a knock at the door, but the guitarist held her tight. "Ignore it," Torrin ordered, voice husky. "They'll go away." *If they know what's good for 'em!*

Another knock, louder and more insistent. Torrin heard a man's voice through the door. Frozen, the woman's dark brown eyes moved between trying to see the door behind her and peering up at the rapidly angering guitarist.

Torrin cursed, pulling the woman's head away. She rose, using her grip for leverage. Feeling movement beneath her fingers, she glared down at the woman. *"Don't* move from this spot," she growled, planting a fierce kiss on ruby lips. Breaking away, she stalked to the door.

Even as she reached it, another round of pounding came. Torrin threw the door open, glaring at the intruder. "What the fuck do you want?" she demanded, scowling.

Middlestead was a little taken aback by her vehemence. He stared blankly at Torrin, his fist in the air from his aborted attempt at knocking.

"Well?" the redhead snapped.

"Uh." He shook his head, dropping his hand. "Sonny's uh … not in here, is she?" he asked, gaze flickering over the smaller woman's shoulder. He caught sight of a naked feminine back, but the hair color wasn't right. *Good thing, too,* he thought with a hint of anger. *I'd have to kill my guitarist if that was Sonny.* His eyes returned to his band mate, finally realizing that her shirt was open and her attributes bared for his view. *So they* are *pierced!* Middlestead blushed, mouth dry, and forced himself to look into Torrin's eyes.

"No," the woman said slowly, as if to an idiot. "She's not here. Nor would she be at …" and she craned her neck to see her alarm clock, "… three-thirty in the morning." Despite her anger at the interruption, she glared at the man and asked, "Have you looked in her room?"

"Yes! Of course, I looked in her room!" the drummer snapped. "When I got home, I went to check on her before bed. She's not in the *house,* Torrin!" Anger and worry fought for dominance. "She's never done this before."

Torrin shrugged. "Maybe she just decided to spend the night at Shelly's. It is a weekend."

Middlestead shook his head. "She's not there. I've spent the last twenty minutes calling all her friends, rousting families out of bed. Nobody's seen her since the dance."

A trickle of worry ran through her like ice water. Flippantly, she shrugged, "Maybe she's making out in the back seat of her date's car." Torrin felt the wrongness even as the words left her lips. "Whatever ... Who was her date, anyway?"

Running a hand through his dark hair, Middlestead winced and looked away. "I don't know. Pete Something, I think."

Torrin's anger flared again. "Your sixteen-year-old sister is out on a date with a high school jock, and you don't even know who the hell it *is*?"

"Look, I'm her *brother,* damn it! Not her parent!" came the defensive answer.

"Well, here's a clue, pal," Torrin said acidly, buttoning up her shirt. "Times like these are when you're supposed to act like a parent. Whether you want to or not." *Oh, yeah, Torry! Miss 'Oh-So-Superior' is now an expert on child rearing.*

Middlestead's face was pained, but he offered no argument

The guitarist took a deep breath and closed her eyes. Opening them, her frustration contained for the moment, she said, "Go back inside and call Shelly again. She'll know what the kid's name is. I'll be down in a minute." She used her chin to indicate the woman behind her. "I've gotta take care of something first."

He nodded in relief before turning and hustling down the stairs.

Torrin shook her head and rolled her eyes. *Men! Can't live with 'em! Can't shoot 'em!* Closing the door, she turned back to her evening's entertainment.

As Middlestead hung up the phone, he heard the patio door closing. Craning his neck from his place in the living room, he saw Torrin approach.

"Find out his name?" she asked, putting on her leather jacket.

"Yeah! Pete Bailey. But Shelly doesn't know where he lives or anything."

Torrin nodded, proceeding towards the stairs.

"Where are you going?" Middlestead asked, frowning. When he got no answer, he followed the small woman up the stairs and into his sister's room. "I told you she wasn't here."

Ignoring him, Torrin switched on the light. *Good thing she's a neat freak,* she thought. On the girl's nightstand was a phone, and she made her way toward it. Opening the drawer, she said, "Bingo," pulling out a school directory.

Middlestead slapped his forehead as she flipped through it. "Crap! I didn't even think of that!"

The woman shrugged and picked up the phone. "No reason you should have," she said as she dialed a number. "You're too worried to think straight right now." She waited for someone to answer. The man behind her paced nervously.

"... Hullo ...?" asked a sleepy male voice.

"Yes, I'd like to speak with Pete Bailey."

"Wha ...? Lady, it's four in the morning," the voice grumbled.

"Yeah, I know. And I'd like to know why my ... *sister* hasn't made it home from her date with Pete." There was a pause before she added, "Unless he didn't come home either ..."

She heard a rustling sound and muffled voices. "Look, uh ...what's your name?"

"Torrin."

"Uh, Torrin. ... Look, my boy's been home since a little after one. I saw him myself. I don't know where your sister is."

"May I speak with Pete then? He can tell me where he last saw her."

It took a moment for the man to process this. "Yeah. Okay. Hold on and I'll get him." The sound of the phone being laid down followed.

When no more was said, Middlestead stopped and said urgently, "Well?"

"Shhhh," Torrin waved him down with a glare. "They're waking the kid now. It's been a couple of hours. A few more minutes ain't gonna make a difference."

"Easy for *you* to say," he grumbled as he resumed pacing.

There were voices on the other end of the line. Finally a young man was put on.

"Hello?" he asked tentatively.

"Pete?"

Middlestead heard a distinct change in Torrin's voice and stopped to gawk at her.

"Yeah?"

"Let's get something clear from the beginning," she said pleasantly. "If *anything* has happened to Sonny, either by your hand or your stupidity, you are going to be in severe need of traction. You don't know me. You don't know what I look like. You'll never know if I'm across the room or right beside you. And whatever I do, keep in mind ... I hold a grudge. Do we have an understanding?"

"Yes." There was a slight pause before the shaky voice said with a rush, "I didn't do anything to her, I *swear*!"

"When was the last time you saw her?"

"Just before I came home. Quarter after one maybe? Give or take a few minutes."

Gray eyes narrowed. "The dance didn't go that late. They would have let your out before curfew. Where did you last see her?"

Silence.

"Keep in mind that your future of having children is on the line," Torrin growled. "*Where* did you last see her?"

"At Washington Park," he answered slowly, the information being forced from him. "There's a place near there ... on a side road, ya know. Where kids ... uh ... hang out."

"You mean make out, don't you?" Not waiting for a response, Torrin asked, "Why'd you leave her there, Pete?"

Audible sound of swallowing. "We ... uh ... We got into an argument. She started yelling and jumped out of the car." His voice raised an octave. "I didn't want to leave her, I swear! She just walked off! I followed her for several blocks, but she wouldn't get back into the car so I could take her home!"

Doing nothing to soothe the teenager's fear, Torrin got the street name and directions from him.

"Um ... Sonny doesn't have a sister," Bailey said, shaken. "Who *are* you?'

There was a long silence. "I could be your worst nightmare," Torrin rumbled.

Middlestead backed away as the woman turned toward him

and the door. An inner fire lit her gray eyes, and her mouth curled in a feral smile. "Where is she? Is she okay?"

"I don't know, but I'm gonna find out." Torrin rattled a set of keys. "I'm gonna take a cruise in whatsername's car and see if I can scare her up."

"I'm going, too," Middlestead insisted, following her down the stairs. The redhead stopped so abruptly that he plowed into her.

"No, you're going to stay here in case she shows up or calls," she ordered.

Despite himself, he took a step away from her intense glare. "But …"

"No 'buts,'" she growled. "You don't know the bus system and I do. I can already tell you two ways she could have gone." Torrin turned and began her descent again, continuing. "She obviously either missed the bus entirely or missed the connection and has been walking."

Middlestead trotted after her, trying to think of a reason to go. "Two cars, two search parties. We could cover more ground in less time," he suggested.

Opening the door, Torrin turned back to the worried man. "Look, Tom," she said, putting a hand on his shoulder. "Best case scenario — I find her and you don't. You keep looking, worried sick, until you come home to find her asleep in her own bed."

Frowning, he considered before standing straighter and shrugging his shoulders, not convinced.

Torrin scowled at him, continuing with an edge in her voice. "*Worst* case scenario — there's been a horrible accident, she needs emergency surgery and your signature on the paperwork. You're not here to get the call. She's dead and you're guilty." She glared at him. "You like *that* one better?"

Middlestead gulped, fear showing in his eyes. He searched the guitarist's unflinching gaze, finally breaking contact and looking down. "No," he said softly.

"I'll probably pick her up inside of an hour. I'll have her call when I do, okay?"

The drummer nodded.

"Okay. Later then." Torrin went out the door.

I swear! All they ever think with is their … dicks! Sonny fumed.

"What *is* it with guys?" she demanded of the night sky. With no answer forthcoming, she pulled the collar of her jacket closer to her neck and dug her hands deep into the pockets. Fortunately, the rain was the standard misty drizzle that was the norm for the Portland area and not a real downpour to soak her. She continued walking.

She'd learned a valuable lesson tonight. *Never, never,* ever *go on a date without twice the bus fare home.* At the very least, she would have had the money for a pay phone and been able to call the bar where Warlord had been playing. As it was, they wouldn't accept the collect call she'd made from downtown, and she'd had to walk. At the time it was far too early to call home, and now that it was late enough, there were no pay phones in sight.

Sonny was in a predominantly residential area. She knew there was a Safeway up ahead about a mile or so — it was on her bus line. *I'll call Tom from there.* A flash of her brother, worried sick and angry, crossed her mind. "Oh, *man,* is he gonna be pissed."

There were headlights ahead, coming toward her. The teenager stood straighter as she strode along, head held high. Alone at this hour in an unfamiliar neighborhood, Sonny knew she wasn't safe. She heard Torrin's voice saying, *"If ya act like you belong, they'll think you belong. Don't be looking at the ground with your head down. You'll have 'victim' written all over you."*

As the car got close enough for the driver to see her, the vehicle slowed and honked.

Sonny's heart pounded, but she kept her head. A glance at the vehicle showed she didn't know who it was. The streetlight overhead was reflecting off the windshield, so she couldn't see the driver. With a nonchalance she didn't feel, the youth kept walking.

The gold late model Buick slowed to a halt with another short honk. When she ignored it again, the driver put the vehicle in reverse to catch up.

Sonny glanced over her shoulder at the approach and gulped, eyes wide. *Crap! Now what?* She looked for a house with a porch light on. *There! Three houses down!* She picked up her pace.

"Hey, sexy," a familiar voice called. "Need a ride?"

The girl slowed and looked over her shoulder in amazement, her fear easing. "Torrin ...?"

"Or you could keep walkin'," Torrin shrugged with a mischievous grin. "Makes no never mind to me." The engine revved.

"No, no!" Sonny said hastily, moving around the front of the car to the passenger side. She clambered into the seat with relief. "I am *so* glad you're here!"

"I'll bet," Torrin responded. Once the door was closed, she put the Buick in gear and drove away. "You okay?"

Sonny put on her seatbelt. "I am now," she said with a grin. "How'd you know where to find me?"

Torrin shrugged, pulling a pack of cigarettes from her jacket. She proceeded to light one, speaking around it as it dangled from her lips. "It was pretty evident once I knew where you'd been and the time."

The brunette shivered as the heater began warming her feet and legs. "And how'd you know that?"

A grin played across the woman's face. "Had a little chat with Mr. Bailey."

"Did he ... Did he tell you what happened?" Sonny asked tentatively. She was glad for the darkened interior, her face feeling heat of a different sort.

Rolling down her window a crack, Torrin took a drag from her cigarette. "Not really, no. Just that there'd been a fight and you ditched him."

"Oh."

There was a long silence, the only sound being the car as it made its way down the street.

It occurred to Sonny that they were still driving away from home. Puzzled, she asked, "Where are we going?"

Torrin pondered the question. "Well, Tom's in a dither, and I told him we'd call when I found you." Gray eyes sparkled. "But I think he needs time to settle down before we get home. His knee-jerk reaction is gonna be to start yelling and screaming. A bad scene." The redhead shrugged and flicked ashes out the window. "We'll call and then give him time to cool off."

"Oh." A seed of dread lodged inside. It wasn't hard to imagine her brother's response to the whole mess. "Good idea," Sonny agreed.

There was a chuckle from the driver's seat.

Eventually they pulled into the parking lot of an all-night diner. After locking the car, they entered the building, stopping long enough to make the proscribed phone call. As expected, Middlestead was at first relieved and then yelling in anger. When Sonny pulled the phone away from her ear with a wince, Torrin snagged it.

"Cool your jets!" she bellowed, gaining not only the attention of the raging man on the phone but two waitresses, three bar hoppers having breakfast, a dishwasher and a chef who rushed out from the back, wiping his hands on his apron.

Sonny smiled weakly at the stares, a lovely shade of crimson. She listened to the guitarist's side of the conversation as people settled down and returned to their business.

"Now look, she's fine and dandy. No more worries. I know. Yeah. *NO*! We're gonna sit down and have a cup of coffee or something." Pause. "Tough! We're gonna have a talk. Yes! You know, it's a *girl* thing." Another pause. Torrin rolled her eyes. "We're gonna have some coffee and dis the entire male population. You sure you want in on *that* discussion?" She smiled at the teenager beside her, drawing a circle in the air next to her ear and mouthing "crazy."

Sonny barely stifled a giggle.

"Yeah. Don't worry about it. Have a beer and try to get some sleep. We'll be home in an hour or so. Alright. Bye." Torrin shook her head in feigned exasperation and hung up the phone. "He is *such* a boy."

As the pair made their way into the diner, Sonny asked, "It doesn't get better with age, does it?"

"Not in the least."

A few minutes later they were comfortably seated in a booth, backs to the window and legs resting along the padded benches. The older woman had coffee, and Sonny opted for a hot chocolate.

"So," Torrin began, sipping at the black liquid. "Gonna tell me what happened?"

The ebony haired teen blushed and dropped her eyes, finding the spoon stirring her drink very interesting. "What exactly did Pete say?" she asked, fishing.

"Nope. Tell me or not. I ain't gonna play that game."

Sonny nodded glumly. After a few moments, she said, "Well, we went up to the park after the dance ..." Her voice trailed off.

"Did he get to first base?" Torrin teased.

Despite her embarrassment, Sonny snickered. She grinned up from under dark bangs. "Yeah," she admitted.

Torrin's eyes sparkled. "Second?" she prodded.

There was a flash of anger. "No. Not second."

The redhead nodded, comprehending. "He gave you shit about it and you bailed," she supplied.

Pale blue eyes flared. "You make it sound so … so *blasé*," she snapped. "When I say no, I mean *no*!"

"Whoa, whoa, whoa!" Torrin said, turning to put her feet down and face the teenager. "That's not what I meant. I was simply stating a fact."

Sonny blew out a breath, feeling the anger and guilt. "I know. I'm sorry." She shook her head. "Guess I'm still mad."

"Sounds like it."

There was silence at the table as the adolescent became lost in thought. Finally, she spoke again. "It was the same thing with Jay last year. Is that all the boys think about?"

Torrin looked into the beautiful, serious face. *Boys ain't the only ones, baby.* "Well, that's been my experience" was her response.

"And it doesn't get any better as they get older?"

The guitarist raised an eyebrow. "Lando."

Sonny scowled. "I might as well just give in and let 'em have it, then."

"No."

The strength in Torrin's voice startled her. She looked into stern gray eyes.

"Sex is one of *the* most powerful weapons you have, girl," Torrin insisted.

Dark brows furrowed. "What?"

"*Think* about it. All those males out there will jump through hoops at even a *hint* of getting into your pants. It's a tremendous tool, a major point of control."

Sonny worked at wrapping her mind around this concept.

"You're still a virgin?" came the blunt question.

"Uh … yeah." The teenager blushed again.

Torrin nodded. "Good. Hold onto it. Use it as the carrot to string the guys along. Don't just give it up."

Wow. She's really adamant about this, Sonny mused. She considered the implications. Dropping her own feet to the floor, she leaned her elbows on the table. "Did you just give it away?"

The question hit Torrin with an almost physical force. She sat back abruptly, mouth open, and stared for a second. Then her training rushed in to protect her. Mask settled into place, she raised a cool eyebrow. "Why do you ask?"

Unsure of what had just transpired, Sonny realized she might have committed a *faux pas.* "I ... I was just curious. You seemed pretty ... It seemed really important to you and all."

Torrin studied the girl for a long moment. *Ya blew it, Torry,* a voice giggled. *Don't tell, don't tell, or you're gonna go to Hell,* it chanted, singsong. *"Show me your love, Torry. You seem to think you have a choice."* Another voice, the smaller one that was seldom heard, whispered, *Tell her the truth.*

"I'm sorry. I shouldn't have pried," Sonny said, dropping her gaze and pulling away.

"No." The guitarist reached out, taking Sonny's hand. "I just wasn't expecting it" She swallowed and wet her lips. "I don't remember losing my virginity, squirt. Simple as that."

"Were you drunk or something?" Sonny finally questioned, frowning.

Torrin shook her head. "No ..." She considered her next words, releasing the hand she held. "It was taken from me by my father when I was really young." The voices in her head took up a clamor, and she busied herself with her coffee cup, trying to maintain control.

Sonny blinked at the woman. A sudden wave of compassion rolled through her, and she reached out to touch Torrin's hand. "I'm so s— "

"*Don't* even say it!" Torrin warned with a glare, pulling her hand out of reach. "It happened, it's over and I don't wanna talk about it." *Yeah! Don't need anybody else to wipe while yer on the pity potty, huh, Torry? Betcha it'd be fun ... crying on her shoulder, her arms around you ...*

The dark girl chose not to be hurt by the woman's brusqueness. *I'd probably feel the same way,* she considered. Another question came to mind. She pondered it, the thing getting bigger and stronger, and she was hard pressed not to blurt it out. *Oh, no. Now is* not *the time ...*

Torrin wrestled her demons and the emotions rampaging through her system. Finally getting herself under control, she spared a glance at Sonny. With mild surprise, she didn't see pity or sympathy. Instead, it appeared the youth was trying to keep her thoughts under wraps – and failing miserably. The guitarist tilted her head and braced herself. "What?" she asked.

"Nothing."

"You don't lie well, Sonny," the redhead said with a growl. "Now spit it out."

There's got to be a way to stop all this blushing! "I was just ... Well ..." Sonny began to fidget and look anywhere but at Torrin.

"Sonny ..." Torrin warned, eyes flashing.

Swallowing, she took the dive. "Is that why you ... you know ... like women ...?" The resulting laughter eased her nerves, and Sonny snuck a peek at the woman.

Torrin chortled. "Oh, no, squirt," she said, wiping her eyes. "I've been falling for gorgeous babes since I was knee high."

Despite herself, Sonny blurted, "Really? How come?"

With a shrug, the guitarist looked with amusement at the curious teenager. "I dunno. It's just always been that way. Boys were for beating up and girls were for kissing." Pause. "Among other things," she drawled, chuckling again at Sonny's embarrassment.

"How are you ladies doing over here?" the waitress asked, a pot of coffee in hand. "Need a refill?"

"No, thanks. We're fine, I think," Torrin said.

"Alright then. You girls have a good morning." She left after placing the check on the table.

Relieved at the interruption, Sonny used the opportunity to change the subject. "How long have you been playing guitar?"

"A while." Torrin shrugged, relaxing. "Got my first one at ten. Been playing ever since."

"You're really good," the brunette insisted, reddening when she realized she sounded like a love-struck fan. "I mean, I heard Tom tell Chris at my birthday party he thought Warlord would make it to the big time for sure now."

Raised eyebrows were the only indication of surprise. "Really?"

Sonny nodded. "Yeah. The band's good. Max and Tom write some pretty cool songs, but I think they've been drifting along, waiting for the right mix of people." Shyly, she peered at Torrin from under her bangs. "I think they found it."

"Thanks, squirt," Torrin said, a slight grin on her face.

"Just call it as I see it," she answered in a stuffy tone. She smiled at the chuckle from across the table. "So, do you think he's cooled off enough yet?"

The redhead pursed her lips and considered. "Yeah, maybe. Ready to hit the road?"

"Yeah, I'm pretty beat," Sonny said, stifling a yawn.

"Let's go then."

As the pair approached the Buick, Sonny asked, "Whose car is this anyway?"

"Uh ..." Torrin searched her memory. "Della? Daisy?" She snapped her fingers as her eyes lit up in remembrance. "Dolly! That's it!"

"And she is ...?" Sonny climbed into the car and shut the door.

Getting in on the other side, Torrin shrugged. "Just some chick I had over when your brother came pounding on my door."

Sonny frowned. "So she let you borrow her car. Did you take her home first?"

"Naw. She's in bed," the guitarist informed her as she started the vehicle. "I told her to get some sleep while I was out."

Number Thirteen.

Sonny's Journal – September 11, 1999

Oh, man, it's been a long night! Thank God, Torrin found me! I would have been walking until dawn before I got home!

We had a talk about guys at the restaurant. She basically told me that guys were idiots to be used. Considering her past history, I can understand her point of view. But I don't think all guys are like that. There's my dad and Tom and Lamont, Max, Chris ... They're all decent men. I guess I'm just not lucky with boys. (Hopefully that'll change!!)

I am amazed though. Torrin left number thirteen to come find me! Tom said she argued him down and wouldn't let him go with her. Wow! Maybe she does like me. Well, that's not exactly what I meant – I know *she likes me. I just didn't know how much.*

We touched a little bit on why she likes women instead of men. I thought it was because of her dad, but she says it's not. After thinking about it, I'm pretty sure she's right. It's hard to explain, but I think she's always been this way, regardless of her past circumstances.

And I have to admit, I'm even more curious about the logistics of it all now.

Maybe I'll check in the library downtown next week ...

Torrin pretended to be asleep. She always did when her new daddy, Louis, came into her room at night.

During the daytime, he was fine enough. Sometimes he would get really mad, but lots of grown-ups did that. After Mommy tucked her into bed at night, Louis became a scary monster. It never happened at naptime, only after dark. The scary monster didn't ever talk when he was there. He was quiet and sneaky, sitting on the edge of her big girl's bed.

At first, he used to watch her for the longest time. That was before Torrin found out he was a scary monster. She thought it was just Louis making sure she was safe and asleep. He would kiss her on the forehead before leaving.

One night he touched her, gently feeling her skin with his fingers. It felt nice and sort of tickled. Even though Torrin pretended to be sleeping, she couldn't help but squirm, a smile on her face. Her Mommy told her that daddies did that sometimes, played with their daughters. Torrin never knew her real daddy. He was dead, hit by a car before she was born, so she'd never had a daddy before Louis.

Things changed after a while. Louis began undressing her, unbuttoning her Superman pajamas and sliding his hand inside to tickle her chest. When he pinched her nipples it tickled in a different way, a scary way. Torrin would squeeze her eyes shut and pretend really hard she was sleeping, hoping Louis would go away.

It didn't work. Soon he was slipping his large hand inside her pajama bottoms, touching her privates through her panties. Not long after, the underwear didn't stop him either, a large finger caressing her. Even though it felt sort of good, it was bad and scary. Mommy had taught her she wasn't supposed to touch her privates. It was bad. Torrin didn't *think* daddies were supposed to play with their daughters this way, but she couldn't be sure since she'd never had one before.

One night Torrin heard Louis at her bedroom door, so she rolled over onto her tummy, hoping that would stop him. That time he hurt her, his finger somehow going *inside* her. That's when she realized that Louis became a scary monster. His breathing got funny, and the bed shook with little jerks until he let out a long sigh.

Torrin pretended to be asleep. She always did when her daddy, Louis, came into her room at night. This time was different. His hand was on her bare chest, shaking her.

"Torry, I know you're awake," Louis said. "Open your eyes."

She didn't want to see what the scary monster looked like, so she squeezed her eyes closed and shook her head.

"Torry," he said, his voice all growling like it sounded before he got mad.

Not wanting the scary monster to get mad, Torrin opened her eyes. She was surprised to see Louis sitting on her bed instead of the monster.

Louis tickled her tummy but he wasn't smiling. "Torry, I have bad news. Your mommy left us."

Torrin frowned. "When will she be back?" she asked.

"She won't *be* back, Torry. She ran away."

Tears came to her eyes and her lower lip quivered. "Like Toby when he ran away to the circus?" It was one of her favorite stories.

Louis nodded. "Yes, just like that."

"Toby missed his family and went home at the end of the story." Torrin sniffled. "Will Mommy?"

His voice was low. "I don't think so, Torry. She seemed really angry with us."

Torrin started to cry. "But why? Did we do something bad?"

"No, we didn't do anything bad," he said, picking her up and holding her in his lap. "I think Mommy got tired of being a mommy. She wants to have a different life."

That confused and scared her. *Why wouldn't Mommy want to be a mommy? She says she loves me. Doesn't she want to be my mommy?* Torrin cried for a long time as Louis held her. The idea of not having a daddy was nothing new, but not having a mommy was terrifying.

When her crying subsided, Louis produced a handkerchief and helped her blow her nose. "We have to stick together now, Torry. We're the only family we have."

Still teary eyed, Torrin hugged her new daddy and nodded.

"You know what that means?" he asked, caressing her red-gold hair.

"No," Torrin whispered, somehow knowing she didn't want to hear the answer.

Louis pushed her away enough to study his adopted daughter. "I've shown you how much I love you at night. You need to show me you love *me* now."

The one constant in Torrin's life had been her mommy, and she was gone. Realizing she couldn't pretend to be sleeping anymore when the scary monster was there, she began to cry again.

Holding her close, Louis rocked, letting her weep. "And you can never, never tell anyone how much we love each other, Torry," he said. "Other people don't understand. The police will think you're bad for your mommy leaving. They'll take you away."

I must be bad for my mommy to leave me, the little girl thought. *What if Louis decides I'm bad and leaves me, too?* She imagined herself like the Little Match Girl, going to heaven because she was all alone in the streets with no one to take care of or love her.

Eventually, Torrin's tears faded, and her daddy helped her blow her nose. Then he kissed her on the forehead and began teaching her how to love him.

Torrin awoke with a start, eyes wide, searching. Several moments passed before she realized it was the nightmare that woke her. Breathing a shaky sigh of relief, she slumped back onto her mattress.

Locked up and tied down,
Do unto others…
TORRIN C. SMITH, "WHAT'S BEEN DONE"

Part III: Senior Year

I can hear your
Persistent poison.
TORRIN C. SMITH, "SHADOW VOICES"

Sonny was curled up in an old armchair, a heavy textbook cracked open on her lap and a spiral notebook crammed into the side cushion. She paused occasionally, pulling a pen from behind her ear to jot down a quick note. Nearby, her brother lounged on what used to be the bench seat of a van, flipping through a magazine. On the makeshift stage, Torrin and Atkins worked on a song. Rehearsal was at a standstill, Hampton having a meeting with someone "in the biz," he had said. His girlfriend, Lisa Foley, was seated on the edge of the stage with another woman as they watched the two guitarists work.

Finally finishing the chapter, Sonny looked up at the stage. The stranger – *Number Twenty-one,* she thought – was drooling as she watched Torrin on stage. Sonny's lip turned up in a sneer. *Do any of 'em have any brains?* she wondered. Shaking her head and clearing it of the uncharitable thought, she set the book to one side of the chair and stretched out her long legs.

At seventeen, it appeared that the dark girl had finally stopped growing. She was already five-foot-eight, looking most of her male peers in the eye. She'd walked with a slump last year, trying to seem shorter for a time. Torrin had made some rude remark about slouching around with a bull's-eye on her forehead, and from that point Sonny had stood tall and towered over the boys. Most had caught up with her this last year.

"How's it going?" Middlestead asked from his seat.

The teenager grimaced and ran a hand through her hair. "Crappy. This chemistry class is gonna be the death of me."

Her brother chuckled. "That's what you said about trigonometry last year and geometry the year before that."

Sonny grinned ruefully. With a little shrug, she said, "Guess I'm just not too logically inclined, huh? Must be the artistic company I keep."

As she stood and stretched, the drummer griped, "You saying

we ain't logical?"

"No! Of course not!" Sonny said, a sparkle in her blue eyes. She took the pen from behind her ear and tossed it onto the chair. "Any clue when Max'll get here?"

"Naw. Said it'd be at least an hour. Maybe more." The man shrugged and went back to his magazine. "Whatever it is, he said it'd be good for the band."

Sonny nodded. She wandered over to the stage and settled down to watch the proceedings.

"No, no," Torrin said over the guitar Atkins was playing. "We wanna start out quiet, just one axe in the beginning. Like this ..." She played a simple melody with an odd half note that elicited strangeness and a vague sense of unease. Then, Torrin began singing, her sweet voice inconsistent with the lyrics.

> Reality is pain;
> it's all I ever feel.
> I would have to hurt myself,
> to prove that I am real.
> I've tried it all before,
> all the drugs and drink,
> My memory's unbroken,
> and I still have to think.

The guitar melody changed to a more conventional tune and Atkins picked it up with his. Torrin continued singing the following stanza. When it was finished, she stopped playing. "And here's where Tom comes in with heavy drums." She pointed at the piece of paper she'd scribbled the music on.

Atkins nodded. He took up the tune, his throaty voice rough and dark. "I can give you everything — I can make you hurt. I can give you hate and pain, I am an expert."

"Yeah!" She began the odd strain again, and Atkins continued on to the following set of lyrics. The two then worked their way through the next chorus and finished the tune.

"Oh, wow!" the groupie gushed. "Isn't Torrin great?"

Hampton's girlfriend smiled politely and nodded before turning away just enough to make a face at Sonny.

The high school senior stifled a laugh, peeking at Torrin to see the expected annoyance on the guitarist's face. *Well, Twenty-one, looks like you're not gonna make it to round two!* she thought with smug satisfaction.

I hate *that shit. Sounds like my mother gushing over Elvis on TV,* Torrin thought. Another little voice made itself known. *Besides, you ain't all that anyway.* "Let's take a break," she growled as she settled her guitar in its stand. "C'mon," she said to the woman.

The groupie seemed to sense she'd made a mistake. She swallowed nervously, her eyes flickering around to look at the others. "Sure, okay," she said softly, collecting her jacket and purse.

As the couple headed for the door, Sonny couldn't help but feel a bit of sympathy for the woman, not to mention a bit of guilt for her own thoughts. *Lord knows I wouldn't wanna be where she is now!*

Hampton chose that moment to walk in. He passed the women at the door and continued toward the stage, unzipping his coat. Glancing back over his shoulder, he asked, "Where's Torrin going?"

"Takin' out the trash," Atkins snorted as he fiddled with one of the strings on his guitar.

"Lando!" Sonny exclaimed in indignation. She leaned forward and slapped him on his booted shin.

The tall man blinked at her. "What?"

Hampton's girlfriend, Foley, rose and gave the bearded man a welcome kiss. "She'll be back in a minute."

"Good," he said as Middlestead approached them. "Got some big news for us." He took off his coat and tossed it onto a nearby chair.

"Any hints?" Sonny asked hopefully.

The shorter man chuckled and rubbed his bald head. "Nope."

"Bummer."

A few moments later, the band was looking expectantly at their bassist/manager. Torrin had returned alone to her stool on stage, and Middlestead was standing behind his sister's chair, arms crossed.

"Alright, Max. Whaddya got?" the drummer asked.

Hampton clapped his hands together and rubbed them vigorously, a smile on his square face. "Okay! I don't know if you guys have noticed, but we're getting really popular in the area. We've got people coming from as far away as Seattle to give us a listen."

"Really? That's cool!" Sonny piped up.

Hampton nodded. "And apparently there are bootleg tapes of our shows all up and down the West Coast."

"Yer shittin' me!" Atkins exclaimed with a surprised grin.

"Nope." The shorter man stepped over to his coat and rummaged through the pockets. A cassette case appeared, and he tossed it to the guitarist. While Atkins looked it over with Torrin peering over his shoulder, Hampton continued. "There's a lot of interest out there right now. I just left a meeting with three guys who own some clubs in Seattle, Portland and San Jose. Between them and their contacts, we could increase our territory with a mini-tour."

Silence, and then everyone spoke at once. Hampton let them go for a couple of minutes before raising his hands to quiet the hubbub. "We could get a guaranteed itinerary of four months from Seattle to San Jose and the surrounding areas. We would make enough money on this venture to top off our savings and be able to record that CD we're always talking about."

"Guaranteed?" Torrin asked.

"Yes. All we have to do is sign an agreement that we will appear on those dates at those venues."

Atkins' face was scrunched in thought. "But what if they cancel on us? Won't we get screwed?"

Hampton shook his head. "The agreement covers our butts, too. It will stipulate that we'll still get paid half the performance fee if they should cancel out on us. Besides, I'll have my sister have a look at it before we sign."

"Sounds good to me," the guitarist said, looking around at his band mates.

"When?"

Hampton turned to the drummer. "Our first gig would be scheduled for December 1 in Seattle."

Middlestead's face deepened into a frown. "No. I can't do it."

"What? Why the hell not?" Atkins demanded.

The dark man looked down at his sister who had whirled around in amazement at his refusal. "Sonny's got school. It's her senior year. I can't jeopardize her chance at a college scholarship by taking her with us. And I can't leave her at home alone for four months."

"But —" the adolescent began.

"No buts, Sonny," Middlestead intoned, shaking his head. "This can wait. Your education comes first." He brought his dark blue gaze up to scan the rest of the crowd. "I can't ask you to wait until summer, so I'll understand if you need to get another drummer. It's cool." He scooped up his jacket and strode out of the warehouse. Everyone stared after him.

"Well, fuck me," Atkins breathed.

Sonny stared after her brother, feeling his heartbreak at such a tough decision. *This is what he's always wanted, what he's worked on for years! I can't be responsible for this. There's gotta be another way ...* She searched her mind and the room for answers, her eyes finally connecting with gray. *Torrin'll help ...*

Sonny's Journal — November 14, 2000

Well, it's been a couple of days since I've written. Guess I'd better catch up here. I've been so busy and have had so much on my mind.

Warlord has a chance at a tour – guaranteed income for four months! But, Tom has nixed it for himself because of me. I can't have that on my conscience. He's been working on this for nearly as long as I can remember!

So, I skipped school on Monday. Torrin took me downtown. We checked the library for books on home schooling first. Found a couple of really good ones. I've only been able to scan the first three chapters of one, but it appears to have tons of educational ideas and resources.

Torrin then took me to Greenhouse, a youth shelter near Burnside. She knows one of the counselors there. Had a long talk with Gladys (the counselor) and she helped me brainstorm some options.

Today I had a meeting with Mrs. Rutherford, my school counselor. I laid it all out to her and what I wanted to do. She thinks it'd be great for me to do an independent study program. Since I want to get a degree in journalism and all, Mrs. R thinks I could do an extracurricular thing for the school paper. Weekly updates on the road with a rock band kind of thing. She says it'd be nothing for me to get the assignments from my classes and do the work on the road.

About the only trouble spots will be chemistry lab and tests. We could do the tests through college libraries and computers. I might have to wait on the lab work, though. It just all depends on where we are and whether or not I can get permission to use a lab somewhere ...

Now, if I can just talk Tom into it. Well, tonight's the night for that. I've asked Torrin to be there and back me up. She could argue Moses out of the Ten Commandments if she wanted!

I hope this works. I have a feeling that Warlord is going to get bigger and bigger now. I don't want Tom to lose his dream because of me.

Hampton stood at the microphone, his bass slung low across his body. His hands were still, holding the instrument under a hot spotlight. The rest of the stage was dark, eerie strains of a guitar the only sound.

There were some hoots and heckling from the audience who had paid to see the next band. For the most part, however, the crowd had been captivated. As Hampton sang the second stanza in a mellow tenor, a few lighters lit up the darkness at his feet.

Reality is pain;
it's all I ever feel.
I would have to hurt myself,
to prove that I am real.
I've tried it all before,
all the drugs and drink,
My memory's unbroken,
and I still have to think.

The guitar melody changed, a second adding its own voice. Hampton began playing his bass, and red spots lit up the stage with somber darkness, showing Atkins and Torrin playing their own instruments nearby.

What have I turned out to be?
what have I become?
What will ever happen to me
when all I feel is numb?

Drums kicked in, hard and slow, pulsing in an almost erotic beat and leading the way for the rest of the band. The guitars picked up in volume and depth, the bass going along for the ride. Stage lights throbbed with the beat. Hampton's voice gained an edge of strength and pain.

I can give you everything –
I can make you hurt.
I can give you hate and pain,
I am an expert.

His voice softened again, in direct contrast with the music

backing him.

> One more time
> around the wheel,
> I'd give my soul
> to once more feel.

He hung on to the final note as the music reached a peak and came down in a crash of sound and light.

There was silence for a split second before the crowd erupted in cheers and applause.

"Thank you, Seattle!" Atkins waved at the audience with a wide grin. Everyone took their bows and trotted off stage. Behind them, the emcee – a local radio disc jockey – came out.

"And that was Warlord, folks! Damn! Can those Portlanders rock or what?" The crowd erupted loudly in agreement, and he went on to introduce the next band.

"That was great!" Sonny exclaimed as the band approached her. She stepped into her brother's arms and hugged him before turning to the rest. "That song is really fantastic, Torrin!"

The redhead's mouth quirked in a grin. "Thanks," she said in an off-handed manner.

Sonny thought she saw a flash of real pleasure at the compliment, despite the superior air the woman was giving off. *You might act like you're all that, but I think I'm beginning to see past it.* "Well, now what?"

"We gotta get my kit and our gear packed up," Middlestead said, his eyes still sparkling with the excitement of being onstage.

"Yeah," Hampton agreed. "Got a gig in Salem tomorrow night. We wanna leave early in the morning." The shorter man looked pointedly at the two guitarists.

Atkins looked offended and Torrin smirked.

"What?" he demanded.

She slapped him in the belly with the back of her hand. "He means we have to stay in the motel tonight."

"Aw, Max! C'mon, man!" the tall man groaned. "There's this girl out front who's been ogling me all night."

"There's *always* a girl, Lando," Sonny piped up. She flushed a little at the snicker from the smaller woman.

Atkins said, "Well, yeah. I know that! But, *this* one —"

"Is going to be without the benefits of your attentions tonight," Hampton ordered. "Or we're leaving your ass here when you don't show up in the morning."

The tall man seriously appeared to be considering his chances of partying all night and still making it to the motel in the morning, and whether or not it made a difference if he didn't make it in time, and what other options he had for getting to Salem for the next performance.

Torrin rolled her eyes. With surprising strength, she reached up, hooked her hand in Atkins' collar and pulled the man down to her level. A quick whisper in his ear and she let him go, staring into his eyes intently.

He blinked at her for a second before a grin broke out on his face. "Okay. Okay, yeah." He straightened and looked at the bassist. "No problem. I'll be a good boy tonight."

A startled expression crossed Hampton's face before he shot a suspicious look at the drummer, who shrugged. "Okay. Let's get the gear and pack it up then."

It was a few minutes of work, the sounds of another band playing on the stage nearby, before Sonny could corner the redhead. "What'd you tell Lando?" she asked, glancing quickly around to make sure they were out of earshot.

Torrin shrugged. With a slight grin, she said, "I just reminded him of all those bodacious California girls that would miss his ... expertise when we get down there."

The dark teenager chortled as she helped pack up her brother's drum kit.

Sonny's Journal — December 9, 2000

We've only been on tour for a week. It's been both exhilarating and exhausting! I've become the one and only roadie for the band, helping set up and tear down the equipment. Because of that, I'm allowed to stay and watch even though some of their gigs are located in bars. I just have to stay backstage in places where alcohol is served.

I've noticed that even on the road, Torrin's songs get the most attention from the audience. Tom's right. She was the spark Warlord needed to make it big. And even though it's really obvious she's the better lyricist, she doesn't laud it over the guys or anything. I wish her songs weren't so violent, though. It's kind of scary listening sometimes. What kind of life has she had to think of these things? I wish I could go back in time and spare her some of it.

She and I are spending a lot more time together now. Since I'm with the band 24/7, we hardly get a break from each other. We even stay in the same motel room when we're not sleeping in the van or car. I really enjoy having the chance to get to know her better. I mean, I've known her for a couple of years, but this is different.

All right, I'll say it. I think I'm falling in love with her.

I don't know that I would have figured it out without Torrin here. I remember having crushes on women teachers in school. At the time, I thought I was just admiring them. But I feel the same way about Torrin. At night when we're supposed to be asleep, I lay awake and watch her, wondering. What would happen if I touched her cheek? Ran my hand through her hair? What do her lips taste like?

It's been a slow process to get to this point. Out of curiosity I began doing some research into the lesbian lifestyle last year. The more I read, the more I feel this ... yearning, I guess I'd call it.

I haven't said anything to Tom. He'll flip, especially if he finds out I want Torrin! Her reputation as a hound dog is secure in the band, and he'll want to protect me. And if I did say something, what would Torrin do? Would she take me to bed like I want and then dump me like all the others? Do I really want to go through that?

Sometimes I wonder what Mom and Dad would say. Dad always said if given a choice between being right and happy, choose happy. I always have. It's much more satisfying. I would hope that he'd accept me, that both of them would. I've read so many horror stories about parents not accepting their children's sexuality. I don't think I could stand that kind of rejection from my parents.

Still, I miss them. I wish they were here.

Torrin tossed her keys on the desk and settled her guitar case in the corner. Sonny followed her into the room, shutting and locking the door behind her before throwing herself onto one of the double beds.

"I'm so tired," Sonny grumbled. "But if we're gonna be in the van together for three or four hours, I'd better get a shower tonight."

"I know *that's* right," the guitarist teased, a look of distaste on her face. She switched on the beat up television, and as she flipped through the channels, a pillow sailed through the air.

Sonny watched as it connected solidly with Torrin's shoulder and side. The woman froze for a second and then scooped it up, turning to her roommate on the bed with a feral smile. *Oops.*

"Little girl wants to play," Torrin purred. She stalked Sonny, detouring long enough to retrieve a second pillow from her bed.

Sonny sat up straighter and grabbed her second pillow, holding it in a threatening manner over her head. She giggled in nervous anticipation, wondering if she should make a break for the bathroom or not.

As if reading her mind, Torrin changed course to get between the youth and the exits. Sonny scrambled off the bed and backed away, holding her pillow out in front of her.

"N ... now, Torrin," she warned, trying to be serious and failing miserably. "I'm sorry. That was uncalled for and a mistake. I didn't me—" The back of her leg hit the second bed, and she stumbled, reaching a hand down to regain her balance.

That was all Torrin needed. Without a sound, she leapt forward and began pummeling her foe with the pillows she wielded. There was a loud squawking as Sonny took the abuse for a few seconds. It wasn't long, however, before her longer reach was used to her advantage, and she began scoring as many hits on Torrin as she was getting.

With Torrin losing one pillow, it ultimately came down to the two of them standing over the bed, pounding on each other, swinging their pillows like baseball bats. Realizing that this could go on all night or until a pillow exploded, the redhead chose to escalate matters.

Bringing her pillow around with full force, Sonny saw her roommate lift her arms and toss her weapon behind her. Unable to stop the swing, the pillow connected with Torrin's ribs. Effectively pinning the pillow against her body by dropping her arms, the guitarist scuffled for supremacy. The pillow began to give a little, and Sonny hastily released it, not wanting feathers all over the place. Torrin lurched backwards to keep her balance, took the pillow from under her arm and tossed it behind her. She then launched herself across the bed.

Suddenly, Sonny found herself on her back, the woman straddling her hips and tickling her mercilessly. She laughed hysterically, trying to wriggle away but unable. Attacking in kind, she tried to give as well as she got.

Torrin laughed as the two of them wrestled around. *Just what the doctor ordered, a little roughhousing to release the jitters.* As the battle progressed, however, she began to feel other things as well. The sudden urge to caress the skin beneath her with more than her hands brought Torrin to her senses. *Gotta get outta this!* After living with Sonny for nearly two years, she knew how to bring a screeching halt to any of the little flirting sessions that had reared their ugly heads. Torrin slowly allowed Sonny to gain the upper hand.

"Hah!" The brunette grinned. She finally had her opponent pinned on the mattress, straddling her hips and holding her hands above her head. "I've gotcha now!"

Torrin's body suddenly lost its fight, no longer struggling. Her gray eyes became hooded, and she said in a sultry voice, "Whatcha gonna do with me?"

Sonny's heart pounded and she flushed at the immediate image Torrin's voice brought up. *Damn it! Get a grip, girl!* Not willing to concede so easily, she tossed her dark hair to one side and said with great courage, "I don't know. Maybe I should spank you for attacking me like that."

Eyes flashed and Sonny barely got her mouth open to yell before she found herself back on the bed, their positions reversed. The redhead leaned close, staring into pale blue ice. Their breath mingled, and the adolescent swallowed, half in fear and half in hope.

"Maybe I should spank *you* for your insolence." An eyebrow was raised in appraisal. *Yes! Do it!* Torrin shook her head, clearing it of the erotic image — red cheeks, tender flesh, wet and willing. She sat up and released her opponent, a cool grin plastered on her face. "Go take your shower, squirt."

Sonny swallowed hard, slowly sitting up. She watched Torrin wander back over to the television and return to flipping through the channels.

Sonny's Journal – January 3, 2001

Well, tomorrow we leave Medford, Oregon, and head into California. It's been snowing in the mountains nearby, so it'll be rough going at this time of year. But so far, so good. Both the Honda and Max's van are still plugging away — no mechanical problems. (Knock on wood!)

We spent the week through Christmas at home. It was pretty nice. I got to see Shelly and Lamont and some other friends. I checked in at school. I also got a lot of my chem lab out of the way. Mr. Elliott was good enough to come in on a Saturday so we could work on it for a few hours. So now I'm officially caught up on that aspect of my education! The rest is pretty much all finished – I've done most of the assignments and turned them in. I took a few tests that were backed up while I was there, too.

The band is doing fantastic. Things are starting to pick up, and they're actually getting people returning to their shows rather than coming to see the band they're opening for. It's pretty exciting! I know that Tom is really happy, too. This is what he's dreamed of for so long. I'm glad I was able to work things out.

Torrin's being ... Torrin, I guess. About the only time she's in the motel room is when we're going to leave the following morning. Or to take a nap before shows. She's hardly ever here. It's worse than when we're living in Portland! I can count on a couple of girls a month at home – not every freaking night!

There've been a couple of times that she and Lando have taken over the other motel room for their orgies. Those are the nights Tom stays in my room. I don't know what Max and Lisa do. Probably sleep in his van.

I don't know what she's trying to prove. I don't know what she's searching for. I wish I did. I see some of the 'babes' she seduces, and frankly, I don't think they're all that great. They don't have what she needs. She needs a woman with intelligence, for one thing. And someone who'll give her a kick in the seat of the pants when she needs it. Someone to hold her at night. Spoil her.

Love her.

I can give that to her.

Torrin drowsed in the back of the van, the sound of the road lulling her. Normally, she'd be lounging in one of the passenger seats, but in all the activity to be on their way, Sonny had ended up in the van with her.

Whatever was going on, the guitarist wasn't pleased. It seemed that whenever the teenager was in close proximity, Torrin couldn't think straight. On the nights she'd stay in the motel room, she got no sleep – preferring to stay up all hours and watch Sonny's face as she slumbered. Her fantasies were more and more consumed with imagined visions of dark hair and blue eyes.

Her control was slipping.

It was a rotten feeling. Rather than be near Sonny and escalate her emotional turmoil, Torrin had feigned a need to work on a tune. She'd used her duffel to make a backrest against all the gear and twiddled with her guitar for a time.

The woman was glad the band was heading south. *It's too damned cold at night here!* she groused. When she could find someone to crash with, she did. When she couldn't, she spent most of the night walking around. *Doesn't make any difference, does it, Torry? You wouldn't get any sleep in the motel either, if you had your wish!*

All in all, it was a very unsettling feeling. The more Torrin put distance between them, the more Sonny found reasons to be near. Like climbing into the van at the absolute very last minute. Not to mention the flirting — there were constant touches and innuendoes by the high schooler anymore, whenever she was within reach.

So fuck her and get it over with! You know she wants it. What's the problem? Torrin grumbled and jammed an elbow into her duffel in an attempt to get more comfortable. *The problem is she's too close. I don't want to hurt her. I like her!* The other voice, Lucifer's, snorted in disgust. *Love is pain, Torry. You know that. It can never be anything else.*

Cracking her eyes open a bit, she could see the elegant profile as Sonny animatedly discussed something with Hampton in the driver's seat. She was using the brush in her hand to underscore a point in her conversation. Her voice was only a low sound mixed with the noise of the road under the wheels. A quiet little voice piped up clearly in the rare stillness of Torrin's mind. *You don't* have *to hurt her.*

Torrin drifted off to sleep, feeling warm arms envelop her and hold her, smelling the scent that was Sonny's own, feeling another heartbeat pulse in time with hers.

Sonny stepped into the motel room, closing the door behind her. Her roommate made a beeline toward the bed farthest from the door, dropping her duffel and guitar before flipping the television on and scanning the channels. *As usual,* she thought, half in vague irritation and half in fondness. *And I thought* I *watched too much TV!*

The dark girl dropped her pack on her bed and settled her suitcase on the luggage rack. They had about three hours before they were due to meet the rest of the band for dinner. *Just enough time to shower, get my hair dry and write in my journal.* Unzipping her suitcase, Sonny rummaged inside.

Several minutes later, a pile of clothes and toiletries in her arms, she grumbled crossly, "Where did I put my brush?"

Torrin, who had sprawled on the bed on her stomach, glanced over. "You had it in the van. Is it in your backpack?"

"Oh, yeah! You're right." Sonny stepped into the bathroom to dump her things and returned to the bed. After several moments of digging, she became irritated at not immediately discovering the item. With a muttered curse, she partially dumped the contents and fished around. "Aha! Found it!" Turning to the woman, she waved the brush in the air. "I'm gonna take a shower. You need the bathroom?"

"Naw, I'll just wait until you're in there," Torrin responded with a wry grin.

Sonny mock glared at her, brandishing the brush. "Don't even think about flushing that toilet!"

The redhead raised a regal eyebrow.

Snorting, Sonny rolled her eyes before turning away. "Whatever ..." She took a final look at the guitarist as she entered the bathroom and shut the door. *I wonder if she'll disappear before I get done ...? I hope not. It'd be nice to spend some time with her for a change.*

Approximately forty-five minutes later, the brunette stepped out of the bathroom, a cloud of steam in her wake. A quick glance into the room and her heart thumped a bit. *She's still here!*

Torrin had changed positions on the bed, sitting up and leaning against the headboard. Surprisingly enough, a book was in her hands, and she was flipping through it with a look of amusement on her face.

Pale eyes widened at this unnatural phenomena as Sonny stopped at her suitcase to put things away. Chatter from a game show was the only sound in the room. Retaining her brush, she sat on her own bed next to the mess she'd left when she'd dumped out her pack.

Sonny glanced again at the woman. The book looked...familiar. Her heart fluttered again, and she quickly scanned the contents of her spilled pack. *Oh, no. Was* that *in there?* With a feeling bordering on panic, she ran a hand through her belongings, searching. Flushing, she looked at Torrin.

Gray fire sparkled at her. Torrin held it up, her thumb holding her place, and said, "Interesting reading material, squirt. They assigning this stuff in high school now?" The book, *Sapphist Dreams,* waggled.

Sonny was speechless. A myriad of emotions ran through her. Embarrassment at her predicament. Worry about what the woman would do in response. An irrational guilt at having been caught at something she'd been researching for nearly a year. And lastly, fear. *Shit! Busted! What do if I do if she bails? What if she tells Tom?* Or worse. *What if she won't have anything to do with me, now?*

As was usually the case when Sonny became scared, she got angry. Her eyes narrowed, and she stood up to tower over the seated woman. "Who the hell said you could go through my stuff?" she asked harshly.

Pale brows raised in surprise. "Excuse me?" Torrin asked, a flash of uncertainty crossing her face before the mask settled.

"Where do you get off going through my stuff?" the youth demanded. She reached for the book only to have it pulled out of reach, furthering her irritation. "Give it back!"

The guitarist's eyes flashed, and she scooted forward on the bed to stand. She was toe to toe with Sonny, glaring back at the taller woman, as she kept the book just out of reach behind her. "I didn't go through your stuff," she intoned in a warning voice. "You left it on the bed— "

"Bullshit!" Sonny exploded in reaction, trembling inside from the knowledge that the woman was right. She made another lunge for the book.

Torrin held it farther down and out of Sonny's reach behind her. She was beginning to get pissed off. If it had been anybody else but Sonny questioning her honesty, that person would have already been on the floor with a bloody nose or worse. Trying another tack, the redhead controlled her temper and said, "Why would you wanna read something like this anyway, squirt?"

"Don't call me that!" Sonny growled. She stopped her futile attempts at regaining the book to glare down at the smaller woman. "I am sick and tired of you acting like I'm a child!"

Jesus! If it ain't one thing, it's another! Torrin rolled her eyes in exasperation. "Alright ... *Sonny*. If you didn't act like a child, I wouldn't treat you like one. *Comprehende*?" She leaned closer, refusing to be daunted by the teenager's size. "I don't know if you're PMSing or what, but back off," she hissed, "before I really get mad."

Sonny's mind cleared instantly. Everything in the room intensified. She could make out golden flecks in the woman's angry eyes, could smell the red-gold hair. Overloud sounds of an enthusiastic television audience crashed against her ears, yet she could hear and feel Torrin's breath on her face.

It occurred to Sonny that everything, from the moment she'd first laid eyes on that red and green-haired punk rocker two years ago, boiled down to this moment, this second of time. She was at a crossroads that she knew could either make or break her. A choice had to be made between the unknown and the familiar, to break out of the box she'd created for her life or to stick to the comfort zone. Remembered thoughts and actions and feelings ran through her mind, jealousies and insecurities and half understood desires. It was on a subconscious level so deep that she could barely acknowledge thought in the split second it filled her mind. She only knew that the time was now.

Sonny made her decision.

As if to make another grab for the book, she reached around Torrin who stood her ground, daring the girl to do something. Sonny wrapped her long arms around the redhead, effectively pinning her arms.

Stiffening, the guitarist broke her eye contact only long enough to look down. She tried to twist to one side and looked back up, snarling, "What the *fuck* do you—"

Sonny silenced her, ducking her head and kissing the woman soundly.

Frozen in shock, Torrin could feel the teenager's mouth on hers, tasting her, tongue exploring her open mouth. This wasn't the kiss of a tentative youth. This was a young woman who was determined to get what she wanted come hell or high water.

Despite any tenuous thoughts to the contrary, Torrin responded, fire pumping through her veins. She pressed up against the lanky frame. In response, a low moan hit her ears and raced directly down to her core. Torrin began actively kissing back, tongue investigating an area only dreamed of before.

Sonny loosened her grip as the smaller woman began responding. Soft lips on hers, voracious tongue and teeth, lithe body pressing into her own forced a low moan from her throat. She brought her hands up to bury themselves in soft hair, its silky strands running through her fingers, tickling. Strong arms wrapped around her waist, and she could feel hands roaming and squeezing her back and sides and buttocks.

The guitarist broke off the kiss, hungrily nipping at the tender neck and throat. Hands in her hair convulsed and held her close to her task. Using Sonny to lean on, she stood on tiptoe to suck an earlobe into her mouth, biting down.

"Mmmm, yes," whispered Sonny, her heart pumping furiously. She shivered at the sudden goose bumps. One of the roaming hands on her back snaked around until it was cupping an aching breast. Moaning again, she pushed against the hand that held her. A throbbing heat developed between her thighs at the seductive whisper filling her ear.

"You like that, don't you?" Torrin squeezed the full breast, reveling in its softness. Her answer was a sudden intake of breath. "I thought so." She smiled. A thumb brushed purposefully over the nipple, raising it to a peak that was clearly visible under the bra and heavy sweater that Sonny was wearing. Squeezing again, the redhead gave the nipple a tweak between thumb and forefinger.

"Oh, God, Torrin," Sonny sighed, feeling a little weak in the knees.

The woman slid her hand downward, reaching for the bottom of the sweater. "I've wanted you for a *long* time, sexy." She looked up into hooded blue eyes that reflected a sunny summer sky. A rush of arousal ran through her and she growled. "And now I'm going to take you."

The lips that eagerly assailed hers smothered any response that Sonny would have made. She rode high on the crest of passion, her belly aflutter and wetness between her thighs. Her skin flushed at the warm hand on her bare abdomen slowly sliding upward.

Everything stopped.

Torrin cursed softly as another knock sounded on their door. She stepped out of the embrace with every intention of reaming somebody a new asshole. Cool reason washed over her. *This cannot happen.*

By the time Torrin arrived at the door, she was in control. Sparing a quick glance backward, she could see Sonny seated on the edge of the bed, facing away. Her sweater was back in place, and it appeared she was watching television. Torrin took a steadying breath and opened the door.

Atkins grinned at her. "Hey, girlfriend! I was on my way to the liquor store and thought you might wanna restock." He jingled a set of keys. "I've got the Honda for half an hour. Whaddya say?"

Torrin pursed her lips in thought. She looked once more at the brunette, almost seeing the ears grow longer. Turning back to her band mate, she said, "Yeah. Sounds good. Just lemme hit the can and get my jacket."

"Five minutes?"

The redhead nodded. "Make it ten." A grin she didn't feel graced her face.

"Okey dokey. I'll go warm up the car."

As she closed the door, Torrin sighed deeply, smile fading. She moved over to sit next to the high schooler. "You okay?"

Sonny was staring down into her lap where she fidgeted with the hem of her sweater. The dark head nodded in mute response.

Torrin felt a rush of guilt. *Horny Torry strikes again!* "Look, squ ... ah, *Sonny,*" she began.

"You can call me squirt," Sonny interrupted quietly, peering up from under dark bangs. "I didn't mean what I said about that."

"Okay," Torrin acknowledged. She mentally screamed for silence in her thoughts. "This can't ... I can't *do* this, squirt."

Pale eyes flashed in pain.

Go, Torry! Go, Torry! Let's see if we can twist that knife now! "It's not you, okay? It's me." When there was no response, she reached down and stopped the twitching hands. "I can't ... I can't give you what you need, Sonny."

Despite her pain, the youth peered at the guitarist. Curiosity burned in her eyes as she asked in a soft voice, "What do I need?"

Torrin's hand moved up to caress a cheek, stopping inches away. She dropped her hand onto her own lap, balled into a fist. "You need someone who can love you, treasure you. Somebody who can make every day seem like the best day in the world." She released Sonny's hand and rose to her feet. "Not someone like me."

Sonny watched as the woman strode over to one of the armchairs and scooped up her leather jacket. "Why *not* you?" she questioned.

Cool gray eyes regarded her, distant and aloof. Torrin pulled out a cigarette. Lighting it up, she squinted through the smoke. "I'll hurt you" came the gruff, adamant response.

Hoping the teenager wouldn't see her hands shaking as she returned the lighter to her pocket, Torrin sauntered across the room. The voices were laughing and cackling, making it hard to think. As she closed the door behind her, she thought, *I need to get drunk and I need to get laid. Not necessarily in that order.*

Now alone, Sonny stopped fighting the tears that had been threatening to overcome her since Atkins had been at the door. She reached for a pillow and hugged it as she rocked gently back and forth, quiet sobs drowned out by a commercial.

Eventually, while the pain did not recede, the intensity of it did, a kind of numbness setting in. Fumbling around in her nearby bag for Kleenex, she found a small travel pack. She blew her nose and mopped her face, an occasional hitch in her breath. Standing, she tossed the wadded tissue into the trashcan by the desk before going into the bathroom and running water in the sink.

Sonny splashed cold water onto her face, shocking her warm skin. She looked up into the mirror, her reflection gazing back with red, watery eyes. A bit fascinated, she straightened, droplets of water rolling down her face and throat. In her mind's eye, she compared herself to the women she'd seen with Torrin.

Her general resemblance to all of them was unnerving — tall, shapely, long hair. Sonny turned to one side. *About the standard bust size.* She turned back and leaned on the counter, getting close to the mirror to search her eyes. *Why am I different?*

Shaking her head, eyes no longer saw her mirror image, ears no longer heard the television echoing from the other room. Instead, she saw gray fire flashing, heard a voice say, "I've wanted you for a *long* time, sexy."

A surprising thought popped into her head and she blurted, "She really *cares* about me!" Which brought to mind what little she'd learned about Torrin's past — loving, no; abusive, most certainly. Losing her virginity to her father at so young an age she couldn't remember. When asked about her mother, Torrin merely said she left them when she was little. Everyone Torrin had cared about in her childhood had either abandoned or hurt her. "She's scared ..."

Sonny was an astute young woman. Raised under her brother's

tutelage, she'd become a bit more knowledgeable of the world and the way it worked than most of her peers. Her father had always taught her that she had a choice in all things. For the most part, she had always opted for being happy.

Now was no different. Her road to happiness was a small, redheaded metal music prodigy who was hell on wheels. When Sonny made up her mind to get something, she succeeded. This would be no exception.

I'll show her what love can really *be like.*

Sonny's Journal – February 3, 2001

Last night was ... It was the best night of my life. And the worst.

I finally kissed her. Oh, man, it was so much better than kissing a guy! I could never understand what the other girls got all worked up about. Wow! I think I've figured it out! (I'm getting all tingly just thinking about it!)

It's so hard to describe – it was soft and rough at the same time. Hot and wet. All those silly clichés in the Penthouse *letters are true! She squeezed my breast and I about fell over, my knees got so weak. It's definitely* not *mutual masturbation! Wowza!*

And then Lando showed up, and Torrin did a fast back pedal. She tried to act all cool and shit about it. She said that she'd hurt me and that I needed someone else to take care of me and treat me right. But she doesn't realize that she's *the one to treat me right.* I know *she won't hurt me – I've known it from that first night at the bus stop. I've just got to get it through to her that she's the* One *(with a capital O, damn it!)*

I'm backstage at some rock club in a little California town. Lando and Torrin aren't jumping around as much as usual – they're both feeling pretty crappy. They left the hotel last night and went to a country/western bar, of all places, to pick up chicks. There was a big fight outside with a couple of the local yokels. Lando ended up with stitches near his eye and his knuckles split. Torrin has a shiner that's so bad she still can't see out of it. They're just lucky that the guys they got in the fight with were troublemakers – otherwise they'd *be in jail and* we'd *be losing money on this contract!*

I think she did it because of what happened. Maybe she was punishing herself for losing control with me, I don't know. Maybe she just had all that pent up sexual energy and needed to release it. I guess a fight would do that.

I don't know how I'm going to do it, but I will. I will *get Torrin to love me if it's the last thing I do. That's a promise.*

Warlord Metal

When you hear my footsteps,
I'm just behind you.
When you think you're alone
do you feel my shadow?
TORRIN C. SMITH, "WATCHING YOU"

Part IV: Eighteenth

An innocent victim;
fear of the hunger -
Will is the master,
blood is the slave.
TORRIN C. SMITH, "SCREAMS"

Sonny stood over the tray of chemicals in the low red lighting. She slid in a piece of paper, using the tongs to fully submerge it, watching a black and white image develop. This one was a picture of the band from backstage. At the time of the shot, Atkins had just leapt into the air, so it was blurred in one corner. Sighing, she removed the photo and ran it through the rinse tray before hanging it behind her to dry. Ten other students were doing the same, developing their first rolls of film. The instructor wandered among them, answering any questions.

So far, there had been little that was usable on her film. *Well, you're only on the seventh exposure,* she chided herself, preparing the eighth. *And this* is *your first roll.* As she continued with her work, she mused over the past four months.

The tour had finished in March. After a self-congratulatory stop at Disneyland, the band had returned home to Portland. By the end of April, they had burned their first compact disc and were now selling copies for ten dollars apiece at the various venues they played.

In May, Sonny had graduated high school with flying colors. Despite several lucrative offers at various institutes, she chose to remain at home, accepting a four-year scholarship at Portland State. She had lasted through two weeks of scholastic freedom before she couldn't stand it anymore. Within a few days, she was working part time at a local shipping delivery company and attending this summer course in photography. Sonny had used part of her scholarship to purchase the camera and accessories needed, putting the remainder in her savings account for the fall semester.

Her goals had changed a bit. No longer interested in becoming a news journalist, Sonny had made up her mind to follow a more unconventional path. She was determined to become Warlord's first publicist – doing photography and articles of the band as they gained in popularity. Granted, there wasn't much call for it now, but the budding photographer was sure the band would hit the big time soon, which was why she had chosen this class. Candid shots of Warlord would eventually fetch a pretty penny. Especially when they became successful and people were clamoring for information from before they had "made it."

The next photo began to develop. Sonny blinked at it. "Oh, yeah. *That* turned out really well." It was a close-up, three-quarter facial of Torrin as she sat in the armchair at the warehouse. The neck of her guitar moved out of focus to her right, a dreamy expression on her face as she worked on a song. With a grin, Sonny remembered the irritated glare that had followed the flashbulb.

"That *did* turn out well," the instructor said, peering into the tray as he passed. "Definitely a keeper."

"Thanks." She grinned, transferring the photo to the rinse tray as the instructor continued on his way. "*Definitely* a keeper."

One thing that had not changed was Sonny's intentions toward the guitarist. The young woman had conducted many comparisons between herself and the standard "Torrin Sexpot" over the last few months. While there were quite a few physical similarities, that seemed to be all Sonny could locate. She'd cornered the few she could get her hands on for impromptu interviews. For the most part, they were all pleasant women with no higher education who adored the Warlord. *Two outta three ain't bad.*

A major point of difference was style. The women usually all wore skimpy outfits and tons of makeup. Sonny wasn't quite willing to concede to that degree. She had taken to wearing light makeup, and her wardrobe had evolved as well. Gone were the typical baggy pants and shirts her peers were comfortable in. Sonny now wore tight fitting jeans and shirts that showed off her attributes. The first time she'd worn a short skirt, Hampton's jaw had sagged open and Lando had run into a wall.

Sonny snickered at the remembered sight, hanging the ninth exposure to dry. The band, in all its glory, had posed for her like a pinup poster in the teen magazines. They were full of attitude and glaring at the camera, dressed in leather and jeans.

As her appearance became more seductive, she'd received

quite a few comments, some of them unpleasant. The only thing that kept her going was the occasional look she would receive from Torrin, a look of hooded desire. At first, when the redhead was caught staring, Torrin would put on a sultry smirk and Sonny would blush, dropping her gaze. As the brunette became more comfortable with her new image, however, she was able to match Torrin stare for stare. In fact, it was the guitarist who had blushed and looked away the last time.

Sonny had also begun teasing Torrin at every opportunity. Whereas previously there had been the simple adolescent flirting, now she blatantly led Torrin on. She had taken to not wearing a bra. If there was plenty of room in a doorway to pass, she'd brush her breasts against the smaller woman. Whenever she needed something in the kitchen, it was always in the cupboard that Torrin was standing at, and she would press against her to reach for the item. It was driving the guitarist crazy.

Continuing to work on her photographs, Sonny dreamt of an older woman, dreamt of new schemes to further her plans and of a future happy time of love and warmth.

The radio played softly in her room, the only sound other than the faint scratching of pen on paper. Sonny was propped against her headboard, a composition notebook in hand. A few times she paused, blue eyes searching for distant thoughts. On the bed beside her were a handful of black and white photos spilling out of a manila folder. One was missing from the pile, having replaced the bedside photo of her parents. The face of the Warlord guitarist stared just off camera as she composed.

Tuned so fiercely into her thoughts, Sonny didn't catch what the radio disc jockey was saying. The word "Warlord" snagged her attention, and she glanced sharply at the stereo on her dresser.

"... So that's this week's Band Brawl, folks. We'll have that one up in just a couple of minutes. Remember, all this week we'll be doing local bands for a change. Let's just see if Warlord's any good."

A commercial started and Sonny was off the bed and out the door like a shot. Running down the stairs, she burst into the living room where she found her brother with Hampton and Foley. "Turn on the stereo!" she ordered, doing just that. A local auto commercial blared into the room.

"What the hell, Sonny?" Middlestead complained loudly with a wince. "Turn the damned thing down!"

"No!" Sonny whirled around with a big smile on her face. "Warlord's gonna be on Band Brawl!" While that got a round of appreciative comments, Sonny frowned. "Is Torrin home?"

"Um, I think —" Before the dark man could finish, his sister flew out of the room and out the back patio door. He rose to his feet and yelled after her, "I think she's got *company*, Sonny!"

"Tough!" floated back on the summer evening air.

Middlestead shook his head, rolling his eyes. He went over to the stereo and turned down the volume.

At the bottom of the stairs leading to Torrin's room over the garage, Sonny paused. For a quick second, she took stock of her appearance, adjusting her blouse before trotting up the wooden steps. She paused at the top and took a steadying breath before knocking.

Torrin threw the door open with obvious irritation. She was wearing nothing but a button up denim shirt, the two buttons at her belly the only ones fastened. Upon seeing her visitor, her manner changed. In self-defense to the outrageous flirting, Torrin responded in kind. She leaned casually against the door, one hand running lazily through her hair. "Yeah ...?" she drawled.

Sonny forced herself to not tremble. *What would Torrin do?* she asked herself. Skin tinting a little, she kept her cool and allowed her eyes to wander slowly down the half clad frame. A slight smile on her face indicated she liked what she saw. She had to fight hard to keep from giggling nervously as their eyes met. "Warlord's playing on KMMP."

It took a moment for the words to register. Torrin blinked at her, dropping her seductive pose. "*What?*" she demanded in astonishment.

Sonny's smile grew wider. "Band Brawl."

Abandoning the door, Torrin dashed across her room. She crawled across the bed, nearly trampling the woman in it, and turned on the clock radio.

As strains of "Shadow Voices" began playing, Sonny entered the room and shut the door behind her. She swallowed the sharp stab of pain at the sight of the woman in Torrin's bed — *my place* —

clutching a sheet to her chest. Steeling herself, she sauntered across the room and sat on the corner of the bed. *I belong here, she does not* ran through her head in a litany.

"Holy crap!" Torrin exclaimed. "It *is*!" She looked at her friend, an amazed grin on her face. With little forethought, the guitarist leapt to her feet with a whoop, grabbed Sonny by the hands and pulled her into an exuberant dance.

At some point, the dance became a hug of joy. Sonny felt the full contact, the lithe body wrapped around hers. She swallowed convulsively at the almost overpowering surge of arousal. Despite her control, she couldn't help but let out a little sigh and nuzzled the red-gold hair.

"Hey!" the woman on the bed exclaimed. "That's one of my favorites!"

Two tempers flared – one angry at the disruption by the interloper, the other irritated over her loss of self-control. Torrin stepped out of the embrace, a physical change once again coming over her as she reverted to the seductive game. She turned away from Sonny, moving back toward the bed. "Thanks," she said, planting a rough kiss on the upturned lips.

Sonny resolutely refused to give the Warlord satisfaction. She buried the rending pain deep inside and smiled at Torrin. "I'm going to go vote for it." She swayed towards the door, pausing to see two sets of eyes watching her. "Are you?" she asked.

Torrin's desire to push the dark woman to the limit battled with the childlike happiness that bubbled up within. Finally, "Yeah. We'll be down in a minute."

There was a slow nod and then Sonny left. She closed the door softly behind her and stopped, leaning against it heavily. Getting her trembles under control, she thought, *God, this is hard.* She inhaled deeply and stood away from the door. *But then, nothing worth having is easy.*

An impromptu party popped up that evening. Someone had called Atkins, who had wandered over with a girl on his arm. A couple of their more hardcore fans arrived with a few cases of beer, and Torrin had come downstairs, her bedmate following her around like a long lost puppy. Everyone had called the radio station to vote for the band. Every once in awhile, the radio DJ would put on a couple of the phone conversations of people voting for or against. All in all, the verdict had been "Winner."

Torrin lounged on the loveseat in the living room, her date on the floor between her legs. The redhead idly stroked the long brown hair that splayed across her knees, occasionally reaching forward to rub the nape of the neck. The woman would shiver and toss a smile backwards. The guitarist was on her fifth bottle of beer and still hadn't attained a decent buzz. *Damn tolerance levels are getting way too high.* She emptied the bottle and set it with the others on the table beside her.

As was her wont these days, gray eyes kept a loose tab on her band mate's sister. The way she looked, the way she smelled, the way she moved. Everything about her was becoming more and more intoxicating as time went by. *It would be so easy.*

She shook herself, annoyed. "Hey." Torrin leaned forward to brush her bedmate's ear with a kiss. "Wanna get me another beer?"

The woman on the floor grinned up at her. "Sure." She rose, stopping long enough to thoroughly kiss the guitarist before wandering off toward the kitchen.

Torrin watched her go, imagining Sonny in her place. Again, she shook off the thought. *It can't happen,* she grumbled to herself. *Sonny deserves a hell of a lot better than you.* She contemplated a future where she allowed herself free reign. Quickly moving past the sexual fantasies – *Like I need to see that* – she could see Sonny curled up into a small ball, hear the sobs, her own voice telling the teenager that she was just a fuck and nothing more. *Can't get too close. Can't let anybody get too close. I don't wanna hurt her.*

A beer bottle pushed into her hands interrupted her thoughts. The guitarist looked up into the other woman's eyes, this stranger that she was sleeping with. With callous disregard she thought, *You I can hurt. What you want doesn't mean fuck to me.* She smiled with a wild hunger. "C'mere," she husked, pulling the woman down to sit in her lap.

From nearby, Sonny heard the woman's giggle as the two roughhoused on the loveseat. A tickle fest stopped short as a coarse kiss was shared between them, and she slid her eyes away from the scene. She took a swig of her beer and tried to focus on the conversation she was having with Foley and Hampton. Their voices seemed to drone on and her ears could only hear the murmurings from Torrin and her date.

"Hey, you okay?" Foley asked, her blue eyes concerned.

"What?" Sonny returned her attention to the bassist and his girlfriend. "Oh! No, I'm fine, really." She held up her bottle. "Must be the beer. I don't drink that often."

Foley nodded, unconvinced. She shared a knowing look with Hampton and tucked her sandy blonde hair behind one ear. With a soft smile, she said, "Well, let me know if you need anyone to talk to, okay?"

The young woman blinked at her for a moment. A flash of pain, of embarrassment crossed her eyes. *She knows!* Swallowing the lump in her throat, she nodded and glanced down. "Okay. Thanks." She took a quick swig of her beer. As the conversation once again resumed, her mind wandered to a time that she would have with Torrin in the future.

Sonny's Journal - July 11, 2001

Well, I've survived another night. Tonight was pretty rough – more than what I'm used to. I actually barged into her room and acted like I owned the place. Not too difficult until it's taken into consideration that there was another woman in her bed.

God, it hurt.

On the up side, I have to admit that she's cut her carousing down a lot from before the tour. In the past four months, I think there've only been a handful of women. Torrin kinda rotates through them, not spending a whole lotta time on any one. Maybe she's finally starting to settle down. I don't know exactly how old she is. She must be about twenty-one by now. (She still doesn't look much older than me.)

I don't even know when her birthday is.

Another good thing ... This cutback has got to be healthier for her. She has less chance of catching some horrid disease or something.

Now, if I can just get her to come to me.

I think she considers it sometimes. I've caught her watching me before, kinda distant, in her thoughts. I don't know what she sees in her visions, but I don't think it's good. She becomes a bit more standoffish, a bit more of that false ego and seductress comes through. For the life of me, though, I can't figure out anything about me that would cause a negative reaction. Well, aside from the fact that I'm a virgin and don't know quite what to do in bed.

I need her. Maybe more than she needs me.

I don't know why I'm continuing with this. I know that there are other women out there, that if I really wanted to explore this aspect of myself, I only have to step out the door. Hell, Gay Pride is this month! It would be nothing to attend the parade and wander through the park afterwards. I'm sure I can meet lots of women who would be interested. I have considered it, but one thing keeps stopping me.

They're not Torrin.

Torrin stared out the office window, listening to the drone of her band mates. Warlord was currently meeting with people from an independent label to negotiate a recording contract. The band's popularity had risen over the last year, and their lawyer, Hampton's sister, had been approached for a deal.

The redhead wasn't really paying attention to the proceedings, however. Even without the downers currently raging through her system, the talks would have been nonsense to her. *It's all legal mumbo jumbo anyway.* Her thoughts meandered as she stared at traffic passing by on the highway outside.

She wished she were back at the warehouse now, guitar in hand. Music always flowed, fast and clean, when she was high. She'd been known to compose until her fingers bled upon occasion. When she was under the influence, whatever muses were roller-skating around in her head would go ballistic. All the guitarist could do in response was try to get it all down and hang on for the ride.

Her fingers twitched feeling an imaginary guitar neck, smooth, polished wood and cool frets moving against her skin. She could almost see the music forming in the air in front of her. It wasn't that she was hallucinating, but that the intensity of the muse was so strong at times like these, she could nearly taste the music. It was almost as good as sex.

Only almost.

"Whaddya think, Torrin?" Middlestead asked. The company men and their lawyer had left the conference room, leaving the band and their own lawyer to discuss their opinions.

Gray eyes regarded the drummer for long moments. "I think," Torrin said, enunciating carefully, "I need to go to the bathroom." Rising to her feet felt like moving in a sea of molasses, a warm sticky sensation. She cocked an eyebrow at their lawyer. "Know where the john is?"

After getting directions, Torrin left the stifling office. Veering left instead of right, she was out on the sidewalk within minutes. Across the street was the beginning of Waterfront Park. With extreme concentration, she crossed busy Naito Parkway. Sitting on the first park bench she came to, Torrin sighed in relief, a warm breeze whiffling her bangs. "*Much* better," she said. If she couldn't make any music, at least she could drift along with the tunes in her head without further interruption.

It beats thinkin'. It beats feelin'.

"Thanks for picking me up at work, Lisa," Sonny said over her shoulder as she stepped into the house. Flipping through the mail, she stepped farther into the living room and dropped her keys on the end table. Her backpack found the floor nearby.

Behind her, Foley stepped in. "No problem, girlfriend. I've got nothing better to do." The blonde woman shut the door before moving into the room and plopping down in an armchair. "Besides, I don't wanna worry alone."

Sonny answered the smile with one of her own and snorted. She dropped the mail next to her keys. "You want anything?" she asked as she headed into the kitchen.

"Yeah, something cool if ya got it," Foley called.

"Iced tea?"

"Sounds great!" She leaned her head back against the chair. "This heat wouldn't be so bad if it wasn't for the humidity. I'm glad you guys have air conditioning."

"So am I," Sonny agreed adamantly. She came back into the living room and handed Foley a tall glass of tea. "Eighty-four degrees feels like a hundred and ten in *this* city."

"Thank you," the blonde said, taking the glass.

Sonny settled down on the couch. The two sat in companionable silence as they cooled off from the dog days of a late August afternoon. Finally, the dark youth broke the silence. "So, you have any clue what their chances are?"

Foley set her glass on a coaster on the table. "Actually, Max says it's pretty good. Tamara looked it over, and it appears to be a standard recording contract."

"But everything's on the up and up?" the brunette pressed, a bit anxious.

"Yeah. Everything's cool."

Pale eyes were distant. "I hope so. They've all worked so hard for something like this."

The women sat in silence once more as they ran through memories of the band's labors over the years.

Foley's thoughts returned to the present. She chewed her lower lip, her face becoming somber and her brows knitting. She glanced over at the oblivious Sonny, working out the pros and cons of voicing her thoughts and questions. Finally, she leaned forward and put her elbows on her knees, peering intently at the dark girl. "You realize, of course, that if they sign this contract today there'll be another party?"

Sonny blinked at her. *Oh, God. Not another one!* A lump formed in her throat, and she swallowed thickly.

Foley watched with pursed lips as shoulders visibly slumped. *Now is the time.* With a determined air, she rose and sat on the couch next to her young friend. She draped an arm over the suddenly stiff shoulders. "Does she even have a clue how much you love her?"

The words were a catalyst to Sonny. Months of pain and jealousy and fear surfaced in the light of another who knew how she felt about the guitarist. Unable to hold back any longer, she broke into ragged sobs as the tears began to flow. Soon she was cradled in caring arms and rocked back and forth as she released her agonies, a hand gently caressing her head.

Rather than ease her sobs, the closeness intensified them. The physical sensation of being comforted harkened back to before Sonny's parents had died. Foley, realizing she was in for the long haul, slowly leaned back, putting her feet on the edge of the coffee table and pulling Sonny with her. The women sat this way for nearly a half hour.

At first, the strength of her weeping scared Sonny. It felt like she just wouldn't be able to stop. She would keep crying and crying until there was nothing left but a dried up shell. It was very disconcerting. As her tears flowed, however, the tension of being alone with her burdens eased, and the pain began to recede. As the tears began to subside, real life began to intrude. Embarrassed at the emotional display, she reluctantly pulled away from the blonde woman and sat up, sniffling.

"Better?" Foley asked, not relinquishing her touch completely.

Her fingers were straightening the long ebony hair down the teenager's back.

Sonny shivered at the sensation, wishing it was Torrin's hands, Torrin's fingers. "Yeah," she said with a slight hitch in her breathing. She rose from the couch. "I'll ... be right back," the teenager offered, blushing. "Gonna go clean up a bit."

The older woman nodded in commiseration and watched her disappear into the bathroom. She sighed and returned to her previous seat as she heard a nose being blown and water running in the sink. "You never did answer my question," she called.

Turning the water off, Sonny glanced at her reflection in the mirror. Her eyes looked an even paler blue when they were bloodshot. She grabbed the hand towel and patted her face dry. "I don't know," she finally answered, stepping back out into the living room with a box of Kleenex. "Sometimes I think so. Sometimes not." She settled back onto the couch and blew her nose again.

Foley digested this. "Okay. What makes you think she does?"

The dark woman shrugged, staring down at her hands as they shredded a tissue. "Well. I kissed her last winter." There was absolute silence, and Sonny risked a glance at her friend.

Foley's eyebrows mingled with her hairline and her mouth was wide open. Blue eyes stared blankly at her.

Despite herself, Sonny chuckled even as she blushed. "Close your mouth. You'll catch a fly or something."

Foley's mouth worked silently for a few more seconds, looking much like a fish out of water before she finally gained her voice. "*Who* kissed *who*?" she asked softly.

"I kissed Torrin." Sonny's smile faded. "She didn't make the first move. *I* did."

Still amazed, the woman leaned forward. "Well? What happened?"

"*Nothing* happened," Sonny snapped. "*Lando* happened. I dunno." She sighed and glared back down at her hands. "He showed up at the door and kinda interrupted ... things." Her eyes cast back through the memories from the tour. "That was the night they got into that bar fight and Torrin ended up with a black eye. Remember?"

Foley nodded. "So *that's* why she got into a fight. Lando said she was pushing for one with that cowboy."

Thoughts confirmed, Sonny nodded. "I thought that's what it was, too, but I couldn't be sure."

"And you haven't talked to her about how you feel?"

Mutely, Sonny shook her head. "She told me that I needed someone who would take care of me and treat me right. That she'd only hurt me."

"When? The night you kissed her?"

"Yeah."

Foley studied the young woman before her, frowning in thought. It was obvious that despite the rejection, she had continued on a path to gain Torrin. *And it's eating her up inside.* Now all the months of outrageous flirting became clear to the blonde. Her respect for the guitarist went up a notch. *Jesus, it musta been driving her batty to have a beautiful babe throwing herself at her.* "Have you considered letting it go? Just walking away?"

"No!" was the adamant response. "I've known from the first time I heard her play that we were somehow connected." Sonny rose and began to pace in agitation. "*I* know that she won't hurt me. But *she* doesn't." She stopped, gazing wistfully out the window. "I don't know why, but I can't walk away. I *love* her, Lisa. There's no one else for me."

"Maybe you should make another move."

Sonny stopped to grimace at Foley. She gestured at her clothing – tight black jeans and a stretchy knit tank top that left little to the imagination. "You think I *haven't*? It's a constant thing when we're in the same room together, Lisa! You *know* that!"

Conceding the point with rolled eyes and a nod, the blonde considered the options. *Flirting hasn't done it. Besides, Torrin's got women around her as thick as stink on shit.* Her eyes narrowed. "So, the only thing that stopped you two before was Lando's interruption?" At Sonny's nod, she asked, "And Torrin responded to your kiss?"

Unbidden, the memory popped into Sonny's head, and she blushed at the intensity of the arousing rush that suddenly pulsed through her. "Uh ... yeah. I'd say she responded. If it hadn't been for Lando ... Well, let's just say we'd have ... um ... done it." She blushed furiously and chewed her lip, but Foley didn't notice.

The blonde picked up her iced tea and sipped it thoughtfully. *With the proper planning and backup...* Her eyes met pale blue, and a slow smile crept onto her face.

Sonny's Journal – August 27, 2001

Warlord now has its first official recording contract! I'm happy for the band – they've all worked so damned hard to get something like this! Of course, it's just a small independent label, a local company. But, at least they'll get more coverage and a little publicity! They're gonna go into the studio and get started sometime within the next month.

Needless to say, a party has already begun to develop downstairs. I've come up here to change and get ready for tonight. Hopefully, it'll be a really good one this time!!

Lisa's promised to help me with Torrin! Wow! She knows how I feel for Torrin. I cried for a long time with her. I think I really needed that. I feel so much better now – more alive and hopeful than I've been in a long time. And, if things work out tonight then ...

No. I won't say it. I don't wanna jinx things. Not tonight.

As the last of the drug seeped from her system, Torrin put the final touches on a sixth song.

After Hampton had found her in the park, they had returned to the stuffy office and signed the paperwork. The redhead's only goal was to get to her guitar. She had been oblivious to anything else since she was deposited in a nearly boneless heap on the living room couch. Sonny had gone to her room and acquired the instrument, a pad and a pen. Torrin had been playing ever since, pausing only long enough to jot down the tunes and lyrics.

Nevertheless, the muse was slowing down, and the redhead was coming out of her drugged haze. The last chord faded and she looked around, taking in her surroundings.

She was still seated on the couch, guitar in her lap, pen and pad on the coffee table before her. Middlestead was parked in his favorite armchair, bare feet resting on the same table and a beer in his hand. On the other end of the couch was one of his friends, and they were deep in conversation.

In the dining room, Hampton and his sister were seated at the table. She had changed out of her power suit to jeans and a T-shirt. It looked like they were playing cards, laughing as they joked around. Foley appeared from the kitchen to place a bowl of aromatic popcorn beside them. She ran her hand across the bald man's shoulders and then turned, spotting Torrin. The blonde smiled warmly before moving out of sight back into the kitchen.

A hand played with her hair, and the guitarist swiveled her head to see one of the women she'd been sleeping with lounging on the arm of the couch. She was a platinum blonde, wearing a skimpy spandex skirt and some sort of halter. As the guitarist's attention focused on her, the woman smiled down at her.

"Hey, baby," she cooed. "You ready for a drink yet?"

Torrin studied her for long seconds. *What the hell is* she *doing here? And do I really want her around?* She realized that at this exact moment the answer was a resounding "No!" The redhead also knew, however, that as the night wore on she would change her mind. *Especially with Sonny here ...*

As if in answer to her thoughts, the budding photographer stepped out of the kitchen. She was wearing short shorts that hung low on her hips and a white T-shirt that had been gathered up and knotted to one side, revealing a tanned belly. Smiling warmly, she reached the guitarist and held out a shot glass. "Trade ya," she said, looking down into the woman's lap.

Gray eyes narrowed before glancing down. *The guitar ... She wants the guitar.* Looking back up with comprehension, Torrin suddenly realized she was very, very thirsty. Without a word, she held the instrument out.

Sonny's smile widened as she took the guitar by the neck. She handed the shot glass over, taking the opportunity to brush long fingers against Torrin's knuckles. "I'll be right back," she said with a wink.

Torrin watched her walk away and carefully lean the beat-up guitar in one corner. Her hand still tingled where Sonny had touched her, and she licked her lips at the erotic image that blasted through her mind. *Down, girl!* she growled to herself. She tossed the shot back, the warm burn of whiskey breaking the spell. With a glance to the woman beside her, she reconsidered. *Maybe it* is *a good thing she's here.*

Hearing the sound of glass against glass, the redhead brought her attention back to her hand. A bottle of Johnny Walker Red was tilted, pouring another shot into the glass she held. Even without visually following the arm up to its owner's face, she knew it was the brunette returned. Torrin inhaled deeply of the teenager's perfume and very recognizable scent.

Their eyes met and locked, time seemed to stand still, and the room was absolutely silent. Something seemed to pass between them before the real world intruded once again.

The woman beside the guitarist reached out and ran her fingers through red-gold hair, distracting her. At the same time, Atkins stomped into the dining room from the backyard, loudly demanding to know where the charcoal lighter fluid was kept.

What the fuck was that? Torrin demanded of herself. She swallowed her immediate irritation at the groupie who had distracted her, forcing herself to lean into the caress and smile lopsidedly at Sonny. *Don't make any difference, Torry. Gotta keep the status quo.*

Did she feel that too? Sonny wondered in confusion. She blinked at Torrin for a second before returning to the game. With a sultry smile, she capped the fifth and leaned over, pressing it suggestively between the redhead's thighs. "Lemme know when you're ready for ... more," she said in a low voice.

Torrin watched her straighten and sidle away, all leg and hip. Her center throbbed with instant arousal. *Wowza!* She knocked back her second drink, but it did nothing to quench the real thirst inside.

"Do you think it worked?" Sonny whispered to the blonde woman in the kitchen.

Foley risked a glance around the corner, noting the flushed skin and the sudden swallowing of the drink. "Oh, yeah," she said. "You did great."

Sonny fidgeted nervously. "Now what?"

"Just wait a bit. Let her get some more alcohol into her system," the older woman said, patting her shoulder reassuringly. "You know she's got a high tolerance."

"And when she's done with the bottle...?"

Foley grinned. "Then we begin Plan B."

As the sun went down and the evening cooled, the party ended up in the backyard. The remains of a huge barbecue were scattered across the kitchen counter and dining room table, and the drinking had now begun in earnest. As word had spread, more people had arrived to help celebrate the Warlords' victory.

To keep things safe, Sonny had gathered the notebook and guitar, returning them to Torrin's room over the garage. At every opportunity throughout the evening, she flirted with Torrin. This time, however, things were different. Before, she would act as a woman who *wanted* the guitarist, and now she behaved as if she already *had* her.

Under Foley's expert tutelage, the teenager had stopped her usual blatant seduction attempts. No more brushing breasts, sultry posturing and hooded looks. Instead, Sonny doted on her – delivered a plate of food, refilled her drink, even lit her cigarette once. And *always* touching. A gentle and familiar sensation – stroking a hand across the back of Torrin's neck when leaning over with the plate, taking the liberty of brushing bangs out of the woman's eyes while cracking a joke, reaching out to touch her knee to gain the guitarist's attention.

Which, of course, didn't sit too well with the platinum blonde who was hanging on Torrin. As the night wore on, she became more and more irritated with the young pipsqueak who was invading her territory. The woman's actions became more outrageously sexual in an effort to keep the guitarist's attention diverted.

Finding her bottle empty, Torrin sent the groupie inside to get something more to drink. The blonde happily complied since the kid had disappeared about a half hour prior. *Maybe the brat went nitey winky,* she thought as she negotiated the grassy yard in heels.

Inside, the only lights on were in the kitchen. The stereo was playing in the darkened living room. In the kitchen, Hampton was rinsing dishes into the disposal, and Foley was putting them into the dishwasher.

The bassist looked up and smiled at the woman in the doorway. "She run outta booze?" he asked kindly.

The groupie smiled and nodded, waggling an empty bottle at the couple. "Yep. Wouldn't happen to have another one of these around here?" She looked about the kitchen.

"As a matter of fact, we do," Foley said with a grin. She wiped her hands on a towel and moved across the kitchen to the refrigerator. While she delved into the cabinet above, she asked over her shoulder, "How's she feeling tonight? No soreness?"

"Soreness?" the woman asked with a confused grin.

"Well, you know how it is," Foley said. "Ah, here we go!" She pulled another fifth of Johnny Walker from the cabinet and turned around. "It was worse last week when the symptoms first came up." She shrugged. The woman handed the bottle over to the groupie.

"Symptoms?" the woman asked, her grin fading.

Blue eyes rolled. "Oh, yeah. It was so bad, she couldn't even pee without having to fill the tub with water to dilute it." A thought seemed to cross Foley's mind, and she peered at the platinum blonde before her. "You *have* gone to the clinic, haven't you? I mean, everybody she's been to bed with should."

"Wha...," the woman croaked. She cleared her throat, setting the bottle down on the counter. "What are you talking about?"

Hampton turned around to blink at her. "The herpes, what else?"

There was a long silence as the groupie took in this new information.

"That little shit didn't tell you, did she?" Foley demanded, hands on her hips. As the blonde shook her head no, she exploded, "Damn it! She is *so* irresponsible! Max! Can't we *do* something about this?"

The bald man grimaced and shook his head. "All we can do is let people know, Lisa."

The woman wobbled a bit, the conversation swirling around her as the couple came up with platitudes to ease the shock.

"It's alright, honey," Foley said. "I've heard it's pretty difficult to get it ... you know ... woman to woman."

"But isn't that how Torrin got it?" Hampton asked in confusion.

The pair watched as the woman excused herself, sharing a grin between them as she disappeared into the living room. A few seconds later, the front door closed, and a car could be heard starting up outside. As it faded away into the distance, laughter filled the kitchen.

Torrin reached for her missing bottle three times before she became annoyed. *What the hell's taking her so long? She drive to fucking Texas or something?* The redhead had a good buzz going and wanted to maintain it for the festivities later in the night. With a grumble, she rose to her feet and headed into the house. Even a beer would keep her level of intoxication up enough before the whiskey arrived.

Her boots scraped against the concrete patio, and she slid the screen door open and stepped inside. The only light was the one directly over the kitchen sink. The dishwasher was humming diligently away and the counters and table appeared freshly wiped down. On the end of the counter was the empty Johnny Walker bottle.

Torrin approached it with a frown. She picked up the full fifth of whiskey standing right beside the empty. She cast around with her senses, but the feeling of being alone in the house was overwhelming. *Maybe she went to the bathroom?*

Taking the bottle with her, she stepped into the dark living room. The streetlight out front gave enough illumination to see the bathroom door yawning open and empty. "Well, shit ..." A quick glance outside yielded no solid answers either, as Torrin wasn't too sure which vehicle the woman had been driving. *So many women, so many cars,* a wry voice quipped.

Returning to the dark patio, Torrin straddled the end of a bench and lit up a cigarette, watching the festivities in the yard.

At some point in the past, a fifty-five gallon drum had been converted to a fire pit. This was where most of the partiers were in attendance. There were still about fifteen people around it, illuminated by the flames as they laughed and drank, bullshitting one another, telling tall tales and playing "Remember When?" They were seated on old wooden benches and cracked plastic chairs. A boom box had been brought out, and it was playing Anthrax's latest CD.

Well, it looks like my *night is shot all to hell.* Torrin cracked the seal on the whiskey and took a long swallow. *You can always fuck your hand, Horny Torry,* one of the voices responded, and she grimaced.

Torrin set the fifth on the ground beside her and lay back on the bench, watching the smoke from her cigarette meander upward until it disappeared in the darkness. Music and laughter drifted across the night air from her left. Another sound intruded on her rare moment of peace. Frowning, Torrin turned her head to look to her right.

In the darkness, Atkins and his date had slunk away from the group and the fire. She was pinned against the wall near the corner of the house, firm legs wrapped around his waist. The tall man was hungrily devouring her neck, a large hand kneading her bared breast. The noises that had gotten Torrin's attention were the soft moans the woman made as Atkins thrust into her.

"Oh, God," the redhead groaned, looking away. "Why me?" As if she wasn't hot and bothered enough, the aural delights from nearby were putting her over the edge. Her free hand slid under her T-shirt, moving upward with tantalizing slowness. A sigh escaped her lips as she caressed her breast, imagining another's fingers, another's moans floating in the night air. She teased her nipple to erection, a stab of fire pulsing through her as the woman nearby groaned louder in unison.

A fresh round of laughter from the yard drew Torrin's attention. It looked like the party was breaking up. People were standing, collecting debris and personal items, talking overloud as they prepared to make their way back into the house. Grumbling, Torrin removed her hand and sat up, taking a long drag off her cigarette. Gray eyes scanned the group of people, not finding anything or anyone of interest. *Wonder where Sonny went?* she thought idly, her gaze traveling up to the younger woman's bedroom window. The lights were out. *Probably went to bed.*

The thought of Sonny naked in her bed fueled the ache between her legs. Taking a final pull off the cigarette, she tossed it into the butt can nearby, shaking her head ruefully. *Time to go jack off and get drunk,* Torrin thought as she rose to her feet. She stopped only long enough to scoop up her bottle before strolling toward the stairs that would lead her to an empty room. *An empty life.*

Torrin paused at the top of the stairs long enough to take another deep draught from her bottle. Opening the door, she got two steps into the room before she froze at the sight before her.

Covering the top of the beat-up dresser she owned, candles of various shapes and sizes illuminated the room. Her gray eyes were drawn to the mattress on the floor. The perfunctory sheets and thin blanket had been straightened out. A few candles had also been placed on the milk crate that served as her nightstand. Windows were open just enough to allow a bit of a breeze to cause the flames to flutter. The scent of roses and soap filled the air. *Soap?*

A warm body pressed against her back, and hands reached up to cover her eyes. Despite her startlement, Torrin refused to jump at the touch. The odor of soap intensified. *Aha! She took a shower and then waited here for me!* Pleased that she wouldn't be resorting to Rosy Palm for relief, Torrin leaned into the woman. "I thought you'd gone," she murmured.

One hand was removed from her eyes, the other sliding over to compensate. "Shhhh," was whispered into her ear before warm lips caressed it. A piece of cloth was placed over her eyes, covering them as the woman tied it off at the back of her head.

Torrin frowned and considered whether or not to allow the blindfold to remain. Several reasons to remove it were screamed from her depths – first and foremost being the issue of control. Still ... It would be a hell of a lot easier to imagine a certain ebony-haired teenager in this woman's place without the glaringly visual evidence to the contrary.

As she debated with herself, the woman behind her continued. The bottle was pried from her fingers; warm hands reached beneath the T-shirt and began a slow massage of lower back muscles. As the hands inched upwards, the shirt was brought with it, laying bare more and more of Torrin's back.

Ah, fuck it, the guitarist thought with a sigh. Leaning back, Torrin could feel erect nipples rubbing her shoulder blades. A sudden rush of arousal followed the imagined sight of Sonny being behind her. "Mmmm ..." she purred. "That feels nice, baby."

The T-shirt was pulled over her head and discarded. The woman readjusted the blindfold and then resumed contact with the smaller woman's skin, massaging her neck, gently moving the red-gold hair to one side. Lips caressed the juncture between shoulder and neck, teeth occasionally nibbling a wet path.

Torrin was aching from the agonizing slowness. As the woman snaked hands around the taut abdomen, she forced herself to wait a little longer before taking control of the situation. One hand reached up and caressed the same breast the redhead had played with moments before on the patio. A nipple was rolled between thumb and forefinger.

Simultaneously, another flash of fantasy caused Torrin to moan thickly – she and Sonny on the side of the house in the same position as Atkins and his date. The image was so strong the guitarist could almost feel the teenager writhing against her as she slowly thrust into her. "Oh, God," she groaned, swallowing with a suddenly dry mouth.

Both hands dropped to the heavy belt buckle, prying the thick leather loose from its fastenings. Soon, the shorts were opened and fingers played amid reddish curls. The woman made a sound as those fingers dipped into wetness – a deep, throaty moan that was echoed by Torrin as the smaller woman rocked against the hand, her shorts puddling at her feet.

Torrin was still standing in the exact spot where her vision had been hampered. The room lay before her, a photographic image against her eyelids in a final flash of candlelight. *I might be blindfolded, but I ain't blind.* With strong hands, she grasped the woman's wrists, removing them from play.

Sonny froze. *Shit! Busted!* Her heart rate, already pounding in her ears, seemed to triple.

It had been risky, this plan of Foley's. She licked her full lips. *But it was worth it.* Very *worth it.* It had all hinged on whether or not the guitarist would accept the blindfold. When she had, Sonny's heart soared before becoming lost in the sensations of soft hair and skin, finally able to hold and taste what she'd desired for so long.

She wondered what she'd done to tip her hand. Not wanting to be discovered by her distinctive voice, she hadn't spoken a word. Foley had suggested a shower to remove all perfumes that could identify her.

The redhead's baggy shorts slipped over burgundy combat boots as she stepped out of them, releasing the woman's hands. In four confident strides, Torrin was at the foot of her mattress. She turned and sat down, working blindly on the laces of her footwear. *I wonder why she's still standing over there,* she mused in puzzlement. *It's not like her to hold back.*

Sonny's heartbeat eased a bit. *Not caught! Whew!* She watched as the smaller woman finished removing her boots before scooting farther onto the bed and lounging back on one elbow. *But, can she see me?* she wondered, having noted the sureness of the woman's steps.

"Playing hard to get?" Torrin asked with a sultry smile. Her free hand traveled up and down her abdomen in slow motion.

Mesmerized, Sonny approached and knelt on the mattress.

Feeling movement on the bed the guitarist reached out and slipped her hand up a smooth thigh. She grinned at the sigh she heard. "C'mere," she whispered, reaching out.

With Torrin guiding her, heedless of the blindfold, Sonny found herself straddling the redhead's hips. Callused fingers moved up her sides, over her shoulders and behind her head, pulling her down for a kiss.

Their lips met, a frenzied melding of tongues and teeth. Sonny's elbows were on either side of the guitarist's head, supporting her weight. The unusual sensation of naked breasts against her own sparked a liquid fire within. Torrin's hands were wrapped tightly in ebony hair as she continued her assault on the brunette's mouth, tongues engaged in passionate battle.

Breathlessly, Torrin broke off the kiss, roughly pulling the woman's head to one side and baring the tender throat. She attacked it with a vengeance, reveling in the deep moan she heard. With little effort, she could imagine Sonny's throat creating the sound, and her body responded with a flash of hunger as she bit down on the pulse point.

Sonny was unable to keep still during this new attack on her senses. Unconsciously, she rocked her hips, wetly marking the smaller woman's pubis, curls glistening damply in the candlelight. She transferred her weight to one side, reaching for a breast. As she massaged the flesh, she heard another growl and felt Torrin push her hips upward against her center.

The guitarist worked her way down the long neck so trustingly offered with lustful abandon. She pulled the woman's head farther above her own until her tongue was able to trace around a puckered nipple. As the woman above her quivered, a salacious smile crossed Torrin's face before she drew the nipple into her mouth and suckled.

"Oh," Sonny sighed. She felt teeth pinching the erect nub while her neglected breast ached with desire. The throbbing between her legs intensified, and she ground down against the woman beneath her, panting.

They moved together, finding a mutual rhythm. As they strained against one another, Torrin released her grip on the teenager's hair. Both hands traveled down to knead full breasts, and she licked a fiery trail toward the second nipple, receiving another moaning sigh for her efforts. *God, she's responsive tonight!* she marveled. *She must be really turned on!*

The guitarist's talented fingers scratched a trail along sensitive sides and there was a gasp, the woman shuddering. Redoubling her efforts, she increased the friction between them. Torrin gripped the woman's undulating hips, visualizing Sonny above her, riding her. *Maybe this blindfold thing ain't so bad after all ...*

Sonny's lower lip hurt from biting down, trying to overcome the urge to speak, to plead, to scream Torrin's name. Sweat glistened on her body in the warm glow of candlelight, and she could see the same was true for the woman beneath her. Torrin's talented hands strayed farther down, squeezing and kneading a pliant rear before slipping around front. As fingers other than her own stroked her center for the first time, Sonny almost growled in frustration at her inability to speak.

Not deprived of her voice, Torrin husked through teeth clenched on a distended nipple, "You are so wet tonight, baby." With expert fingers, she located a spot that seemed to drive the woman above her to further distraction. She gently rubbed the sensuous flesh between the hard distended clitoris and the woman's vagina. *Score!* she cackled to herself. *Now for some fun!*

Sonny wasn't sure she could take much more. Just when she thought she'd reached her limit, a fresh wave of carnal delight would envelop her, bringing her to the next plateau. She was a ball of oversensitive nerves, unable to think – only able to feel.

Fingers busy, the sudden bucking of the woman's hips excited Torrin immensely. She released the heavy breast above her and used her free hand to clamp down on the rocking hips. "Stop," she ordered in a firm voice.

The dark woman froze, her heart in her throat. *She knows!*

Torrin's fingers slowly circled in slick warmth. When the woman tried to rotate her hips in response, she applied further pressure to the hand holding her down. "Don't move," she grated in warning.

Even as she forced herself to remain still, the fingers stroked Sonny's center, evoking wave upon wave of fiery need. Her body seemed to have become one large organism of craving. For the life of her, she didn't know what exactly she had to have. All she could do was obey the order given and hope that her desires would be rewarded.

The guitarist continued her activity, eyes closed behind the blindfold. The woman had returned to both her elbows above her and Torrin could hear the ragged breathing, could smell the musky scent of arousal drifting between them, could feel the muscles quivering as the woman fought her natural instincts. If anything, the woman became wetter the longer Torrin played her, breathing becoming more and more erratic. A drop of sweat splashed against her collarbone and she growled at the sudden vision of Sonny's face above her own, distorted with lust.

Every movement, every sound, every smell seemed to be connected to one place, one spot within Sonny's body. She lost herself in the sensations, unable to be coherent in thought or awareness. Only one word rambled through her mind. *Almost.*

"You know what I want from you," Torrin whispered, licking her lips.

Pale blue fire stared down at Torrin as Sonny tried to comprehend, to come up with some sort of lucid response without blowing her cover.

When no answer was forthcoming, the guitarist frowned. "Playing hard to get again?" With a quick movement, she flipped them and continued teasing the woman's genitals. "Give it to me."

Sonny was startled at the sudden change of scenery. The redhead was now straddling one of her thighs, hand still planted between her legs. Involuntarily, her hips moved and all motion stopped.

Her fingers barely touching the hard nub of flesh, Torrin froze at the woman's movement. "You know better than that," she admonished with a growl. "If you move again without permission, I'll stop." The resulting loud gulp from the woman brought a grin to her face. "Now, let me hear it."

Hear? Oh, shit! Sonny swallowed again, mind racing. *What the hell am I gonna do now? What does she want to hear?*

A bubble of irritation rose. Torrin stroked the woman again, hearing a gasp and feeling the muscles beneath her tremble in restraint. She paused, and there was a whimper. Leaning forward until she could feel the tickle of hair against her cheek, Torrin whispered, "I want to hear you beg for it. Or it stops now."

Beg. The word ran around Sonny's mind for a split second as she realized the implications of that statement. *Beg. Speak, converse, talk, plead.* She swallowed again, hard, trying to figure a way through this obstacle.

Torrin was beginning to get annoyed at the recalcitrant woman. In retaliation for the silence, she grasped the woman's clit in her fingers and simply held it, not moving.

Sonny's eyes closed, and she groaned at this new torment. The pulsating between her legs intensified to a point almost beyond her. To not move at the onslaught was almost impossible. "Please ..." she whispered.

"What? I didn't hear you." Torrin applied more pressure to the button.

"Ohhh," Sonny moaned thickly. "Please ... Oh, please ..."

Torrin considered the request and decided that further torture was in order. She nuzzled the ear, tracing it with her tongue. The woman's heart was pounding so hard she could almost hear it. *This is so much fun.* With a low purr, she said, "Please ... *what*?"

Sonny frantically cast around in her mind for a response. *What? What does she want?* She felt the guitarist above her press against her thigh, leaving a wet trail on her tanned skin. *Oh, God, this is killing me!*

Again Torrin rocked against the thigh between her legs, easing her own ache. She sucked the earlobe into her mouth and bit down with a growl. Between clenched teeth, she demanded, "What do you want?"

Having spent a year of research on the subject, Sonny was still at a bit of a loss. *What do I want?* she asked herself for perhaps the first time. Her heart felt like it was going to explode, her sex was throbbing so hard she was sure she'd have to use ice to remove the swelling, and the warm, wet breath in her ear was almost too much for her overloaded senses to bear.

The woman's mouth opened as she panted, chest heaving. Torrin heard the magic words.

"Please ... take me."

The voice was so like Sonny's, and the fantasies she'd been playing in her head all night fueled the inferno within. With a savage smile, Torrin released her hold on both ear and clitoris. Even as she devoured the woman's lips and tongue, she plunged two fingers deep inside, swallowing the cry that came up.

There was a sharp stab of pain as Torrin pushed past Sonny's maidenhood, and she cried out into the mouth that was ravishing hers. Then the sensation of being filled and of movement deep inside took over, and she began rocking against the redhead in a full body movement of wanton rutting. Sonny's long arms wrapped around the smaller woman who was thrusting against her thigh at the same time, and she lost all conscious thought.

Torrin's experience with virginity was nigh on nonexistent. To her knowledge, she had never bedded any woman who hadn't at least been with other men, if not other women. Her own deflowering had happened at such a young age, she couldn't remember it clearly. When her fingers met and broke the barrier within the woman beneath her, it took her a few moments to figure out what had happened. *What the hell?* Even as she moved against the firm thigh, her mind came up with the only possible answer. *But that would mean ... She is ... was ...*

"A *virgin*!" Torrin exclaimed. She pushed up until she was on her knees, using her free hand to whip off the blindfold. Before her was every wet dream she'd had over the last three years. A beautiful naked Sonny writhing on the mattress, dark hair splayed across the pillow, hooded pale eyes regarding her. There was fear in those eyes as well.

Even as the guitarist rose to her knees, Sonny grabbed her hand, keeping it in place within her. "Don't stop. Don't stop ... please," she begged, groaning as she thrust her hips against the trapped hand. "Oh, Torrin ... please ... take me. I've wanted you for so long."

A myriad of emotions coursed through the smaller woman. Gratitude, tenderness, anger, desire, passion, apathy, self-hate all swirled around with the wildness that was Torrin's soul. As the young woman continued to buck against her, her nostrils flared as passion gained the upper hand. *It's too late now, Torry,* a voice whispered in her depths.

Sonny was nearly incoherent as she pleaded for her lover to continue, to bring her to climax. She saw the flash of savagery in the gray eyes above her and shivered, a tendril of fear flickering through her. It seemed to increase her own desires, and she moved against the woman's hand, moaning.

The decision was made almost before Torrin could acknowledge the thought. A rush of arousal that followed in the decision's wake almost caused her to come on the spot. With a feral growl, she fell upon Sonny's body, fingers thrusting powerfully, pressing against a well-muscled thigh as she devoured the succulent neck.

"Oh, God!" Sonny cried out in response to the renewed attack. She bucked against the guitarist, reaching new levels of sensation, hands digging into the other woman's hips, pulling her closer. A thumb expertly began brushing her clit and she suddenly fell over the edge, calling Torrin's name into the night as she came.

Feeling Sonny clutching at her, hearing the contralto voice calling her name, the guitarist slicked across the strong thigh. She added her voice to her lover's in harmony.

Sonny's Journal — August 28, 2001

It's not quite dawn, yet. I've doused all but this one candle. Torrin is asleep beside me. She looks so peaceful. More at ease than I've ever seen her awake.

Lisa's plan worked. This night has been absolutely incredible. I feel so different now, even though I realize that there isn't anything noticeable.

I cried after the first time. I'm still not entirely sure why. I just couldn't help myself. Kinda corny, if you ask me, but there ya are. It was kinda hard for Torrin. She didn't know what to do – whether to comfort me or run shrieking in the opposite direction. She held me, though. I think I scared her. She didn't know why I was crying anymore than I did.

We talked. No major protestations of love or anything, but we cleared the air a bit. It's true that she has wanted me for a while. So, at least we have that in common! Ha ha ha!

I don't know what's going to happen now. I realize there's a good chance that Torrin will move on and continue her 'liaisons' with the other women she's been with. It'll hurt tremendously, I'm sure – just the thought of it is killing me! But I'll take what I can get at this point. Maybe I can eventually get her to understand that I'm the only one for her.

We made love several more times before she finally drifted off to sleep. I simply can't imagine anyone else making me feel the way she makes me feel! I hope I satisfied her. I know I'm a novice at this. I don't want her to toss me to the side because I don't know exactly what to do.

I've got to talk to Tom. Soon. I'm not going to hide anything from him – I haven't before. There's no reason to start now. I'm pretty sure he's gonna be furious.

Well, I'm going to go to sleep now. It's so novel having someone else in the same bed with me. And I can't wait to wake up in the morning with Torrin by my side.

Worthless, empty, soulless, angry,
I will bring you down.
TORRIN C. SMITH, "ULTIMATE TRUTH"

Part V: Responses

Doesn't matter how far,
it's always just behind me.
TORRIN C. SMITH, "BLATANT NEEDLE"

As consciousness slowly returned, Sonny snuggled closer to the soft, warm body beside her. "Mmmm." Outside the open window she could hear birdsong attesting to the fact that it was now morning. Pale blue eyes opened and blinked.

She was curled up on her side, head pillowed on Torrin's shoulder, one arm draped across the well-toned abdomen. Beyond the mattress, Sonny could see out the window. It was gray outside – a typical Portland day any time of the year. The cloud cover appeared high and non-threatening. *Probably burn off by this afternoon.*

It was a bit cool in the room and she shivered. Reaching down, the brunette pulled the blanket up to her shoulder. Several seconds passed before she realized she had help, a callused hand adjusting the covering around her. Quickly looking upward, gray eyes met her gaze. Sonny felt an almost physical jolt in her chest at the visual contact.

Torrin quashed the wary look just before Sonny glanced up, replacing it with a captivating smile. She tucked the blanket around her lover's shoulders. "Good morning."

A bit unsettled at this new intimacy, Sonny colored a little but kept eye contact. A smile graced her and she said, "Hi there. Have you been awake long?"

Reaching over to brush dark tresses from a sleepy face, Torrin responded, "No. Just woke up myself." *Yer a liar, Torry!* a mean spirited voice crowed. *But that ain't nothing new ...*

Sonny closed her eyes and leaned into the caress with a sigh. *I hope every morning is like this,* she reflected, snuggling closer to her lover in contentment.

Despite her better judgment, Torrin couldn't help but hug Sonny closer in response. *It feels so good, so different from the others.* A grimace crossed her face. *But you don't deserve it.* Composing herself, she kissed Sonny's forehead. "You have class today?"

Basking in the closeness she'd worked so hard for, Sonny said, "Yeah. But I'm off work – the benefits of part time employment." She turned her head to kiss the skin near her mouth, marveling at its soft texture. Receiving a slight hug, she felt a hand trace idle circles on her back. "You have rehearsal today, of course."

"Yeah." Torrin closed her eyes as Sonny's hand began to wander along her hip. "We play at the Orestes tonight, too."

"Bummer. I can't go." Sonny nuzzled lower, kissing the redhead's skin where it met the edge of the blanket. A small bubble of pride welled up as she noted a span of goose bumps. *I did that!* Trailing lower, the long hand slipped along the curve of Torrin's hip and on to the thigh.

Torrin closed her eyes and, regardless of her misgivings, caressed Sonny's hair, gently tracing the ear. "You can always get a fake ID," she suggested. *What the hell are you doing, Torry? Let's just see if we can't get her to mainline crank eventually, too, okay?*

Sonny's hand stopped moving as she thought about the suggestion. Moving out of the embrace, she propped herself up on one elbow and looked down at the guitarist with a contemplative face. "Ya know, I never thought of that before. Do you know where I can get one?"

Mind working overtime to come up with an answer, Torrin felt the hand reach its apex and begin tracking upward on the inside of her thigh. Her eyes closed against the sudden ache that filled her. "Ummm ..." she said, licking dry lips.

Delighted, Sonny watched the guitarist respond to her attentions. *Wow!* Her fingers just missed Torrin's sex, veering at the last moment to follow the crease of leg and torso. The quickened pulse in the neck beneath her was evident and she leaned forward to kiss it. "You still haven't answered my question."

What is wrong with me? Torrin demanded. Lips, so soft against her skin, delicately strolled northward until they were nibbling her chin.

"Well? You *do* know where, don't you?" Sonny prodded, fingers combing reddish curls.

"Uh, yeah," Torrin answered breathlessly, her reward a long, slow exploration of her mouth.

Sonny broke off the kiss. "I can't seem to keep my hands off you," she whispered, her expression a mixture of desire and trepidation.

Who's complaining? Turning on her side, the smaller woman pressed Sonny close, pulling a thigh up over her hip. "Feeling's mutual," she rumbled before losing herself in the sensations.

Torrin watched the door close. With a sigh, she sat up, blanket pooling around her waist. She had a languid upper body stretch, combing one hand through her hair before settling, cross-legged, in the cool room. A pack of cigarettes and a lighter were near her "nightstand," and she reached for them.

The guitarist lit one, drawing smoke deep into her lungs. As she exhaled, she slumped a bit, leaning against the wall at the head of her bed. Her mind returned to the memories of the night before.

Entwined, the women climaxed in a frenzied outburst of passion. They lay in the lethargic afterglow of sex, bodies cooling in the night air. When Torrin's brain finally kicked into gear, she realized that it wasn't sweat on her neck and shoulder; Sonny was crying. *Oh, shit! I hurt her!!* Heart in her throat, she gently disengaged herself and pulled up onto one elbow.

Tears fell freely from closed lids. As Sonny realized Torrin was watching, her tears intensified and she blushed. *What's wrong with me?* She turned further into Torrin, burying her face once more against the older woman's shoulder with a small sob.

Sonny tried to analyze the whirlwind of emotion that blew through, none of which could account for this uncontrollable display of emotion. Confusion, relief, fear for the future, happiness, sadness – all vied for a piece of her. Crying was cathartic, however, cleansing and refreshing as the tears carried the last of her concerns away. It seemed to be a milder form of the weeping she'd done in Foley's arms the afternoon before.

The guitarist trembled in her indecision. She'd obviously hurt Sonny, but for the life of her, she didn't know what the hell to do about it. Part of her was irrationally angry at this emotional display, viewing it as weak and stupid. Another wanted to take responsibility, make amends, *do* something. She was furious with herself and absolutely terrified by the idea of causing the young woman pain.

Torrin was a doer, not an idler – her mind focused on what to do. Different avenues of action availed themselves and she flashed across each one. Run screaming into the night? Finalize this pain by ending it, here and now, rejecting the woman? Get the whiskey bottle? Just forget the whole thing? Give her something to cry about? Cut her losses and leave the room, the house, the band?

Then Sonny's arm reached up, hooking behind the redhead's neck and pulling her close. All the doubts and insecurities and anger seemed to fade, the voices becoming whispers before finally disappearing altogether. The guitarist did the only thing possible.

Torrin adjusted herself on the mattress, cuddling Sonny closer. She began rocking with a gentle motion. "Shhh ... It's okay. I got ya."

Sonny clung to the guitarist as the unidentifiable emotions passed over and through her. As the cloud of tears lifted, she kissed the graceful neck near her lips in thanks.

Seeing Sonny's crying subside, Torrin pulled away a bit, cradling the dark head in her arms. She reached up to wipe wetness from a high cheekbone. "I'm sorry," she said, haunted look in her eyes. "I didn't mean to hurt you. I won't do it again."

With a watery chuckle, Sonny said, "You didn't. I'm just ... I dunno ... I'm not sure what this is." Her hand was buried in red-gold hair. Voice gaining strength, she continued. "You didn't hurt me. It felt ... God! It was the end of the world! The beginning of my life! It was *fantastic*!"

A tentative smile crossed the older woman's face. "End of the world?"

"Fantastic," Sonny repeated in a low voice, eyes focusing on the lips above her. The hand on her cheek smelled strongly of ... *me!* Her face tinted and she wondered what Torrin smelled like, felt like, tasted like. Tears forgotten, she put pressure on the guitarist's head, easing her closer. "C'mere," she husked.

Torrin felt an awakening in her groin at the carnal memories, bringing herself back to the present. Her cigarette was burning the filter, stinking up the air with toasted synthetics. With a muttered curse, she stabbed it out in a small plastic ashtray on the floor. Scrubbing her face for a moment, she inhaled deeply before rising to her feet, her naked body shivering in the cool air. *Time to get a move on.*

After more stretches, she got down to the business of stomach crunches and pushups. Twenty minutes later, Torrin used her tiny bathroom to relieve herself and clean up. A shower would be nice, but she wasn't ready to see Middlestead. It was going to be difficult enough getting through rehearsal and the gig.

Torrin dressed in her boots, baggy gray shorts that hung below her knee and a black tank top. Glancing at her bedside clock, she figured she had about fifteen minutes to catch the bus – enough time to walk the four blocks to the stop while having another cigarette. Torrin shrugged into her leather jacket, stuffing her cigarettes and lighter in a pocket. Her guitar, placed carefully in its case with the music she'd written the night before, was scooped up and slung over her shoulder.

At the door, Torrin turned and surveyed her room. Open windows, cold and melted candles on every flat surface, the bedding tangled and strewn about. There was a liquid clatter as she moved her foot. The whiskey bottle, still nearly full, had toppled.

The guitarist picked it up, studying the Johnny Walker label for long moments. A corner of the bed could be seen through the amber liquid. Shoulders shrugging, she uncapped the fifth, took a healthy swig and resealed it. The bottle made its way into her jacket pocket.

Just another fuck-filled night, she thought, leaving the room. A troubled voice responded, *No. It was* more *than that.* Torrin viciously squashed it and clattered down the stairs.

Sonny moved slowly down the stairs. She couldn't quite explain the feeling she had. It was like she saw the world through completely different eyes, eyes that held a bit more wonder, a bit more awe. *Is this how it feels when you love someone?* she wondered idly.

With no other situation to compare it to, she was at a loss. At the bottom of the stairs, she looked over the yard. It was still trashed from the party the night before. The barbecuer hadn't been cleaned, and there was some garbage near the fire pit. Clouds were prevalent in the sky, and a cool breeze ruffled her dark hair. Sonny inhaled deeply, smiling.

The noise of someone whistling and rummaging around in the house interrupted her peaceful interlude. Pale eyes opened and the smile faded a bit. *Tom.* She inhaled again, a bracing breath, as she mentally girded her loins for battle. *Time to go have it out with him.*

Middlestead puttered happily about the kitchen, cracking an egg into the frying pan. Life was good. A new CD was in the works, which meant another tour and more money, more publicity. Warlord was finally getting somewhere. He sent silent thanks to whatever god had blessed him with such a talented crew.

Vaguely surprised at not finding Sonny reading the paper when he came downstairs, Middlestead wondered what was up. He could only count a handful of times she'd slept in later than him – all requiring her to be up way past her usual bedtime. *Musta been writing pretty heavy last night,* he conceded. Though he could have sworn that her light had been off when he had trudged up to bed.

The sliding glass door opened and he glanced up, a surprised look on his face. "Morning. I didn't know you were up," he said to his sister. He quickly glanced out the kitchen window. "What were you doing outside?"

Sonny closed the screen. Unconsciously, she raised her chin a little as she stepped forward, sitting on one of the stools at the breakfast bar. "I was with Torrin."

A puzzled expression crossed her brother's handsome face. "Torrin?" He proceeded to flip the eggs. "What's wrong with Torrin?"

"Nothing."

"Okay ..." Middlestead shook his head. *Women.* Pulling the fry pan off the heat, he slid the eggs onto a slice of bread. He brandished the spatula at her and asked, "You want a sandwich?"

Sonny shook her head. Her stomach was tying itself in knots and food was *not* going to help.

The dark man shrugged, setting the pan on the stove and turning off the burner. He finished preparing his plate and wandered into the dining room.

Well, now what? Sonny asked in exasperation. *"Hey, Tom, I got laid last night. You know. By the guitarist? She's the one I want to spend the rest of my life with."* The imagined response from her brother both amused and worried her.

Chewing thoughtfully, Middlestead studied his sister who was fidgeting on the stool. *Something's up. The longer she's quiet, the more nervous she gets.* With a sigh, he set down his sandwich. "Okay.

What's up?"

"What ...?" Sonny asked, looking startled. "What do you mean?"

"I mean you're shaking so much, the tremors are going to bust that stool into a dozen pieces." He chuckled as she stilled, eyes wide. "So, what's bugging you, Sis?"

Sonny swallowed. "*You're* bugging me. Something wonderful has happened and I don't think you're going to be happy about it."

Well. Nothing like a different approach. A frown came to Middlestead's face as he tried to conceive of things that would make him unhappy with his sibling. "You dropping out of college before you even start?"

"What? No, of *course* not!" Sonny shook her head, dismissing that particular worry. *Where'd that come from?* She opened her mouth to speak, but he interrupted.

"You've become involved with some weird religious cult?" Before she could respond, he continued, "You wanna buy out my half of the house and kick me out? You've decided that a life of crime is worth it?"

"Where do you come up with this stuff?" Sonny demanded in exasperation.

Middlestead grinned. "You'll never know." Returning to the topic – *or lack thereof* – at hand, he asked, "C'mon, Sis. What is it?"

The moment of truth. Sonny gulped, blurting, "I spent the night with Torrin." *There! I said it!* She watched her brother carefully.

Frowning, he initially couldn't figure out what Sonny meant. *Why would she stay up there? Sonny. Torrin. Torrin's room. All night ... Sonny and Torrin ... Torrin's room all night?*

She watched Middlestead's face grow dark, his shoulders seemed to become wider as he swelled up with anger. *Ah, jeez, he's pissed!*

"You spent the night with Torrin," he repeated in a dangerous monotone. At her nod, he added, "The two of you. Alone. In her *bed*?"

"Yes."

A fist thumped the tabletop, rattling the plate and the centerpiece. "That *bitch*!" he snarled, rising to his feet. The chair toppled over, but he ignored it, taking a step towards the patio door.

Sonny flew off the stool, intercepting him. "Oh, no you don't,

Tom! Where do you think you're going?"

Hardly looking at the woman, he glared out the door as he grabbed Sonny by the shoulders to forcibly put her aside. "First I'm gonna fire her. Then I'm gonna evict her. And the best part, then I'm gonna *kill* her!"

"*No*, Tom!" Sonny refused to move, struggling to keep her feet. "It's not her fault! I tricked her!"

"Tricked her?" Middlestead bellowed with an incredulous look. He focused on his sister. "I'm sure it didn't take a whole hell of a lot, Sonny! She's a fucking *slut*!"

There was no conscious thought, only the resounding ring of flesh on flesh. Middlestead was left with a hand-shaped imprint reddening on his left cheek, eyes wide in surprise.

"Don't you *ever* call her that again," Sonny warned in a low, menacing voice. She shook her stinging hand. "And for your information, it did take a lot. I've been working on this for months!" The brunette felt tears of stress and anger well up, but she fought them down. *Not yet! Not yet!*

Middlestead blinked. *Where the hell is my sister and what have you done with her?* Calming himself, he tried another tactic. "Look, Sonny," he said, voice full of common sense. "Torrin's a ... she's ... got a lot of experience. I don't think you'd be able to 'trick' her. There had to be some point where she knew what was going on." An irrational curiosity overcame him. "Was she drunk?"

Sonny blushed, not expecting to have to discuss her strategy with him. "Blindfolded," she muttered.

A dark eyebrow arched before he remembered that he was furious. "Anyhow, there was a point in time that she knew. And she didn't stop." *So, I get to kill her.*

Coloring further, Sonny rolled her eyes. "Trust me, Tom. There ... wasn't much opportunity to stop things."

"Whatever." He sighed deeply, his stomach roiling with tension. Running hands through his hair, he sighed. "Fine. I won't kill her. But she's outta the band, and I want her outta the house."

"*What*?" Sonny exploded. "Why? Because I slept with her? She's the best thing that's happened to Warlord and you know it!"

"She took advantage of you, Sonny! She waited until you were legal age and then ..." He shook his head, banishing *that* particular image.

Eyes narrowed. "Let's set the record straight. *I* took advantage of *her*. Not the other way around." Seeing she wasn't making any headway with her older sibling, Sonny tried another direction. "What if I had just told you that I had slept with Lando?"

"What?" The change confused the man and he struggled to catch up.

"If I told you I'd slept with Lando, would you be acting like this?" Sonny demanded. "Would you be so bent outta shape?"

"That has nothing to do with it," he sputtered, shaking his head. "The reality is that it's the other way around!"

"I think it has a *lot* to do with it!" the woman insisted. "I think you'd be pissed off, but you'd let it go if it was what I wanted!" She shook her head in frustration. "Don't you dare drop Torrin because of this! The band will fall!"

"We'll get by without her," Middlestead grumped, nose rising in the air. "We've done it before." He ignored the thoughts that argued the point.

"Fine!" Sonny turned away and marched toward the doorway leading to the stairs. "Then you'll get by without *me*!"

The man trailed after her. "C'mon, Sonny! What are you talking about?"

Whirling around, Sonny's eyes snapped with energy, and she pointed a warning finger at her brother. "If she goes, I go. Got it?"

There was a long pause before he nodded.

Sonny spun around and stomped up the stairs. Middlestead could track her progress in the upstairs hall before hearing the slam of her door.

"Shit!" he said, face sour.

Torrin stepped off the bus, a fresh cigarette dangling from her lips. She dug out her lighter and lit it before walking away, paper cup in one hand, cigarette in the other. The guitar, strapped comfortably on her back, swayed back and forth over her right shoulder as she sidled along in the industrial area of southeast Portland.

Six blocks later, she arrived at the warehouse. It was late afternoon and clouds remained in the sky. Torrin fished her keys out of a pocket just as she heard a familiar motor.

A beat-up, rust brown van pulled into a parking spot on the

side of the street. The engine cut off and Hampton hopped out. "Hi," he called, opening the side door and retrieving his bass.

"Hey," Torrin responded. She unlocked the warehouse and waited for him to join her.

As they entered, the bald man glanced at her. "Have a good night?"

Innocent curiosity met Torrin's sharp gaze, and she mentally kicked herself. *Chill, Torry! It ain't common knowledge.* Pause. *Yet.* She shrugged and said, "Yeah, it was okay. You?"

"Pretty good." *No complaints about her lady friend pulling a disappearing act. In-ter-est-ing ...* "You must have gone to bed early. I didn't see you after we went inside." He jumped up onto the stage and began tuning his guitar.

Torrin colored so slightly, it was hardly noticeable. "Yeah. Well, I was tired," she offered, putting her cigarette out in a nearby ashtray. She took a long swallow of her soda, the Johnny Walker within warming her, soothing her.

"So, you were doing a lot of writing yesterday?" Hampton hinted, deciding to drop the subject for now.

Back in her element, the guitarist chuckled. "Yeah, I got some stuff. Hold on." She unzipped the guitar case and pulled out the pad of paper, handing it over to the eager man. "No guarantee that they're legible," she warned. "I haven't looked at them since last night."

"S'okay," the bassist shrugged. "I've got you here to translate."

They looked over the songs for the next half hour, deciding which seemed workable. Lyrics were cleaned up, and they began working on the melody.

"I dunno," Torrin said. "We could speed it up a bit. Maybe make it a little rougher." She sang out a couple of lines, keeping time by tapping on her guitar.

Nodding, the bald man said, "Yeah. That'd work." Hampton turned when the door slammed. "Cool, Tom's here. We can see what kind of rhythm to put on it."

Whatever enjoyment Torrin got from the collaboration evaporated. She coolly regarded Middlestead, noting the angry stance and intense blue eyes glaring back. *Great. Might as well pack up and move out now.* She picked up her cup, sipping the melted ice water and dregs of her whiskey. *Fuck him!* another voice growled.

Shit happens and he needs to get over it!

"Hey! You got here just in time," Hampton said with a grin. "We're trying to figure out the beat on this song." Brown eyes noted stiffness in the man and woman, the very evident anger lurking just beneath Middlestead's demeanor. *Oh, yeah,* he thought. *If there was any doubt about what happened last night, it's gone now!*

Middlestead grimaced. "Another Torrin Smith Billboard Hit?" he asked in a snide voice.

The redhead stiffened but refused to be baited.

Frowning, Hampton answered, "No ... Another half decent song for us to work on. You know, we *do* have a CD to burn next month."

"Whatever." Middlestead stomped up onto the stage to check his kit.

Craning his neck to follow the drummer, Hampton noted the flexing jaw muscles of the woman beside him. *Gotta get this out in the open.* "What bug crawled up your butt?" he asked Middlestead.

Dark blue eyes narrowed. Rather than answer, he began playing the drums, loosening up. *I* can't *kill her,* he reminded himself.

Hampton sighed, looking askance at the ceiling. Arching an eyebrow at Torrin, he asked with a voice loud enough to carry, "Is there something I should know?"

Teeth grinding, Torrin shrugged sharply. She set her guitar aside and the music next to her cup on the floor. "You'd better ask him. He's the one with a problem." Torrin rose and stretched before stepping off the stage and toward her jacket.

Middlestead's baleful eyes followed her. *Why her?* He pounded on the skins, wishing it were Torrin. *Would it be different if it were Lando?*

At an impasse, the bassist listened to Middlestead beat his drums half to death and watched Torrin light up another cigarette before moving away. He sighed deeply and set his bass in its stand. *Now what?* he wondered, rubbing his bald head. *Something's gotta be done. Preferably today!* For lack of anything else to do, he stepped from the stage as well, parking himself on the old bench seat.

Torrin wandered over to the armchair she favored and slumped into it. *What the hell do I do now?* she scowled. *Back to the streets, back to hustling and squats and eating out of dumpsters until another gig comes along? This fucking sucks!* She smoked in silence. *Well, he hasn't kicked you out, yet. Maybe he just needs to work things out.* Snort. *Yeah! Working out the best way to kick my ass for fucking his little sister!*

As usual, Atkins was late to rehearsal. He pulled the door open, almost drowning in the crescendo of a drum solo. With a huge grin, he strode in, waving at Hampton and Torrin.

Behind him, unnoticed, Sonny entered.

"Sorry I'm late," Atkins said as he approached the pair. "Sonny wanted me to pick her up." He glanced at the stage. "What's up?"

The bassist watched the younger woman carefully. "Nothing. Might have some problems, though." *She looks kinda pale*, he thought, concerned.

"Really?" the tall guitarist asked, looking around expectantly. "What kind?"

Hampton nudged his chin toward the drummer. "Trouble in paradise." At the confused look, he shook his head dismissively. "Don't worry about it. We'll get it worked out. He just needs to get over being mad."

Atkins nodded sagely, trying to look like he understood the cryptic comments.

Sonny stopped inside the door, surveying the situation. Her brother was taking his frustrations out on his drum kit, a dark cloud over his head. The two other men chatted quietly, with many glances towards the stage. Torrin sullenly put out a cigarette and immediately lit another. *Not good.*

Inhaling deeply, Sonny steeled herself before sauntering into the room. She could feel her brother's eyes on her but ignored him. A warm smile and a slight wave to Hampton, a wink at the tall man beside him and then the seated woman captured her attention. Sonny slid onto the arm of the chair, leaning her right arm on the backrest. Startled gray eyes looked up at her, and she gave a sly little smile as she bent closer for a kiss.

Lost in thoughts of doom and gloom, Torrin hadn't seen her lover enter. She was mentally pursuing a bleak future when a warm body settled next to her. She looked up into sparkling eyes and a crooked little grin that said, *I understand. I'm here now.* Their lips met, soft and warm and steadying; nothing sexual, simply a reminder of their time together.

Suspicions confirmed, Hampton grinned. *Now maybe Sonny'll calm down. This constant jealous flirtation is getting on my nerves.* As the kiss broke off, he became privy to a gentle look in Sonny's eyes. *And maybe she'll be happy.* He turned to Atkins. Backhanding the taller man's stomach, he said, "Close your mouth, nitwit. Haven't you seen Torrin kiss anybody before?"

"Wh ... But ... Wh ..." Atkins sputtered, eyes rapidly flicking back and forth between his band mate and this public display. "But ... but that's *Sonny*!"

"You're quick." The bald man chuckled.

A resounding crash startled everyone.

Middlestead cursed, his face flushed, as he fought with a snare drum. In his anger at the blatant display, he'd put his stick – fist and all – through the skin. Freeing himself, he jumped from the stage and strode toward the group, blood in his eyes.

"Uh oh," Atkins said.

"Did I mention trouble in paradise?" the bassist asked, stepping to intercept Middlestead.

"I think so." Atkins followed his lead.

Seeing Middlestead's approach, Torrin pushed her lover far enough away to get out of the chair.

His friends blocking the way, the angry man stopped, glaring at the women. "What the hell are *you* doing here?" he demanded of his sister.

Sonny stood, taking a step forward. "I skipped class. Torrin and I have an errand to run after rehearsal," she said, peering regally down her nose.

"Yeah, I'll just bet," he responded acidly. "You gonna bed all her little dyke friends, *too*?" As the words left his lips, a flash of pain crossed his eyes and Middlestead wished them back. *This isn't how it's supposed to go!*

The superior air vanished as Sonny stared at her brother in abject shock. *He's never spoken to me like that!*

Silence filled the room.

Pain swelled in Torrin's chest. Circling her lover, she placed a hand on Sonny's shoulder, the other reaching up to caress a cheek. Their eyes met and she mentally questioned, *Are you going to be alright?*

The brunette's eyes stung with unshed tears, and she nodded, biting her lower lip.

Assured that Sonny was okay for the moment, Torrin turned to face Middlestead. Her presence filled the room as she bristled. She was standing in front of her band mates in two strides. With a quick glance, Atkins and Hampton stepped away.

The drummer felt like a bug under a microscope as he was studied. There was a flash in his mind's eye of a woman on a throne examining him with cold, calculating eyes. Then it was gone.

"Your problem isn't with Sonny, it's with me. At least be man enough to admit it."

Dark blue eyes flashed. Middlestead growled," Got *that* right, bitch!" he agreed. "You took advantage of my sister. If left to me, you'd be dead already."

"Tom!" Sonny interrupted. "That's *not* what happened!" She was cut off by a sharp glance tossed over her lover's shoulder.

Returning her attention to the man before her, Torrin nodded. "You're right. I did."

An immediate hubbub of murmurings was drowned out by Sonny's plaintive denial. "*No,* Torrin ..."

"*Yes,* Sonny," Torrin insisted in a firm voice, eyes never leaving Middlestead's. "I could have stopped. I had the choice."

Hearing his suspicions confirmed the drummer seemed to deflate. Somehow, he thought it would be harder to get the guitarist to admit it. Now that she had, he was at a loss.

Torrin scrutinized him a bit longer, mind racing. "You think I'm going to treat her like the others," she stated.

Middlestead's eyes hardened, but he didn't answer.

"I don't think that's possible," the guitarist continued with a slight smile. Turning, she regarded Sonny, her demeanor inviting everyone in the room to have a look, as well. "She's not like them. Not by a long shot." Her smile widened at the blush she detected.

Middlestead looked at his sister, not seeing a gangly youngster anymore. She was a beautiful young lady with the thoughts and feelings of a woman. Comparing her to the women Torrin usually bedded, he recognized one very basic difference. *She loves Torrin.*

Turning to Middlestead, the guitarist's smile faded to sternness. "Shit happened, Tom. Deal with it." She leaned forward, her voice dropping low enough for only him to hear. "And if you *ever* hurt her like that again, you're a dead man."

Middlestead pulled back, a little surprised at her vehemence. Looking at her small frame, he had no doubt that his longer reach and fifty-pound advantage would do him no good in a confrontation. He nodded mutely.

"Go apologize to her."

He nodded again and stepped past Torrin, a part of him wondering *When the hell did I start taking orders from her?*

Hampton breathed a sigh of relief. "Glad that's over."

Torrin seemed to dwindle to normal size. "Me, too." She blew out a breath and ran hands through her red-gold hair.

"You know, I'm honor bound to kill you now," Atkins said, half in jest.

Torrin nodded with a tight grin. "Yeah. I know."

"Hell, girlfriend! You lasted for longer than I woulda, and that's a fact!" He clapped her on the shoulder, shaking his head.

With a rueful grin, she said, "That's because women have more staying power."

Rolling his eyes, Hampton shook his head at the innuendo. "I'm gone," he said, hands raised in surrender as he turned toward the stage. "Okay, people! Let's get this mess cleaned up and some music played!"

Torrin turned her attention to the siblings as the others headed for the stage.

"I just don't want to see you get hurt," Middlestead was saying.

"I know, Tom," Sonny responded with a sweet smile, a reassuring hand on his shoulder. "But if I get hurt, it's my choice. Do you understand?"

He nodded reluctantly.

The redhead watched them, grim thoughts returning. *Oh, you'll get hurt, alright, little girl. You shouldn't play with fire.*

Sonny's Journal — August 28, 2001

I am so drained. This entire day has been a roller coaster ride.

I was right. Waking up with Torrin was wonderful, sweet, sexy. I could get used to this!

And she's so wise! She got Tom over being mad at us without resorting to violence! I fully expected him to fly off the handle and smack her. Good thing he didn't, because then I'd have to hurt him myself.

It was hard, though. Quite a few nasty things were said. I think that if I were bedding Lando, Tom would have accepted it much faster and with better grace. He's raised me from eleven years old – that's gotta put pressure on a person. Nobody would want their kids or siblings to go through the crap that gays and lesbians do.

I don't know where the boldness came from, but I marched right into the warehouse and kissed Torrin in front of God and everybody! So, everybody knows now. I still don't know what all this is going to mean for our ... my future. Torrin and I haven't discussed it. Don't know that we will anytime soon, either. I think she's afraid to say anything because she might not be able to hold up her end of any commitment.

And, if she did make a commitment to me, I don't know that I could believe in it. Not that I would expect her to outright cheat on me or anything. But I know how she is – I can't imagine that she'd be able to keep a promise like that. At least, not right now. Maybe in the future ...

We went to a friend of hers. I've now got an ID that says I'm twenty-two. Torrin said that with a little bit of makeup, I could pass fairly easily. And I did! I was able to get into the Orestes tonight and watch Warlord! (Yet another reason Tom wasn't happy tonight) I love watching them play! And Torrin ignored all the women vying for her attention, spending her breaks with me! That felt really good.

Excuse me while I yawn! I've gotta get some sleep!

Sonny backed through the glass door and into the lobby, arms laden. She carried her pack on her back, a camera case slung over her shoulder and an armload of fast food bags. Grinning at the receptionist, she asked "Hi! They in number three again today?"

An older woman looked up, smiling, a stylized logo of a horse gleaming starkly white against a deep blue background behind her. "Yes, they are. How are you today?"

"Great!" Sonny propped a bag on the corner of the woman's desk and fished out a cup of coffee. "Here ya go. Thought you could use the extra caffeine dealing with those yahoos." A handful of sugar and creamer packets were sprinkled on the desktop.

Surprised, the woman thanked her as she took the steaming Styrofoam cup.

"No problem!" Sonny repositioned the bags in her arms with a smile and a wink. To the left of the reception desk were a pair of double doors, and she went through them in search of Warlord.

The technician closest to the door heard a rattling of the knob.

He frowned a bit, keeping his aural attention on the guitar strains as he rolled his chair over a couple of feet and opened it.

"Thanks," Sonny breathed in relief. She made her way into the recording booth, hearing the door click softly behind her.

Standing waist high, shelves to the left held recording equipment, above them was the company's logo. Sonny settled her packages on a small table and chair in the back corner. To her right were several soundboards, currently manned by two technicians and the producer. Glass filled the rest of the area in front of them, a picture window looking into the studio. Music filled the room, and the three men conferred as they adjusted switches and mixed the sound.

Sonny removed her camera bag and backpack, rotating her shoulders in relief. Settling down in the chair, she finally afforded herself a view of the other room. As usual, the first sight of her lover caused an almost physical jolt.

Torrin and Atkins were laying down the guitar tracks of a song. Their eyes were closed as they flowed with the music in their headphones. The other two band members were watching from their places, headphones on as well. The woman's hair was pulled back out of her eyes in a ponytail. She wandered the realms of inner darkness, interpreting what she saw into sound. Her tattoo seemed to flash ominously in the fluorescent lighting overhead.

The song ended with a flourish, followed by a few seconds of silence before a tech flipped a couple of switches. An older man with gray hair, the producer, leaned in with a smile and said, "That's a wrap, folks. Sounds great!"

"Break time?" Sonny asked.

The producer glanced at her. She held up a hamburger and waggled her eyebrows with a grin. Smiling, he said, "Sure." Turning back to the microphone, he said, "Half hour break, kids. Looks like dinner's here."

There was hooting and hollering in the studio at this announcement. The band began setting things down and turning off equipment.

Torrin took a few seconds to gather herself. She could hear her lover's voice in the control room. Torturing herself, her eyes opened, but she refused to look through the glass.

Part of Torrin was damned glad she'd finally gotten to bed Sonny. It'd been a part of her masturbatory fantasies for months. She'd hoped that by achieving the fantasy, the intensity of her feelings would mellow. It'd happened before when she'd finally bagged someone who'd been seemingly unattainable. Given a couple of days, fucking like bunnies, the infatuation faded. Real life intruded. The woman was then left on the side of the fast track Torrin traveled.

The guitarist was unprepared for what happened. The longer she was involved with the dark-haired beauty, the stronger the attraction became.

It was terrifying.

"Hey, sexy," a low voice insinuated itself into her thoughts.

Torrin set her guitar in its stand and turned to regard her lover who had long since entered the studio, handing out food. Her eyes swept up the long frame.

Sonny was still in her work uniform, khaki shorts and short-sleeved shirt. Sturdy walking shoes were on her feet, and the shirt was unbuttoned to where it disappeared beneath her belt, revealing a white tank top. Her dark hair was pulled back at the temples, exposing a long, graceful neck.

The slow burn of lust sparked deep in Torrin's belly.

Sonny set food and drink containers on a folding chair. She straightened and stepped forward with a smile. "I got you a chicken sandwich," she said.

Torrin stepped into the woman's space, not touching. She let her eyes roam the tall body before her, inhaling deeply as she leaned close. "I'm hungry," she rumbled before nibbling the inviting flesh at the edge of a khaki collar.

Shivering, Sonny sighed and closed her eyes, knowing Torrin didn't mean food. "*Now*?" she asked, half chagrined and half hopeful.

The guitarist closed the fractional distance between them, pressing her body against the taller woman. "Now," she confirmed.

Sonny blushed, imagining all eyes on the two of them. She swallowed nervously.

Sensing Sonny's hesitation, Torrin pulled back a bit to look into sky blue. "Unless you'd rather not ...?" she offered in a low voice. *Schyeah, right! Like you're gonna let a little thing like her modesty stop you!*

Irresistibly drawn, Sonny nodded, the excitement overriding her need to keep things low key.

That was easy, Torrin mused as she led the brunette out of the studio. *Wonder what else I can get away with?*

Everyone watched them leave, the techs in the booth openly gaping. Hampton surveyed the drummer, checking his response. Middlestead was a bit grim, but he continued to eat his hamburger.

The photographer allowed herself to be led toward the restroom. Sometimes this was the way things were with the redhead. Torrin would get a wild hair, and Sonny would find herself being ravished in all sorts of places. It was exciting and dangerous. She enjoyed it immensely.

Sonny had been raised in a house that frowned on blatant displays of sexuality. Torrin's free spirit had fascinated her from the first. For some reason, it never occurred to Sonny that by being Torrin's sexual partner, she'd be treated in much the same way as the other women. Not that some aspects of it weren't welcome, just unexpected.

The two women entered a small room with a toilet and sink. Torrin led the way, tugging the younger woman behind her. As Sonny got past the door, Torrin pushed it closed, trapping her lover against it. She hit the lock and pressed firmly against the dark woman, pinning her to the cool wood.

Mere seconds swept past before Sonny's top was pushed up to her chin, bra following close behind. Torrin attacked a nipple with voracious intent, teeth biting, hands roaming the writhing body, a strong thigh clamped between her lover's legs.

Sonny groaned at the sudden infiltration, moving against her lover. It was always this way with Torrin – a sultry look followed by a passionate strike that left her breathless, wanting more.

Torrin turned to the other breast, treating it in the same manner as she rubbed against the taller woman's thigh. There wasn't going to be much time for more, but Torrin had to take the edge off her ravenous sexual appetite or go insane.

One hand buried in red-gold, Sonny arched into the eager mouth, her other hand convulsively grasping the demon-eyed tattoo.

The guitarist unfastened khaki shorts, delving inside. She reached her goal, feeling warm wetness on her fingers, but the angle wasn't right for anything further. Growling in frustration, Torrin released the dark woman's breast, pulling back to grasp the flared hips. With a quick movement, she spun Sonny around and pressed up against her from behind.

Sonny found herself pushing against wood, its gentle chill against her cheek and breasts. Again hands slid netherward and she gasped and moved at the contact.

Atkins walked down the hall towards the studio and food, nerves relieved now that he'd had his nicotine fix. As he passed the restrooms, he heard a slight thump.

With a frown, he stepped closer to listen. The sounds of movement, heavy breathing and soft moans reached his ears. He grinned a little and shook his head, resuming his walk.

"You are so hot," Torrin grated, her hand buried in liquid warmth. Her other hand snaked up to massage a breast, hardwood brushing against her knuckles. "You drive me crazy with need."

Sonny let the words wash over her, exciting her, drawing her closer to the edge.

"All I can think of doing when you're near is fucking you." There was an answering moan. "Like now," Torrin whispered.

The woman against the door redoubled her efforts, the flesh beneath her lover's hands reaching the pinnacle. Then she came, almost explosively. She could feel the shorter woman thrusting harder and harder against her until she climaxed as well with a deep growl.

They stood there, holding each other up, catching their breath.

Torrin leaned her forehead between the dark woman's shoulder blades, shaking her head slowly. "What you *do* to me, woman," she muttered, not altogether happy.

Sonny smiled in contentment.

Atkins entered the studio and made a beeline for the piano. "Looks like they're at it again," he announced, scooping up a container of french fries.

"Kinda figured," the drummer said in a low voice. "I mean, when *aren't* they?" He sighed deeply, wishing things were different. *I'm not cut out for this parental shit,* he thought. *Knew that when Mom and Dad died.* But Hampton's older sister, fresh out of law school, won him custody of an eleven-year-old girl. *I just hope things work out for her.*

Sonny's Journal — September 14, 2001

Warlord's almost finished with the CD. I've heard part of it. Of course, it sounds great! Mike Hoffman, the producer, says that things are going smoothly, and it's been a snap working with the band.

I was working on my photo portfolio while they were recording. Mike saw my pictures – not just the artsy fartsy ones, but the ones I have of the band as well. He's going to look into what White Horse has scheduled for a CD cover. Maybe my photos will be added! Cool!!

The band's playing at Orestes this weekend. It's an early gig and they should be finished around ten p.m. Torrin's taking me dancing! I've never been in a gay bar before. It should be interesting! I can't wait!

Things are still a little strained between Torrin and Tom. I can't blame him. He's been raising me since I was a kid. It's gotta be tough. I'm just glad that he's not being a jerk about the whole thing. He's just being protective.

I've seriously been considering getting a tattoo or something. I'm not sure I want to pierce my nipples or anything, though Torrin's suggested it. She says that it increases the sensations in them. But, jeez, it musta hurt! She says that it did, but not for long. I dunno ... Still gives me the shivers, just thinking about it!

I don't know if it's just me or not, but I've noticed that Torrin's been drinking significantly more lately. Maybe she always did and I didn't realize. Now that we're practically living together, though, I see a lot more. I'm worried about her.

I await no future, laughing screams,
I've made my path through shadow
And found my insanity.
TORRIN C. SMITH, "IN SANITY"

Part VI: Popularity

Where do you think you're going?
This is far from over.
I've led you through the dark -
You are mine.
TORRIN C. SMITH, "9/10THS OF THE LAW"

"Mitochondria," the Hispanic man across from her stated, his book across his chest.

"Small granular bodies found in the cytoplasm of the cell," Sonny responded. The woman next to her scribbled furiously in her notebook.

Reynaldo turned to the other woman at the table. "Mitosis."

Hazel eyes rolled and she nervously tucked short brown hair behind her ears. "Oh ... man! I'm gonna flunk this final, I just *know* it!"

The man sighed and reached to snag a french fry. "You will with *that* attitude," he predicted, readjusting his wire frames as he glanced into his biology text.

"How do you do it?" the woman asked her dark companion. "How do you remember all those technical terms and stuff?"

Sonny shrugged, finishing her carton of milk. "I dunno. I've just always been good with tests." She wiped her mouth with a napkin. "Have you thought of taking one of the study skills classes, Miranda?"

The woman shook her head. "You think I should?"

Shrugging, Sonny answered, "It couldn't hurt."

As the trio took a break, another young man approached. He dropped a heavy shoulder bag on the only empty chair. "Sorry I'm late," he said, grabbing another chair from a nearby table. "Had to finish that term paper for Writer's Comp." He straddled the folding chair and rested his elbows on the back.

"S'okay, Steve," Sonny said. "It looks like we're taking a little breather."

"Frigid!" Steve said. "In that case ..." He pulled a compact stereo and a CD case out of his bag. "I picked this up before class today. I've been wanting to hear it."

As the new arrival set up the music, Sonny's brow furrowed. She picked up the empty case and studied the familiar cover. "Hey," she said with a grin, "that's my brother's band!"

"Warlord?" Steve asked. "Rock *on*! They're hellacious!"

"No way," the other man scoffed. "Your brother isn't in Warlord."

"Yes. He's the drummer. Tom Middlestead." She handed the case over to her friend. "Check the credits."

The young man adjusted his glasses as he scooped up the case and pulled out the inner front cover. Meanwhile, Steve set up his player and began the disc, strains of a guitar swelling in the immediate area of the college cafeteria. Hampton's voice began singing.

"Wow, he's good," Miranda commented, eyes wide.

"They're kickass," Steve agreed. "My friend got it last week – that's where I heard 'em." Turning to Sonny, he asked, "Think you can get me autographs?"

The brunette almost choked on her sandwich. When she was able to speak, she exclaimed with amazement, "*Autographs*?"

Steve shrugged. "Yeah. If these guys do well, it'll be worth some money, ya know?"

"Hey," the other man interrupted. "Says here that photo credits go to Sonny Middlestead." He looked at the young woman. "You?"

Sonny blushed. "Me."

"How much did they pay you?" Steve asked.

"Two hundred and fifty dollars."

Reynaldo looked sour. "Well, *that* ain't much."

"No," Sonny agreed. "It isn't. But, the band's not big yet. When they get more popular, my pictures will sell for more."

"How about an autographed picture?" Steve asked.

Sonny chuckled. "Okay! I'll see what I can do!"

"Cool!"

"Now, can we get back to work? We've got a test on this in two hours."

With good-natured grumbling, the group returned to their studies.

Middlestead looked up from a magazine when the front door

opened. His sister stepped in, dropping her pack and closing the door with a sigh. "How'd it go?" he asked.

Sonny nodded speculatively. "Not bad." She tossed herself onto the couch. "Had a little trouble with cell separation, but that's about it."

"And that was your last one?" Middlestead set the magazine on the coffee table, resting his elbows on his knees.

"*Last* one," the student confirmed with a grin. "No more headaches for two weeks. How was your day?"

"Not bad. Finished that song I've been working on. I hope we can have it ready to perform in a couple of weeks."

"Great."

The siblings sat in silent contemplation.

Sonny straightened with a broad smile. "Hey, can I get the band to autograph a picture for me?"

"What?" The dark man frowned. "What are you talking about?"

"An autographed pic! Some guy at school wants to know if he could have one."

"You're shittin' me, right?" Middlestead asked with a grin and a raised eyebrow.

Sonny shook her head with a smug look. "Nope. He bought the CD, and we were playing it while we studied."

"Huh." The drummer contemplated the news, a mixture of suspicion and joy flowing through him. "Well, I don't see why not," he finally allowed. "I'm sure the others will go for it."

"Fantastic!"

Silence again. Middlestead was shaking his head slightly in wonder. His sister sat back and propped her feet on the edge of the coffee table.

"Have you seen Torrin yet?" Sonny asked.

Middlestead shook his head no. "Not since last night. I think she's still in bed."

The dark woman nodded. "You guys play at La Luna tonight, right?"

"Yep."

"Cool." She put her feet on the floor and sat up. "I'm gonna go take a shower. I'll wake Torrin after that."

Middlestead furtively scanned his sister. She appeared happy with her choices in life. He'd noticed, however, that the longer she and Torrin saw each other, the more the guitarist was flirting with other women. Middlestead wasn't sure, but he thought Sonny was aware of it – Torrin didn't blatantly do it in front of her, though.

He blew out a breath and leaned back in his armchair. With feigned nonchalance, he asked, "So, how are things going with you and Torrin?"

Sonny stopped her attempt to rise and peered at her brother.

Her face was closed to the drummer, and it wrenched something deep inside. "Look, Torrin and I got along just fine before ..." and he waved vaguely, "... this. I'm just concerned for you, you know that."

She considered his comment, nodding. Coming to some sort of decision with herself, she offered, "Things are okay."

Dark blue eyes regarded her a little sadly. "Only okay?"

Sonny thought about a response. *I don't want to hurt him. But I am by not talking to him.* She sighed and searched her mind for an answer. "Yeah. Okay. It's not like we're a couple or anything." Deciding to take the bull by the horns, she continued, "Frankly, I'm surprised I haven't lost her interest yet. It *has* been over six months."

Middlestead nodded. "True. I'm surprised too. It's not a Torrin thing." He examined his sibling carefully. "So, what happens if she does?"

Sonny gave a sharp laugh. "Don't you mean *when*?" Her derisive humor vanished as she shrugged her shoulders. "Simple. I'll deal."

The man's face became grim. *You, of all people, don't deserve this, Sis.*

Shaking off the maudlin mood that was developing, the dark woman smiled and stood up. "I'll be okay, Tom. I'm a big girl now."

Middlestead put on a false smile. "I know, kid. You're a tough bitch."

"Yep. That's me!" Sonny scooped up her pack and headed for the stairs. "See you in a few."

The scowl returned to the drummer's face once she was gone.

Sonny sat at the bar with Foley. Nearby, the two women who had come with Atkins tittered and giggled together. As usual,

Sonny's attention was focused entirely on the stage.

Her lover was onstage with the band, guitar wailing a melody. A fine sheen of sweat covered her body, her only clothing being boots, shorts and a flimsy black tank top. She and Atkins were leaning against each other, back to back, her head barely coming to his shoulders as they slammed out the song's finale.

It was pretty crowded, an indicator of Warlord's level of popularity. The floor in front of the stage was hopping in beat with the music, a mass of humanity that seemed to have no beginning and no ending.

"Hey, can I buy you a beer?"

Sonny blinked, glancing to her right.

A fairly good-looking young man smiled warmly at her. When she didn't respond, his grin widened and he waggled his bottle. "A beer?"

She gave a slight smile, shaking her head. "No, thanks." She returned her attention to the stage where the band was preparing for a break.

Sensing her apparent fascination with the people onstage, the man leaned forward. "Which one are you watching?"

Sonny chuckled, tossing a rolled eye at Foley. "The guitarist," she answered.

He nodded sagely. "Ya know, I *know* those guys. I could maybe introduce you."

Foley chortled as the young woman raised an eyebrow.

"*Can* you?" Sonny asked.

"Oh, yeah!" the man bragged. "Me and Joe go way back."

"Joe ...?"

"Joe Prescott," he explained, gesturing toward Atkins.

Grinning, Sonny said, "Actually, I was interested in the *other* guitarist."

The man frowned, trying to make the connection. "You mean Hank?" he asked, looking at the shorter man.

Sonny snickered, feeling the waves of laughter from the woman beside her. "No, not 'Hank'. The redhead's more my ... type."

As Romeo tried to fathom this, the band clambered off the stage for a break. When Hampton arrived at the bar, he gave his girlfriend a hug.

"Hey, Hank."

The bassist looked into her laughing eyes. "What? Who's Hank?"

Romeo became flustered. Before he could extricate himself from a potentially sticky situation, Torrin arrived.

Sidling up to them, she snaked an arm about Sonny's waist, eyeballing the blushing man. "He bothering you?" Torrin asked with implicit menace.

Romeo opened his mouth, but Sonny cut in. "He was offering to buy the beer." She grinned angelically at the man, who was now sputtering.

An eyebrow raised and Torrin appeared impressed, her threatening demeanor fading. "Thanks!" She pounded on the counter to gain the attention of a bartender. "Hey! A round! On him!" she pointed at the man.

He paid the tab, especially when he found Atkins and Middlestead behind him, before melting back into the crowd.

Sonny had a tough time not laughing. "That was good." She giggled as he disappeared.

Torrin took a drink from her beer. "Yeah, it was. *Always* good to have fans." She felt arms around her waist, long legs straddling her, and she relaxed.

Sonny sighed, enjoying the closeness while she could. Sometimes her lover didn't allow this in public venues. Torrin's stage presence slopped over into real life, and she would become macho, preferring to be the one to initiate contact.

Nuzzling the long neck, inhaling the scent of roses, Torrin said, "Was he bothering you? I can still go break his legs." She grinned as she felt Sonny tremble in laughter.

"No. No need to break legs."

As Torrin drained her beer bottle, the bassist clapped her on the shoulder. "Time to get back to work," he announced.

Amid good-humored grumbling, Torrin placed her bottle on the counter, leaning into Sonny for a quick kiss. "See you in a bit, sexy."

"Okay. Give 'em hell." She smiled, watching her lover lead the way back to the stage.

Halfway through the crowd, Torrin nearly ran over a woman who turned abruptly into her path. The guitarist reached out, grabbing her arms to keep them both upright. "You okay?"

"I am *now,*" the woman said with a broad smile. Her eyes ran illicitly over the smaller woman. "You are a killer guitarist."

Raising an eyebrow, Torrin recognized the speculative look. "Thanks," she answered with a crooked grin. *Play the game, Horny Torry!*

Without warning, the woman leaned forward and captured Torrin's lips in a rough kiss.

Having spent years sampling the wares of women along her path, Torrin responded. Allowed entry, their tongues explored each other, her hands gripping the woman's arms firmly. *Gotta get back to work.* Torrin backed out of the kiss in increments.

Sonny's stomach dropped when the woman kissed Torrin. She noted the fact that the guitarist hadn't initiated the intimacy but also that she hadn't stopped it either.

When the kiss broke, the woman said in a low voice, "I hear you're killer in bed, too."

Torrin smirked. "Shouldn't believe everything you hear, babe," she said, resuming her trek to the stage. When she arrived, she was acutely aware of her band mates' eyes on her.

Atkins climbed up beside her. "What the hell was that?" he demanded, retrieving his guitar.

"*What*?" Torrin settled her guitar strap on her shoulder. "It was a girl, Lando. Ain't you seen one before?" She rolled gray eyes in disgust. "Shit, man, it's not like I'm married! Or a nun!"

Her friend pursed his lips in disapproval. Hampton set his instrument up, acting as if nothing happened.

Middlestead was last to the stage. He saw the kiss and was not happy. A quick glance at his sister verified that she'd seen it as well, her face pale and Foley holding her hand. Glaring daggers at the redhead, he wanted to say something, but she wouldn't look at him.

I didn't do a damned thing wrong, Torrin growled, adjusting the guitar. *Fuck somebody for a few, and suddenly you're inseparable,* a voice complained. Another piped up as she glanced across the sea of faces to see a pale, dark-haired woman at the bar. *Horny Torry strikes again!*

It was bound to happen sooner or later, Sonny thought, the pain in her chest seeming to deafen her. She glanced at Foley, seeing sympathetic eyes and feeling a hand take hers. The nausea passed and numbness set in.

The band began their set, and Torrin's eyes met hers across the room. It saddened Sonny that only the mask was shown. *Does she know? Does she care?*

Playing another forty-five minute set, the band filled the area before the stage with a hyper crowd. Atkins did his usual hot-dogging, leaping about and careening from one side of the stage to the other, while the bassist and Torrin played in a more sedate demeanor.

Middlestead pounded on his drums with more power than necessary. He'd learned his lesson months ago and didn't attack his kit with enough force to break them. *No, I'd rather break someone else,* he scowled, baleful eyes following his sister's lover. *The bitch is going to two-time my sister I just know it! It's only a matter of time.* Feelings of helplessness washed over him and were the absolute worst. He hadn't felt like this since right after his parents had died.

The look of heartbreak on Sonny's face ... Middlestead growled, banging his cymbals with extra strength. Torrin had completely ignored him since the set started, not even glancing his way for tempo cues. *She knows she's gonna do it, too.* That thought put his anger on a whole different level.

Deep inside, however, there was hope. Hope that Sonny's emotional suffering wouldn't be in vain. Hope that she'd let go of this path, this woman, and find someone who would at least take care of her and love her. Hope that Torrin would leave his sister alone and go fuck her little sluts instead. Buried beneath that was a secret, dark hope that he refused to acknowledge within himself – hope that this was just something Sonny was experimenting with and she would come to her senses and find a nice young man.

Warlord finished with a flourish, basking in the applause. Hampton, who'd been singing the lyrics to their last song, spoke into his microphone, "Thanks, folks! And have a good night!"

Last call was half an hour past. People on the floor began making slow way out of the establishment, finishing their drinks, gathering jackets and scarves. A few approached the stage to give their thanks for a great time and were met with gracious smiles as Warlord began dismantling their equipment.

It wasn't long before most people had left. The band was on stage, their voices echoing in the empty room as they packed their gear. A couple of the diehard fans/friends were helping Middlestead with the drum kit.

At the bar, Foley and Sonny sat with Atkins' dates, watching. The dark woman's face was worried as she studied a small cluster of groupies who hadn't left. One of them was the woman who kissed Torrin.

"What am I gonna do, Lisa?" she asked the woman beside her, voice hushed. "I haven't had to deal with this before."

Foley sighed, her lips pursed in thought. "Is she worth fighting for?"

Blinking in surprise, Sonny frowned. "Of course she is!"

The blonde nodded. "Then you'd better do something to remind her you're here." She studied the gaggle of groupies. "Give me a minute to think."

Sonny nodded, watching the women as well.

Warlord finished putting gear away, and Hampton left to bring the van to the stage door. The drummer "accidentally" bumped into Torrin several times during the packing, each time getting a little rougher. As the subtle abuse continued, Torrin's scowl deepened. Atkins played it smart, steering clear of them.

Torrin crossed the stage, attempting to step down and walk to the bar. Simultaneously, the groupies nearby began drifting toward the stage.

Foley gauged their trajectory, grabbed Sonny by the elbow and boosted her off the stool. "Interception," she said, heading for the women.

Swallowing, Sonny nodded in understanding.

Before Torrin could get off the stage, Middlestead took the opportunity to "bump" her again with a shoulder, putting her off balance and causing her to stumble.

All right! That's it! She whirled, hands fisted at her sides. "Just what the fuck is your problem, Tom?" the guitarist demanded.

Dark blue eyes narrowed. "*You* are my problem." He faced her fully, puffing up in anger. "You're going to hurt my sister. You're messing her up more and more each day." He leaned closer, his voice lowering in menace. "She thinks she loves you. And you're gonna break her heart."

Sonny, seeing the beginning of the exchange between her brother and lover, veered from the groupies and picked up her pace. *Uh oh!*

Seeing her course change and the tension surrounding the stage like a cloud, Foley continued on her original path to intercept the groupies before they got there to muddle things further.

She loves *me!* Torrin's tension increased at the whirlwind of emotions that the comment stirred up. Gritting her teeth, she growled, "What of it?"

"What of it?" the drummer yelled, his face flushing. He trembled, holding back from hitting her. Middlestead sputtered, his anger overcoming his ability to think and speak.

"Yeah. It's not your life. It's hers." *She can't love me! Can't! She's not that stupid!*

Middlestead pulled back, fist clenched and aching to come into contact with the grim young woman before him.

"Tom! Stop it!" Sonny ordered, jumping onto the stage. She reached up to grab his shoulders and stepped him backwards.

"Stop it? She's as much as admitted that she's going to hurt you, Sonny!" Middlestead's face was a mixture of fury and confusion. *Why is she defending her? Why can't she see?* "You need someone who will love you. Can't you see that?"

"Torrin does love me ... In her own way," Sonny insisted. "If I get hurt, it's my own problem. Not yours!"

Torrin could hear the voices in her head, cackling. *What the hell is there to love? She loves me, she loves me not, she hates me, she wants me to rot.* Sonny's last comments filtered through and Torrin blinked in shock. *I* don't *love her! No!* The darkest voice, Lucifer's, the one that guided her for years, piped up. *Guess you'll just have to show her how wrong she is, huh, Horny Torry?*

Mask firmly settled in place, Torrin took two steps to be within reach of the siblings. She reached out to touch Sonny.

Sonny looked over her shoulder, seeing the cool aloofness in her lover's eyes. Her heart leapt into her throat, knowing instinctively that something wasn't right, something ominous was happening.

"He's right, you know," Torrin confirmed. "You *are* going to be hurt." To prove her point, she scooped up her jacket and jumped from the stage.

Foley was trying to talk the groupies into leaving, but the altercation on the stage kept their attention. She was surprised when Torrin was suddenly beside her.

With great purpose, the redhead thoroughly kissed the woman who waylaid her earlier in the evening. "You got someplace?" she asked, voice husky.

The delighted woman blushed in anticipation and nodded happily. "Yes, I do."

"Let's go then." Torrin led her and her entourage out of the bar.

A gleeful feeling overtook Middlestead when he saw the guitarist kiss the groupie. *Yes! Maybe now she'll listen!*

Sonny watched, first in amazement, then heartrending sorrow. She seemed to deflate before her brother, turning away from Foley's sympathetic look. After Torrin left, Sonny returned to the bar to get her jacket, shoulders drooping.

Middlestead returned his attention to Sonny, and his face fell, realizing the extent of her pain. Anger drained from him, leaving him feeling hollow and empty.

Hampton entered through the stage entrance, wondering at the strange tableau he found awaiting him. "Where's Torrin?"

The tall guitarist sighed heavily. "Don't ask," he warned, watching the no longer volatile Middlestead return to his gear with a lost expression on his face.

Rubbing his bald head, Hampton looked to his girlfriend who approached with a concerned look on her face.

Sonny's Journal — March 16, 2002

I've been sitting here for half an hour, and I still don't know what to write.

I'm in Torrin's room. I know I probably shouldn't be here. God knows what'll happen if she brings that woman here and finds me. But I need to be close to her. And this is as close as I can get right now.

The woman ... It hurt so much when she kissed Torrin. I know that Torrin didn't start it. But she enjoyed it – I could tell. I don't know if I should feel jealous or not, or which one to be angry with. At least Torrin didn't pursue the matter initially. I think she would have come to me if Tom hadn't interfered.

I can't even look *at Tom. I realize that he's only looking out for me. But damn it! He's complicated things* so *much with his idiocy! Pushing Torrin like that! And then expecting me to just say, "Oh, sure, Bro. You're right. How silly of me."*

I'm not sure what set Torrin off. I don't think it was Tom saying she would hurt me. She told me that a year ago. I hope it wasn't anything I said ...

Anyway, I couldn't even be in the same room with Tom afterwards. Max and Lisa drove me home. I brought Torrin's guitar up here and have been here ever since. I don't want to see Tom right now.

I just want Torrin. To tell her it's okay. To tell her that I don't have to like it, but there's nothing tying us together except some good times.

I wish there was more than that. Maybe that's why I continue this farce of a relationship. I want so badly for her to love me that I can't let it go. Is it obsession? Addiction? I have to laugh that I can be addicted to Torrin just as she's addicted to alcohol.

God, I miss her.

Torrin lay naked in a strange bed with a strange woman wrapped around her. It wasn't anything that hadn't happened a multitude of times before. Casual sex had been her byword for so long, she couldn't remember when it hadn't been. This time, however, it was different.

This time Torrin didn't want to be there.

The woman – *I don't even know her name* – was soundly asleep, her head resting on the guitarist's shoulders. Her arm was around Torrin's waist, and she cuddled the Warlord in her sleep.

Torrin couldn't close her eyes. Each time she did, she saw Sonny's face crumbling. Sighing, she craned her neck to read the bedside clock. The numbers proclaimed it to be precisely 3:12 a.m. Even as she watched, it changed to 3:13.

I can't stay here. She looked down at the sleeping stranger's face. With slow, methodical movements, Torrin eased herself out from under, wrapping now empty arms around a large stuffed bear that had been tossed to the floor during their frenetic activities.

Finally free, Torrin stood at the side of the bed, glancing about. They had stripped each other as they made their way to the tiny bedroom. The light from a single lamp in the main room gave enough illumination to see dark shadows on the floor. Torrin followed the trail, donning her clothes in the reverse order of losing them.

At the door, Torrin shrugged into her leather jacket, her hands digging into the pockets reflexively. Smooth glass met her fingers, and she pulled out a tiny vial and studied it.

Torrin weighed the pros and cons before shrugging her shoulders. She found the bathroom and entered, shutting the door and switching on the light. Checking the medicine cabinet, she pushed aside various vitamin bottles and toothpaste. Further search of the vanity drawers yielded a razor blade and a handheld mirror. *Bingo!*

With experienced hands, Torrin poured a small amount of white powder onto the mirror. She used the razor to cut and form the powder into two thin lines. The redhead made a straw from a dollar bill to inhale the methamphetamine.

Torrin's nose burned, tears sprang to her eyes. She used a wet fingertip to pick up the rest of the powder on the mirror, licking it clean. The mirror and razor were then rinsed and put away.

A quick glance in the cabinet mirror told her that she didn't have anything on her face. Torrin ran hands through red-gold hair, already feeling the bizarre sensations of her fingers against her scalp. "Much better," she murmured, sniffing a little.

In a matter of minutes, Torrin let herself out of the apartment.

Moving around the side of the house in the dark, Torrin opened the gate leading into the backyard and the stairs to her room. Closing it quietly, she stepped onto the patio, looking up at Sonny's dark windows.

Three days had passed since she'd been home. Three days of a meth binge designed to let her forget. It didn't work.

Despite the euphoria of the drug in her system, Torrin didn't want to go to her room. There was too much of Sonny there. *Ain't* that *a laugh?* She shook her head ruefully, settling on a bench. Her breath steamed in the chill March morning, and she fished out her cigarettes, her heel tapping restlessly.

A dog barked in the distance. Lights came on at the neighbors' as they began to prepare for another day. It was cold, the temperature in the low forties, but Torrin's jacket was open, sweat on her skin.

She jerked upon hearing the screen door behind her and her eyes narrowed.

Middlestead stepped from the house, zipping his jacket and closing the door behind him. He sat on the other end of the bench. There were long moments of tense silence before he finally spoke. "Got a cigarette?"

Torrin blinked. "You don't smoke."

The dark man shrugged. "First time for everything." He glanced sidelong at her. "Well? Do you?"

Wordlessly, Torrin slid her pack and lighter across the bench to him. She continued to fidget as she watched him light one and inhale deeply before breaking into dry coughs. Raising an eyebrow, she asked, "Feel better?"

Knowing she wasn't talking about the smoking, he scowled. "No. Do *you*?"

Torrin debated about being honest. *What the hell. Whaddya got to lose, Torry?* She sighed and looked away, legs bouncing. "Not in the least."

Middlestead nodded and the tension between them eased. They smoked quietly for a while, the only sound a car engine as the newspaper deliverer made his rounds, the only movement Torrin's fidgeting.

Perversely, the guitarist asked, "How'd Sonny take it?" She tossed aside her cigarette and lit up another.

"Not well," was the gruff answer.

Torrin nodded. "It's for the best."

The drummer chewed the inside of his mouth, his stomach acid. "I don't think so," he finally said, the words almost dragged from within.

"What?" Torrin regarded him with suspicion. "It *is* what you wanted, isn't it? Sonny to be away from my 'evil' influences?" *And you haven't even begun to corrupt her, ya dog!*

Middlestead rolled his eyes, blowing out a breath. "Yeah, yeah, it's what I wanted." He tossed the half-smoked cigarette into the nearby butt can. "But it's not what Sonny wants."

"Oh, *there's* a surprise," Torrin responded. "What gave it away? Her telling you to back off?" *Dammit! Shut up!* she ordered herself. Unable to sit any longer, she rose and walked a few steps away.

Stiffening in anger, the dark man glared at Torrin's back. He forced himself to look at the situation, accepting his culpability in it, and dropped his gaze. "Yeah, I'm dense. No big surprise there. If she hadn't told me to begin with, I would have never figured out you two were an item."

Torrin considered. "I think it might have been obvious the first time I planted a big ol' wet kiss on her." She shook her head and turned to face him. "Look, Tom, *you* know I'm bad news. *I* know I'm bad news. Even Sonny's gotta know I'm bad news. Shit, she's seen the women come and go as much as anybody else."

Middlestead recalled a fifteen-year-old on a wet October morning finally discovering that the bevy of women weren't homeless. Despite himself, he let out a dry chuckle. "No ... I don't think she knew you were as bad as all that. She thought you were having slumber parties when you first moved in."

There was a long silence. Torrin snorted. A vision of the groupies doing a slumber party gig was hilarious. Her laughter was infectious, and soon they were both holding their sides with tears streaming down their faces. Eventually, their laughter died down and they were quiet, Torrin still jittery.

"I'm sorry for being such an asshole. She's all the family I've got, and I don't want to see her get hurt."

Torrin shrugged. "Don't blame you. She's a good kid and deserves better."

A speculative look crossed Middlestead's eyes as he regarded her. "I don't know."

The guitarist raised an eyebrow. "Look, Tom, there's one major problem here. I'm not a man." As he opened his mouth, she overrode him, moving closer and towering over him. "No, now listen to me! I'm not saying you're prejudiced. Hell, if you were, I wouldn't be in the band, would I?"

Frowning, the dark man shook his head. "No. You wouldn't."

Torrin waved her arms and shrugged. "She's your sister. It's understandable. Even if I *were* a man, there would be friction between us over the whole mess. But it woulda been a hell of a lot easier for you to accept."

"Do you ..." Middlestead stopped and considered. Forging onward he asked, "Do you think she's gay? Really?"

Eyes lost focus as Torrin thought. She scooped up her cigarettes, dumping them in her pocket. "I don't know for sure. She's had crappy luck with boys. I can't say I've ever seen her lust after any of them. Schoolgirl crushes, yes, but nothing more." Again she sat on the bench, foot tapping to the unheard beat of crank. "The men she hangs out with are friends. I haven't seen a romantic attachment." *That's 'cuz she's already attached, Torry. To you!* Pause. *Would it have been different if I had stopped that first night?* A tiny voice whispered, *I don't know.*

Middlestead nodded solemnly in understanding. "I know what you're talking about. I haven't seen anything either."

Torrin snorted. When he glanced at her, she said, "Buddy, you didn't see her throwing herself at me for the last year either." She snickered at his chagrin, imagining a blush in the dark. She stuck her hand out towards him. "Truce?"

The drummer regarded her for mere seconds before taking her hand. "Truce."

They sat for a few moments in silence, Torrin's body in a constant state of motion, letting the feud between them settle into the concrete beneath their feet.

Middlestead finally glanced at his watch. "Damn. Already nearly five in the morning. I've gotta get some sleep."

"Yeah. Me, too," Torrin lied. They stood and regarded each other. "Night, Tom."

"Night, Torrin."

Torrin moved quickly up the wooden steps to her door. Behind her, she could hear Middlestead going into the house. Slipping inside, she closed her door, leaning against it briefly as she scanned her room.

Her eyes needed no adjustment, a single candle burning in the window, illuminating the space in golden hues. Torrin stepped further into the room, shrugging off her jacket and dropping it onto the floor before she saw the form in her bed.

Sonny was asleep, breathing easy. Her long frame was wrapped around one of Torrin's pillows, hugging it close in her slumber.

Torrin moved closer, movements stealthy. She squatted down, staring at the dark woman. The meth in her system screamed to keep moving, and her hands twitched on her knees. Ignoring it, she forced the desire down, refusing to respond. It was torment, but nothing she didn't deserve.

Watching her lover sleep peacefully, Torrin remained still. No matter how hard she tried, Torrin couldn't fathom what made Sonny tick. Her mind worried it like an old bone, her thoughts racing as she tortured herself by not moving, not risking awakening her.

Hours passed. The gray light of morning overcame candlelight;

Torrin watched dawn play across her young lover's face.

"Hey, sexy," a low voice said in her ear.

Sleep disturbed, Torrin growled and rolled over, pulling her pillow over her head. She heard a soft chuckle and felt the sheets shifting as someone slid beside her.

"Time to get a move on," Sonny said, caressing her lover to wakefulness.

Torrin grumbled, "Don't wanna." She had finally begun crashing early the previous morning, barely making it to bed to sleep most of the last two days away.

Hands on Torrin's body were warm and inviting. The post-high depression had lifted somewhat, but her eyes hurt, and her skin seemed to crawl with itchiness.

Sonny grinned as her lover squirmed, trying to burrow unsuccessfully into the bedding. She snuggled closer.

When the brunette had awakened two nights ago to find Torrin peering down at her, she thought her heart would explode. Neither of them mentioned the absence or the night that had triggered it. Instead, Torrin made gentle love to Sonny, as close to an apology as she would receive. The tension and animosity had fairly disappeared between Torrin and her brother, so Sonny was certain the two had talked through their difficulties.

Stroking her lover's arm, Sonny felt the tattoo against her fingers. *Almost like it's trying to get out for real.* She continued her subtle attack. "C'mon. You've got a meeting."

There was a groan from under the pillow. "Go without me," Torrin mumbled, knowing that it wasn't an option.

"Nope." Sonny slowly pulled the pillow away, revealing tousled hair and firmly closed eyes. "Betcha they're wanting to organize a more extensive tour for the CD."

Torrin sighed. *No rest for the wicked.* She cracked open an eye to gaze at her tormentor. "I'm awake," she growled, rolling onto her back.

With a suspicious look, Sonny studied her. "You sure?"

"Lemme prove it," the guitarist said. She reached up and grasped the back of her lover's head, forcing her closer for a rousing good morning kiss. *Fuck morning breath!*

Small and crowded, the meeting room held not only Warlord, but also Sonny and their lawyer. Representing White Horse Records were the producer, Mike Hoffman, two of their lawyers, an executive vice president named Jonathan Allen, a publicist and a secretary taking notes.

Torrin lounged in her chair, mirrored sunglasses on to protect her sensitive eyes from the overhead fluorescents. A couple shots of Jack Daniels before leaving the house had helped make her feel a little more human. Beside her, Sonny watched the proceedings with intense curiosity, having never been privy to the business side of the band's dealings.

The VP tossed a magazine onto the table with a grin. "Here ya go. Warlord just debuted on Billboard at number thirty-seven."

"Thirty-seven? No shit?" Middlestead asked, eyes wide.

Allen's grin widened. "No shit," he echoed. As Hampton reached for the magazine, he continued, "Seems that 'Violation' is getting a lot of airplay."

"Far fucking out!" Atkins exclaimed. He leered at Torrin across the table. "Must be my singing expertise."

"Yeah, right," the redhead snorted. "You keep telling yourself that."

"So," the bassist interrupted, passing the magazine to Middlestead. "What's that mean for us?"

"Well, frankly, we weren't expecting it," the VP said, rubbing the side of his nose. "The CD's been out for five months. A few play dates and we called it good." He glanced to one side and the publicist took her cue.

"We don't know what happened," she said with a delighted smile. "Your fans have been generating requests at radio stations up and down the coast." She pointed at the magazine. "Considering it debuted at thirty-seven, we think there's some room for further options."

"Which is why we called you in here," Allen finished.

Tamara Hampton, the band's lawyer and sister to the bassist, spoke up. "My clients have already fulfilled their part of the contract they signed in September of last year. What do you have in mind?"

"A new contract," the VP stated with a smile. "Another release of the CD with a new cover. A wider distribution and a national tour of one hundred cities."

"Do you have the contract handy?"

"Certainly." Allen waved at one of his lawyers who produced the document.

"Why did you ask *me* here?" Sonny finally asked. She'd never been involved with the business aspect of Warlord and couldn't figure out what her purpose was in this meeting.

The producer, Mike Hoffman, smiled at her. "*I* asked for you. I suggested to Janet here," and he nodded to the publicist, "that we have a wealth of information, talent and photos available for a new CD cover and merchandising."

"Merchandising?" the photographer nearly squeaked, eyes wide.

Janet stepped into the conversation. "Yes, we'll need to consider T-shirts and such, photos for autograph sessions, a program book ... Have you ever been to a large venue concert with a big name band?" At Sonny's nod, she continued. "Then you recall the various sales. Merchandising brings in quite a bit of income when done properly."

Torrin frowned. "So you want to look at her portfolio and buy photos like you did for the last CD cover?"

The VP cut in. "Yes, that and to offer her an opportunity to do some freelance photography during the tour."

Sonny openly gaped at the man.

Chuckling, her lover sat forward and nudged her. "Close your mouth," she said. As Sonny complied with a snap, she returned her attention to the White Horse negotiators. "You have a contract for her as well?"

"Certainly!" The second lawyer produced a document and slid it over.

Looking up from the first contract, Warlord's lawyer said, "I'd like some time with my clients to go over these." She swiftly intercepted the one for Sonny. "Perhaps we could meet back here this afternoon?"

"Of course!" Allen exclaimed cheerfully. "Why don't I have my secretary make a lunch reservation for you? Say, Monty's on 10th? My treat."

Middlestead's eyebrow rose, and he looked meaningfully at the bassist beside him. The bald man shrugged slightly.

"That would be fine," the lawyer said with a smile. "We can meet here around four?"

"Of course," the VP agreed.

"Whaddya think, Tamara?" Middlestead asked as their lawyer put the documents down.

"It's a pretty good contract." She took a sip of her tomato juice and blotted her lips with her napkin. "With very little editing, you've got a good thing here."

"What kind of editing?" her brother asked, dipping a piece of bread into the garlic butter of his escargot.

"Well ..." She flipped through the contract. "They've tried to gain rights to the songs on the CD again." A pen was pulled from behind her ear, and she drew a line through that section. "And full copyrights on the photos." Another line. "The tour looks pretty good, though I'd ask for some sort of compensation in the event that venues are cancelled. They don't have a clause for that."

"Sounds good." Hampton nodded. "Let's do that."

As their lawyer scribbled along the bottom of a page, the drummer looked at his sister who was working on a salmon filet. "What about Sonny's contract?"

The lawyer swapped documents with a smile. "Actually, pretty good. Aside from the copyright crap." A line went through another clause. "They've nearly doubled the amount they paid for photography usage. They've also offered an advance to set her up for the tour." She frowned. "Again, I would ask for a lump sum in compensation should they decide not to use any of your work during the tour. Plus pay your way on the tour, regardless."

Sonny nodded.

"But when would the tour be? Do they have any indication there?" Middlestead asked with a frown.

"Well," the woman sighed. "Looks like they're aiming for an immediate one. They want to have a go at it somewhere toward the end of next month. You're looking at six to nine months of touring."

The dark man looked pointedly at his sister. "What about college?"

Sonny sighed and stared off into space. "What about college?" she repeated to herself. *Go to college and stay home for the next nine months? Or take a hiatus and do what I've wanted to do for over a year now – be the band's first publicist?* Her eyes fell on her brother, and she could feel Torrin watching. "There's hardly a choice, Tom. I go with you guys."

"Are you sure?" For so long she'd babbled about going to college and becoming a writer. Middlestead hadn't gotten used to the course change that had occurred over a year ago. "Won't that mess up your scholarship?"

She shrugged. "Possibly. But I've got money in savings still. If they want it back, they can have it. I can pay for the next semester I attend with the trust fund."

He nodded solemnly. Glancing at Torrin beside his sister, he mused, *Like there was any doubt.*

To the lawyer, Sonny said, "Count me in."

Sonny's Journal – April 17, 2002

Well, tomorrow's the big day! We open for Silverdust here in Portland and then we go with them for the next eighteen tour dates on the west coast! After Silverdust, I'm not sure who they'll hook us up with. It's gonna be cool hanging out with other bands. I'm really looking forward to it.

We got to see the tour buses. Wow! Totally amazing! Pretty ritzy living for a road trip. I can imagine why, too. All the comforts of home. We've got two of them. We'll be traveling with four drivers, a couple of security people, the tour manager and his assistants.

The CD cover is looking mighty fine, if I do say so myself! Ha ha ha! It's been released all over the United States and has already shown great sales. It hasn't gone gold or anything, but Jonathan Allen says it looks pretty promising.

Tonight we're having a dinner party at Lamont's Place. He's closed down for the night and having it catered in celebration! I think there're about a gazillion people on the guest list!

I've gotta finish packing! Then get ready for the party!

Don't turn your back on me;
my love is a dagger
and I will use it.
TORRIN C. SMITH, "REALITY BYTES"

Part VII: Turbulence

You know I want it,
know I need it;
abuse is my only pleasure.
Exquisite pain.
Rape me!
TORRIN C. SMITH, "VIOLATION"

A warm, sunny June day could be seen through the bus windows as the miles went by. Currently en route to Des Moines, Iowa, Warlord now opened for an East Coast band called Manslaughter.

Their latest concert in Kansas City sold out, everyone returning to the hotel in high spirits. It had taken a while for them to unwind, of course, as they partied into the wee hours. The early morning departure had been particularly enjoyable for the harried hotel staff watching groggy, disgruntled people shuffling out to the buses.

Middlestead decided to take a nap around ten in the morning. It wasn't long before his sister took his cue and wandered off to the small bed she shared with Torrin.

Sonny removed her jean shorts and curled up under a thin sheet. Sunlight fell over her from the window, the play of light and shadow dancing across the lanky form. She was having the most wonderful dream.

They were on the beach in Texas where their bus had broken down. The water was warm and a crisp blue-green. Instead of the band and crew cavorting around in the waves, it was only she and Torrin. No one could be seen for miles.

After playing in the surf, the two trotted back to the blanket they had spread on the sand and applied suntan lotion to each other. The lotion sparked a hotter fire than the sun overhead. Soon, they were naked, their swimsuits tossed with careless abandon into the warm sand.

Sonny felt firm hands on her body, caressing, tickling. Hungry lips claimed hers. The dark woman sighed, pulling her lover closer, burying her hands in red-gold, guiding those magic lips and tongue farther down.

Her breasts received careful attention before Torrin moved on, licking and tonguing the lithe torso. Sonny felt like she would go insane with the languid pace. It was both excruciating and delicious.

Finally the redhead was teasing her lover's sex, stroking with an expert tongue, tasting salty sweetness. Here, in the dream, Sonny moaned aloud.

"Shhh," Torrin urged before continuing.

The dream continued with the guitarist thoroughly loving Sonny, easing her up through the thin clouds above them, the sandy beach far below.

Between Sonny's legs the texture altered. Something hard slid in her wetness, and Torrin's face was above her, gazing down with lust filled eyes. Sonny recognized the sensation and felt a tightening in her belly before her lover thrust into her.

The sudden sensation of fullness pulled Sonny completely awake. She groaned deep in her throat, clutching at the warm body above.

"Shhh," Torrin whispered again in her ear. She rotated her hips, enjoying the surprised gasp.

"Tom ..." Sonny whispered, licking her dry lips.

"Is asleep. And if we're quiet, he won't wake up," Torrin assured her. With agonizing slowness she withdrew the strap on dildo that was buried within her lover. She felt the pull of the piece inside her in response and bit back a moan.

Panting, Sonny glanced to the thin partition at the head of the bed that separated them from the rest of the bus.

Torrin reached her apex and just as slowly returned her toy to its nest. "Everybody is playing poker," she added, her voice husky. Her hands grasped the dark woman's hips as she pushed in to the hilt. "You want me to stop?" she growled, nibbling at the tender neck.

Sonny's legs wrapped firmly around her lover's hips and she pressed closer in response

Chuckling, the redhead murmured, "I'm gonna fuck you long and slow, sexy. It's gonna take forever."

As their lovemaking continued, Sonny unsuccessfully tried to coerce her lover into speeding up. The guitarist remained true to her word, prolonging the sweet agony for as long as she could, leisurely sliding in the wetness between them. Torrin smothered her with ravenous kisses to quiet the brunette's moans.

Both sweated profusely, trembling in their efforts to hold back. Torrin pulled her lover closer to the edge of the bed, her toes digging into the carpet for better traction. Sonny still had one hand tangled in red hair, the other having reached around to play with a nipple ring, twisting and squeezing as she panted.

Torrin picked up the pace, smoothly thrusting and rolling her hips. Her lover's heavy breathing was harsh in her ear, and she heard a whispery moan. The dildo nestled within her increased its friction with each movement, urging her higher.

Sonny strained against her lover's hips, clutching at her with firm legs. She was beyond thought, the toy stroking her with strong purpose, Torrin's hands digging into the soft flesh of her hips, mouth passionately blazing a trail to encircle an aching nipple. She growled deep in her throat, tossing her head back. Above her, she saw blue sky through the window and passing tree branches.

The redhead slid her hand down a taut, sweaty belly and began massaging Sonny's erect clit, biting down on a nipple. As the younger woman cried aloud, Torrin climaxed, convulsing against her with a deep groan. Sonny suddenly stilled, sensations rolling over her as an orgasm welled up and overtook her.

They lay a few moments in silence, hearts slowing; the only sound the wheels on the road beneath them.

"Now, *that* was a great dream," Sonny said, smiling. She combed her fingers through red-gold hair.

Torrin chuckled. "Interrupted a dream, did I?" She swirled her hips, enjoying the gasp it elicited from beneath her.

Breathless, Sonny said "Oh, yeah."

"Couldn't help it," the guitarist explained. "I came in here to get something, and you looked so delectable I had to have a taste." She slowly withdrew and rose to her feet.

Sonny scooted further onto the bed and lounged on one elbow, watching her lover remove the toy. "I'm glad you did," she said.

"Hmmm ... So am I," was the response. Torrin set it to one side and climbed onto the bed. She lay on her back, gathering her lover into strong arms.

For a time they lay together, the summer sun playing across their nude bodies, cuddling. Both women were silent.

Eyes closed, Torrin relaxed into the embrace, her mind strangely at peace. The voices were silent more often than not when she was with the dark young woman. It was strange, but she took what inner stillness she could get. Only when she was drunk or high did the voices not torment her.

Sonny's silence was based on fear. She enjoyed the physical closeness with Torrin. Time and again, when she began the tentative foray into an intimacy that was not physical, she was rebuffed. Sometimes it would take days before her lover would come back, to hold her and not have a haunted look in her eyes. There was so much she wanted to tell Torrin – a world of emotions and wonder and love. But it couldn't be. *Not yet, anyway,* she mused, fingers mentally crossed.

Sonny traced intricate patterns on skin. "Know how long before we get there?" she finally asked.

Torrin shifted a bit, glancing at her watch. "'Bout an hour," she said, returning her hand to ebony hair. "We get dropped off at a record store for a signing. Everybody else checks into the hotel and sets up the show."

"How long are we in town?"

"I think three days. We've got two gigs, and I'm pretty sure Craig was talking about a day off before we head to Dubuque."

Sonny nodded at the reference to Craig Tramuto, the tour manager. "That'd be nice." She paused for a moment, chewing her lip. "Think maybe we could do something together on your day off? You know ... a picnic or something?"

Picnic? Yeah, right! And don't forget the little clapboard house with a white picket fence, Torry! the derisive voice popped up.

Feeling the woman tense, Sonny inwardly cursed. *Dammit! I wish I knew what's setting her off!* Rather than allow Torrin to pull away from her again, the photographer squeezed her in a hug. "Or maybe we'll just barricade ourselves in the hotel with strawberries and whip cream," she suggested flippantly, appealing to her lover's libido.

That was rewarded with a lascivious chuckle, and Torrin's body relaxed. "I'm liking that," she said, thoroughly kissing Sonny before rolling out of bed. Torrin slipped her shorts on and reached for her sports bra, her clothing of choice during summer months. She scooped up the dildo and moved toward the door.

"Wait! Where are you going?" Sonny asked, eyes flickering nervously to the toys in her lover's hands and then to the partition door.

Torrin grinned at the developing blush. She waved the items in the air. "Gotta go clean these up."

"But ...!" Sonny paused and swallowed anxiously. "But ... they'll *see*," she whispered, looking pointedly at the partition.

"Sexy, they've already *heard*." The guitarist laughed. "You weren't very quiet towards the end, ya know."

Sonny groaned and pulled the sheet up over her head in embarrassment. "Oh, *man*." She heard her lover rummaging in a drawer. Peeking over the sheet, she saw Torrin grabbing a plastic baggy.

Turning around, Torrin realized she was being watched. "Almost forgot what I came in here for." She grinned, wiggling the baggy with several black capsules in it.

"What's that?" Sonny asked.

"Black Beauties. I'm not gonna be worth *shit* tonight without a pick-me-up." Torrin kissed her lover senseless before heading for the tiny bathroom.

As the partition door opened, Sonny heard the poker players in the other room with their raucous comments. She groaned and hid underneath the sheet again in embarrassment. "God, I hope Tom didn't wake up."

The tour buses pulled up outside a downtown record store. Posters covered the windows with album covers and various recording stars, two-dimensional faces looking out onto the street. Outside the establishment two dozen women, aged fourteen to their mid-thirties, loitered. As the bus slowed, they began to chatter excitedly and drift closer. It was plain they had been waiting for Warlord.

"This is so unreal," Hampton said as he eyed their fans from a tinted window.

Surprisingly, Atkins agreed with him. "You ain't a-kiddin'."

The tour manager climbed aboard. "Okay, folks!" he called. "Let's get a move on!" Craig Tramuto was a stocky man with thick black hair that wasn't quite kinky in its curl. "I've got Beth and Ignacio running security. Sonny? You stayin' or goin', honey?" he drawled.

"I'm staying," Sonny confirmed, shouldering her camera bag.

"Great!" Tramuto exclaimed. He handed over two boxes of photographs, a box of black markers on top. "If you'd be so kind as to be their gofer this afternoon ...?"

"Sure, I'd be glad to."

Relieved of his burden, the manager rubbed his hands together. "Alright, then. There're a hundred rabid fans inside, so be careful. They seem polite enough, but you know the score." He bent over and peered out the window at the business' door. "Okay ... Looks like they're ready for ya."

The band was ushered out of their relative safety, the two security guards taking over and helping Warlord get to the record store.

The tour manager stopped Sonny, the last off the bus.

"We'll drop your stuff at the hotel. Tell 'em we'll send a car to pick 'em up in about two hours, okay, honey?"

She nodded confirmation and was out the door. The buses pulled away as she followed in the wake of the band.

Inside, the store was cramped, the crowd making it feel smaller than it was. It looked like the band had been placed at a table all the way to the back. Even as Sonny eased her way through the throng, she heard someone over a loud speaker.

"Hey, Des Moines, look who *we've* got visiting us!" There was a smattering of applause and whistles. "It's Warlord, folks! Straight from their gig in Kansas City!" After the next round of cheering died down, the announcer continued, "They're here in town to put on two shows for us at Maxwell Smart's! Let's give them a big welcome!"

More applause and Sonny reached the table. She scooted behind it, the female security guard stepping back to thwart a hopeful fan. With quick precision, she opened the boxes of photos as the announcer asked people to organize themselves for the signing.

Their CD began playing, and there was the steady hum of activity as fans approached. While the band was busy signing, Sonny poured them each a glass of water from the pitchers provided. Everything settled, she pulled the camera out of her bag and set.

So far, the Warlord publicist was averaging two rolls of film per city. A pen and notepad was slipped into her hip pocket for notes on each exposure. Lately, Sonny was experimenting with different types of filters. Her favorite was the color filter that caused everything to appear in sepia tones like an old-fashioned photograph.

Today let's try the soft focus, she decided as she dug into her camera bag. The filter and flash were quickly attached, and Sonny stepped out from behind the table, scanning for angles.

"Man, how long you been playin' drums?" a teenaged boy asked Middlestead, handing over his CD for an autograph.

The dark man grinned and shrugged. "All my life." He raised an eyebrow as he paused, pen to cover.

"Oh! Ummm ... Make it to Matt."

"Sure thing, Matt." He scribbled a platitude as he continued, "I was banging on pots and pans in the kitchen at a fairly young age. It was just a matter of safety for the cookware ..."

The youth snorted as a fourteen-year-old girl at the opposite end of the table shyly asked Torrin for a picture. Smiling, Torrin pulled one from the top of the box, a shot of the four of them doing a 'pin-up' pose for Sonny.

"Would you put it, 'To Marcia, love, Torrin'?" the girl asked.

The guitarist nodded and began writing. "You bet, Marcia."

"Oh, *I'm* not Marcia! It's for my best friend." The teenager leaned forward with a conspiratorial air. "Her mother wouldn't let her come down here today."

A red-gold eyebrow rose. "She wouldn't, huh? How come?" Finished signing, she handed the photograph to the girl. When the kid rolled her eyes in exasperation, Torrin remembered the same expression from her lover at about that age. A strange nostalgia crept over her.

"She thinks you're evil or something." A pert nose wrinkled and the youth shook her head. "She says that your songs are bad and won't let Marcia listen to your CD!"

"Really?" A spark of anger burned. *What a fucking bitch!*

The girl nodded. "Uh huh. Pretty mangled, huh?"

"Yeah. Pretty mangled." Torrin glanced next to her to see if Hampton heard the story.

The bald man pursed his lips, shrugging slightly. "Well, they *did* put a warning label on it," he murmured as he signed an autograph. "Some parents just don't let their kids listen to that stuff. Nothing personal."

"Whatever," she grumbled. *Good thing you didn't have* that

problem growing up, huh, Torry? A dry wind blew through her soul. *Yeah, damned good thing.*

As Sonny became more experienced, she planned her shots. By the time the signing was over and the owner locked the door, she'd only used about a dozen exposures, catching three or four of the crowd and the remainder of the band as they interacted with their fans. Her expertise had increased to the point that she was confident most of them would turn out well.

"That was a blast!" Atkins exclaimed, rising to his feet and stretching. He picked up several pieces of paper, putting them in his wallet. "I think I've got at least nine phone numbers here."

The security guard, Ignacio, clapped him on the shoulder with a wry grin. "A woman in every port, eh, Lando?"

The tall man snorted. "Only one? I don't think that'd be enough, Iggy!"

Sonny snickered as she put her camera away. A strong arm reached out and grabbed her by the waist, pulling her backwards. She spun as Torrin rose to plant a long, wet kiss on her mouth.

"Hey there, sexy," she said.

Smiling, Sonny snuggled closer, holding her camera to one side. "Hey there, yourself. Have a good time?"

The shorter woman shrugged slightly. "Alright I guess, for being an exhibit in a zoo." She pulled back and looked into Sonny's eyes. Torrin seemed to be ... *searching* for something, and there was a long silence. As her lover's brow furrowed in puzzlement, a voice in her head screamed, *What the fuck are you doing?*

Sonny frowned. There was something elusive in her lover's eyes, and she couldn't quite catch it. Then the mask was in place, and Torrin stepped out of the embrace. The dark woman watched her swagger over to one of the counter people, asking for a restroom. As Torrin left, Sonny returned to putting her camera away, mulling over the strangeness of what had just transpired.

Closing the bathroom door firmly behind her, Torrin leaned against it and closed her eyes. *You're getting too close,* she warned herself. *You're looking for something that's not there.* A whispered, *But what is it? And what if it is there?* She thumped the back of her head against the door. "I don't know" was the plaintive response to an empty room.

Several minutes passed before Torrin stepped to the sink,

vigorously washing her face with cold water. Peering into the mirror, bloodshot eyes stared back. Torrin frowned and reached for the paper towels, drying her face off. She dug into her pocket, pulled out the baggy of pills and dry swallowed two of them before stashing the rest. With a sigh, Torrin squared her shoulders and left the bathroom.

She found Middlestead on a ladder behind the counter, signing a section of wall. The storeowner was talking excitedly with Sonny and Hampton.

"What's going on?" Torrin asked as she sidled forward.

Sonny grinned and waved her arm at the wall behind the counter, a long expanse of white peppered with signatures in varying colors. "Mr. Thanapolis asks everyone who's popular to autograph the wall." She excitedly took her lover by the arm and urged her down a few feet. "Look! See!? He's even got Stephen Beckworth's signature!"

Torrin nodded solemnly, noting the autographs of Sonny's favorite band "Not bad." *Yeah? Big fuckin' deal,* a voice grumbled. *Who gives a shit anyway?* Torrin mentally shook off the voice. She heard her name and turned, seeing the bassist waving her over to the ladder. "Guess I'd better add my name to the wall too, huh?" She smirked at her lover. *Oh, yeah ... Horny Torry the Superstar.*

Sonny grinned as they walked over to the ladder.

Rather than the usual rental car or van picking them up from their publicity spots, a limousine awaited them at the back door, the driver standing attentively nearby. The band was sufficiently impressed, circling the sleek white vehicle before piling inside. On the road, Middlestead and Atkins spent most of the trip standing in the open sunroof, whooping and hollering at passing vehicles and pedestrians. Sonny wondered how long they would have the car and whether or not she would be able to get a few shots of the band in it.

The limo pulled smoothly into the parking lot of a large nightclub, passing through a chain link fence watched by four security guards. Several fans were there hoping to catch a glimpse of their favorite band and called out to Atkins, who waved. Additionally, there were three picketers to one side, holding signs reading "Warlord is Evil!" and "Just Say NO to Violence Against Women!"

Once everyone was through security, the group moved to the main stage. The headlining band was finishing their sound check, the various speakers and equipment set to their specifications and dutifully marked.

Looking for the security chief, the two guards with Warlord moved away. Still excited by their unexpected set of wheels, the band bounced onto the stage to began their sound check. Middlestead's drum kit was rolled onto the stage as a hoist lifted the other band's drums to the ceiling.

Sonny settled into a seat four rows from the stage. She decided to forego any photographs for the time being, pulling out her journal and pen. A good half hour passed before the tour manager slumped into a seat to one side and a row ahead of her. Tramuto sighed deeply and rubbed at his face. "How'd it go at the record store?" he asked, peering at her.

"Pretty good," Sonny reported, setting her pen inside the notebook. "They were all quite nice. No riots or anything."

"Good, good." The stocky man idly watched the band go through the onstage motions. "What'd they think of the limo?"

She chuckled. "Loved it! Torrin perused the wet bar while Tom and Lando hung out the top, heckling people." Sonny leaned forward, elbows on her knees. "Why'd we get it?"

Tramuto grinned, a glint in his eye. "You'll find out after the concert tonight," came the cryptic response. "Oh!" He removed a packet of papers from his vest pocket. "Here are your hotel keys."

"Thanks." Sonny stuffed them into her camera bag.

"Craig?" an older man interrupted with an apologetic grin. He poked a thumb behind him, indicating a group of newly arrived security. "The locals are here. Doug wants you to go over the war plan with him and the new meat."

Tramuto sighed and forced himself to his feet with a groan. "I'm off ... In more ways than one." A chocolate brown eye winked at the woman. "Have a good night, honey."

"I will. You too, Craig."

For the millionth time, Sonny considered investing in a video camera as Warlord played for the crowded stadium. *Or maybe four or five of them.* She recalled a video on a national music station that had been shot from the band's point of view as they played a concert. *From publicist to video director!* She chuckled, shaking her head.

She was standing to one side of the stage in an area blocked off from the crowd. A wide mass of people in front of the stage was moshing to their hearts' content. Looking at the audience, Sonny could see that the nightclub was nearly sold out; the only seating available was in the nosebleed sections.

It had been an uphill roller coaster. As time went on, the venues they played were getting larger and larger, the crowds more and more excited by hearing Warlord than the band they opened for. There had been a week stopover in Burbank as the group taped a video of "Violation," the song that was getting the most airplay on the radio. Their popularity had risen exponentially ever since.

Sonny's attention returned to the stage. Even as she watched, a young woman was boosted onto the stage from the left and made a dash for Hampton. A burly security guard in a yellow T-shirt neatly scooped her up and rushed her offstage.

The band finished its song, the last of the set, with a flourish. The bassist thanked the crowd and Warlord trotted offstage. House lights came up, though not as bright as they'd been before the concert began.

Sonny watched in amusement as the crowd went ballistic, stomping and clapping and screaming. As expected, her brother and his band mates came back out, the cheers rising to a crescendo. The lights went down, and a spotlight hit Atkins who had moved to stage front.

"I guess y'all wanna little *more* ...?" he asked with a seductive grin.

A collective yell came from the audience.

The guitarist tossed his head, long brown hair moving over his shoulder as he glanced around at his mates. When everyone appeared ready, he turned and nodded to Middlestead.

The sound of ripping cloth filled the stadium and the audience quieted down. Middlestead began the beat, followed by Hampton's accompaniment with bass. Guitars kicked in and Atkins stepped closer to the mic. His smoky voice spoke the lyrics to their hit, "Violation".

Spectators jumped up and down in time with the music, and Sonny watched with a mixture of amazement and humor. She frowned when she saw a banner raised from the farthest seating – "Just Say NO to Violence Against Women!" Looking around, she got the attention of the security chief, pointing at the banner.

Sonny kept an eye on the situation as she listened to the now familiar lyrics. When the chorus was sung, she heard Torrin's voice mixing with Atkins' before the rest of Warlord joined in. She shivered, not liking the words of the song but realizing that the fans loved it. Hearing Torrin's voice calling out, "Rape me," wasn't pleasant. *But, hey ... It probably helps her to write about this stuff. Get it out of her system.*

The area around the banner was converged upon by several security guards, and the sign pulled down, the people responsible herded toward the exits. Oblivious, the crowd continued cheering and singing along with their favorite song.

Another surprise awaited the band at the hotel. A guest service aide met them as they piled out of the limousine. She escorted the band through the lobby and to the elevators. "We've got everything set up for you. Your rooms are on the sixteenth floor, right near the elevators. If you need anything, just give the front desk a call."

Puzzled by her attentiveness, the band members thanked her with confused smiles. Atkins stopped long enough to ask for her phone number.

"C'mon, Lando!" Torrin called from the crowded elevator. Warlord, her lover and three security guards surrounded her. "I wanna catch a shower before we go out tonight!"

The tall guitarist jumped into the elevator, grumbling. "Alright, alright!" As the doors closed, he glanced at his diminutive partner. "She's a cutie, isn't she?"

Torrin shook her head with a snicker, and the rest of the occupants chuckled as well.

They reached their destination, stepping out onto the sixteenth floor. A sign indicated the directions to different rooms and the Concierge Lounge down the hall to their right. Directly across from the elevator was a set of double doors with their room number on it.

Sonny dug out the keys that Tramuto had given her earlier. While the three guards wandered off to their own rooms on that floor, she handed out the room assignments. "Looks like they've got you, me and Max in this one," she said to Torrin, approaching the double doors, puzzled. "Tom and Lando each have their own rooms."

Rolling her eyes, Torrin snorted. "So much for privacy."

Hampton used his keycard to unlock the door before him. "Never stopped you before," he said with a smile as he opened the door.

Sonny blushed scarlet.

The lights were on in the short hall. They stepped inside, Hampton leading the way.

"Whoa!" he muttered.

Two couches were in the suite, and every table had assorted flowers. To the right of the living area was a large dining table that was covered with food. The television was set to a video station, popular music floating through the room. There were three other doors in the room: one on either side wall near the windows and a set of French doors.

Sonny poked her head through a door off the hallway. "Wow!" she exclaimed as she turned on the light. "This bathroom is huge!" She stood in the center with amazement. "And it's got two toilets!" she called out. Directly across from her was another door.

Just as Sonny peered out the new door, Torrin opened the French doors on the right, revealing a king-sized bed. "Hot damn!" she said with a lecherous grin and a wink for her lover. She then looked over her shoulder at the bassist. "We got dibs on the bed!"

The brunette giggled as Torrin jumped onto it and splayed out on her back.

"Oh, *yeah,* I could dig some strawberries and whip cream now," the guitarist said with a suggestive wink.

As Sonny joined her, the door in the far corner of the dining area opened, and Middlestead looked in. "Hey! I thought I smelled food!" He looked around as he entered. "Damn, but this rocks! Wonder if they gave us the wrong rooms or something?"

As the drummer began filling a plate, Torrin called from the bed, "If they have, let's not tell 'em until tomorrow."

"You've got the right rooms," a new voice said.

"*Lisa*?" Hampton stared at his girlfriend. A grin broke out as he rushed forward to envelop the blonde woman. "What are you doing here?"

"Surprising you," she responded with a happy smile. "Is it working?"

Atkins stepped into the room from the other connecting door. "I'll say! How ya doing, girlfriend?"

There were hugs and kisses between them as everyone sought to welcome Foley to their suite. Food was dished, a minibar cracked open, and everyone settled down to fill their bellies and catch up.

"They flew me in for the weekend," the blonde woman said as she sliced her steak.

"So why all the hoopla?" Sonny asked. "I mean, we've ridden a limo twice today and now a suite with connecting rooms? What's going on?"

Foley grinned secretively. "Can't tell. It's a secret." She waved her knife and fork in the air at the sudden verbal attack from all sides. "I ain't *saying*!" she insisted. "Craig swore me to secrecy. He'll be here as soon as they've finished preparing everything for tomorrow."

"Are ya gonna be traveling with us now?" the drummer asked, scooping up a mouthful of green beans.

"No," the woman said with a sad smile. "I've still gotta work. Besides, who else is gonna watch the house while you're gallivanting all over the countryside?"

"Bummer," Sonny said.

Foley's expression agreed as she looked at her lover with apologetic eyes. The bassist reached over and squeezed her thigh in understanding.

It wasn't long before Tramuto showed up. Torrin answered the knock and followed him into the room.

"Well, I see y'all found the food," he drawled with a dimpled grin. A glance at Torrin and he added, "*And* the booze."

Torrin settled down next to Sonny, tossing back her whiskey with a smug look.

"So what's this all about, Craig?" Middlestead asked, setting his plate aside and eying the covered item under the tour manager's arm. The rest of the group piped up as well.

Tramuto waved them to silence. Running his free hand through curly hair, he said with his best Texas twang, "Well, kids, y'all done good. White Horse decided to give ya a bit of a surprise." He waved expansively around the suite. "Ya got this for the weekend. We'll do a show tomorrow at Maxwell Smart's, and then y'all get the next day off."

"Not that I'm looking a gift horse in the mouth, no pun intended," Hampton said. "But what the hell for? Why now?"

The manager's face broke into a wide smile. He pulled the package from under his arm and uncovered it with a flourish. "Because yer CD just went *gold*!" He held up the plaque with a gold record and a brass plate shining in the lamplight.

There was absolute silence.

A frown crossed Tramuto's face. "Well? Say *sumpin'*!"

After a long pause, Foley said, "I think they're in shock."

Sonny's Journal — June 9, 2002

This weekend has been absolutely incredible! Warlord has really hit the big time now! Their record went gold last week, and it's been nothing but a party since!

Friday after the show, we finally got to the hotel room. Lisa was here! It was so good to see her! White Horse flew her in to surprise us. (And, boy, was Max surprised!!) And a huge suite! Catered meals! A limousine! Wow!

I don't remember much of Friday, though. Yesterday I spent a lot of time with the toilet. I'll never drink that much again! Yick! I don't see how Torrin does it! She drinks and smokes and pops pills and stuff ... She doesn't seem to suffer from hangovers, though I can usually tell when the drugs wear off.

She's been doing a lot of speed lately. Staying up late, partying, getting up early for interviews, photo shoots and the like. I'm really getting worried. Sometimes she's so wired, she can't come to bed, can't sit still long enough for me to hold her. I think that's why she drinks the alcohol, trying to counteract the speed. It doesn't work.

I just know I don't ever see her 'straight' anymore. It's getting scary.

Speaking of scary, there are people out there who definitely do not *like the songs! I've seen people boycotting the concert! Waving signs and stuff!! There were even some at Maxwell Smart's Friday night! (Maxwell Smart's! What a name for a nightclub!) It's the song — 'Violation'. I haven't figured out if it's the point of view of the rapist, or the victim's idea of what the rapist is thinking. In any case, a lot of people don't like it.*

Small wonder. Even I don't like it. Maybe because I know Torrin and what her dad did to her. Sometimes I wish I could just go back in time and stop him from hurting her like that. She must have been so scared and alone. It's no wonder she's turned to drugs and alcohol. I hope she'll finally realize that I'm here for her.

As Sonny awoke, she felt sunlight warming her body where it filtered through the bus window. There were sounds out in the main area, people murmuring, the clinking of metal against plastic. The bus was running, air conditioning keeping a tolerable temperature in the mid-August heat of New York City. She inhaled deeply, smelling coffee and the unfamiliar odor of bacon. *Wow! Breakfast? That's a surprise!*

She stretched, luxuriating with feline grace. Eyes opened then widened in surprise as she sat up abruptly.

Sonny was surrounded by a riot of metallic color. The alcove she shared with her lover was filled with a huge bouquet of helium balloons in all shapes and sizes. With a delighted smile, she pulled an unusually large Mylar heart toward her, turning it to read the writing. 'Happy Birthday!' read the cheery letters.

"Oh, wow!" she breathed. "They remembered!" Stealthily, the partition inched open, and Sonny turned to watch with a curious smile.

A gray eye peered in. The brow lowered in a scowl, and Torrin turned to the rest of the bus. "She's *awake* already. You guys are making too much noise." Grumbling at their denials, Torrin used a booted foot to slide the partition open and stepped into the tiny room, carrying a tray laden with breakfast.

"This is fantastic." Sonny smiled, shifting in the bed and pushing balloons aside. "Thank you!"

Torrin shrugged, reddening. She settled the tray on the photographer's lap and bent for a kiss. "Well, we aren't in a hotel, so I couldn't very well order room service."

Sonny looked over her food, grabbing silverware and a napkin. "Who's idea was this?" she asked, reaching for some toast.

"*Hers*!" a voice from just outside the doorway answered. "You decent, Sis?"

"Hold on!" Sonny called. Torrin scooped up a T-shirt from the foot of the bed, and the dark woman put it on, almost losing her tray in the process. She giggled as Torrin juggled the food. "C'mon in, Tom."

Middlestead, wearing only jeans, leaned smugly against the doorway, arms crossed. "Don't let Torrin fool ya," he said, eyes sparkling. "Deep inside that bitchy exterior beats a heart of gold."

"Bite me," the guitarist grumbled, looking out the window.

He held up a thumb and forefinger about a centimeter apart. "A *little* one."

Sonny chuckled, picking up a mug of coffee. A quick sip and she grimaced, handing it to her lover. "Yick! This one's yours."

Torrin rolled her eyes and rescued her mug. "Sorry. Mine has less sugar and more alcohol."

Smacking her lips in distaste, Sonny eyed her lover. "*Way* more alcohol ... Is there any coffee in there?" She'd meant it as a teasing remark, but immediately after the words slipped from her mouth, she wished for them back.

Gray eyes flashed. Torrin peered into her mug, teeth grinding on her immediate response. "Well, you know how we musicians get," she said with a feigned grin. "Gotta have something to write about in our obituaries." Seeing Sonny flinch, she felt both furious at herself and bitterly happy she'd scored a point.

"Well, *that's* a pleasant way to start your day," Middlestead said, trying to lighten the mood. Turning, he called over his shoulder, "Hey, guys! Get in here!"

The rest of the occupants crowded around the doorway and sang an enthusiastic "Happy Birthday." Oblivious, Sonny reached for her lover's hand only to have Torrin shift until she was inaccessible. While it appeared natural, the separation was not lost on her. *Swell. If this is how my birthday starts ...*

Torrin's day was going from bad to worse.

First the near mob scene when she had gone into that Mom and Pop grocery store for a half dozen eggs. Some teen punk with dreadlocks, tattoos and piercings had recognized her. Before Torrin knew what was happening, she was surrounded by a handful of skaters demanding autographs.

And then this shit with Sonny, she grumbled to herself. Torrin glanced across the limousine at her lover who was talking with Tramuto about photographs from an overhead crane during the next concert. *She was just teasing. You're being too sensitive,* a quiet voice whispered from her depths. "Whatever," the guitarist growled.

"You say something?" Atkins asked her.

The redhead shook her head, slumping farther into her seat. She glared out the window at passing scenery, ruminating over her bad day.

To top off the morning, she discovered she had used the last of her uppers the night before. Her connections among the roadies hadn't been able to score since they'd hit New York State. She could feel the depression setting in. Alcohol wasn't helping, and Torrin knew better than to take downers when she was feeling this way. *Dammit! I need a boost!*

The limo pulled into a parking structure off the famed 42nd Street. Warlord was headed to a television interview. They were required to film a couple of commercial spots plugging the cable station, do the interview, sign a few autographs and the like – all the publicity stuff that Torrin was not in the mood for. Even as the vehicle parked near an elevator with four people waiting, she could hardly keep her eyes open.

The band, three security guards, Sonny and Tramuto exited the limousine. Introductions were made; the individuals waiting for them included a junior vice president, his aide and a couple of technicians. The crowd climbed into the elevator and took off. Torrin purposefully avoided Sonny, putting herself into a crowded corner with one of the techs and the aide. Her expression was cross, and she focused on staying awake until this fiasco was over. The voices chatting back and forth washed over her, irritating her further.

"You okay?" the tech asked, peering at her.

"Fine," the woman snapped.

Nonplussed, he shrugged, watching her. "You look like you could use a pick up or something. Have a bad night?"

Torrin's eyes narrowed. "Something like that."

The elevator reached its destination and the doors opened. In the activity of people getting off, the technician reached out and shook her hand. "Well, lemme know if you need anything else, okay? I'm *sure* I can be of assistance."

Torrin felt warm glass in her hand and raised an eyebrow. She accepted the handshake, palming the vial. "Thanks." *Yes!*

"No problem," he said with a warm grin before turning to join the rest of the crew preparing for the interview.

As everyone was briefed on what was expected of them, Torrin got directions to the women's room. Upon her arrival, she found a large expanse of room with several stalls to the left. Torrin went to the farthest stall and stepped inside, anticipation coloring her thoughts.

She pulled the vial from her pocket and studied it closely. *Looks like crank.* Unscrewing the cap, she covered the small opening with a finger and tilted it, looking closer at the powdery substance on her fingertip. A light dab to her tongue brought a familiar, bitter mental taste of the high that would follow.

Yes! Cackling gleefully, the guitarist glanced around the stall, finding a folding shelf just behind the door. She pulled it down, using her elbow to keep it from springing back into place. Torrin poured a small amount of the precious powder onto the metallic surface.

She heard the outer door open and froze for half a second. The call of the meth was not to be denied, however. The guitarist pulled out her wallet, glad that the substance was more powder than crystal, and pried out her identification card, using the edge to form lines. The stall walls shook as another woman entered nearby and used the facilities. A dollar bill was removed from the wallet and made into a straw. As the other toilet flushed, Torrin snorted the crank deep into her nostrils.

The initial euphoria was mild, but to her tender nerves, it was ambrosia. Torrin exhaled and slumped in relief, her forehead resting against the cool surface of the door. She took a few moments to savor the feeling. The door shook as the other occupant left the stall followed by the sounds of running water and paper towels being crumpled.

Torrin waited for the woman to leave. Once the outer door thumped closed, she raised her head and took a deep breath. Sniffing, she wiped at her runny nose before cleaning the shelf and letting it snap back into place. Torrin stepped out of the stall and went to the vanity. The door opened behind her, and she looked into the mirror to see her lover's reflection.

Smile breaking out on her face, the guitarist turned off the water and turned around. “Hey, sexy,” she greeted as she pulled paper towels from the dispenser.

Sonny smiled too, though she studied the redhead intently. “Hi. I've been sent to find you.” *She's high again. Why'd she wait until now?*

Torrin tossed the used towels into the trash and swung her

arms open wide. "Well, here I am! They ready?"

The taller woman nodded. With little prodding, she sank into the embrace, smelling leather and soap. "About this morning ..."

"Nope. Don't say it," she rumbled, her hand caressing the back of Sonny's head. "My fault. I was being overly sensitive." Before her lover could argue or make further comment, Torrin kissed her soundly, reveling in the sensations that were altered by the drug in her system. "C'mon, sexy. They're waiting."

Sonny allowed herself to be led out the door.

The institute was fairly pleasant as mental hospitals went: a score of white buildings on a hill encircled by a few acres of well-kept grounds. A tall chain link fence surrounding the property was the only thing that looked out of place, clashing with the old Southern plantation feel of the property. On sunny days, the inhabitants came out to play or sit on conveniently placed park benches to enjoy the occasion. Various nurses and doctors and aides were also seen, interacting with their patients, observing their behaviors or having lunch meetings.

It was raining today, however, the cool drizzle speckling the windows and keeping everyone inside. There were rooms where group therapies were going on, individual office sessions, staff meetings. There were also common rooms where many of the residents gathered. Here they were vegetating, fidgeting, rocking repetitiously or talking to themselves and others. Games were being played, pictures drawn, jigsaw puzzles worked on and television watched. Additionally, it was visiting day, which increased the hospital's population a bit, though sadly, not by much.

A woman sat in front of a rainy window. Her hair, dark with a smattering of gray, was cut into a short, manageable style. She wore a pastel blue button up shirt and tan slacks, a beige sweater draped across the back of the wheelchair she was perched in. Staring into space, she appeared to be looking out the window, but her blue eyes never moved, only blinked occasionally.

Nearby sat two women – an older and younger version of the patient. The elder, the patient's mother, prattled on about family news as she worked on a needlepoint project. The younger, the patient's sister, listened idly and watched, occasionally interjecting her own comments. Their voices droned on and on, never impinging on the inner horrors their relation held close. Nothing and no one ever made it through the walls she erected five years ago.

A voice did work its way through the thick barrier, however. It was the voice of her personal demon, her horror. Most times it would only be inside her head, driving her to bouts of violence, but lately she began hearing the voice outside her head, tickling her ears, pricking at her barriers, dredging up memories and terrors.

Slowly, ever so slowly, the woman's head turned. Her eyes rolled in her head, straining from their lack of use, searching.

Nearby a ratty television set and a cluster of donated couches and chairs held a handful of the residents. One was a young man with stringy black hair, smoking a cigarette and avidly watching an interview. His body vibrated from the constant tapping of his slippered foot, and he held himself close, pulling at his upper lip between puffs. It was *his* television time and he'd chosen a music video station. His mother had told him that Warlord would be interviewed, and he'd been an absolute angel all week to obtain the privilege.

The woman in the wheelchair focused on the television screen.

"So how is success treating you?" a blond young man with a nose ring asked. The members of Warlord sat to his left.

"So far, so good," Torrin responded exuberantly. "It's been a wild ride!"

"We've been on tour for ... what? Five months?" Middlestead looked to his band mates for confirmation. "It's definitely been an interesting progression."

Nosering nodded. "And how's the tour doing? You're opening for Bloodsport right now. Is it any different than when you were opening for other bands?"

"Well, yeah," Atkins answered. "Different bands have different ... *flavors*, ya know?"

"Well, I haven't heard it put *quite* like that before, but I know what you mean," Nosering laughed. He shook unruly blond dreadlocks from his eyes. "According to the credits on your new CD, "What's Been Done," many of the songs are penned by Torrin. How do you come up with lyrics, and do you guys work well together?"

Hampton pursed his lips. "I think we work really well when it comes to writing songs. I mean, yeah, most of the lyrics are Torrin's, but when it comes down to creating the music for it, we all kind of come together to hash things out."

"From all reports, your song "Violation" has been the most popular. I'm kinda curious. The song appears to be about a rape. Is it?"

There was silence for a moment. Finally, Torrin spoke. "Yeah, it is."

Torrin's demeanor cued Nosering that he was treading on very tender ground. The baleful gazes directed at him, not only from the diminutive guitarist but the young woman behind the cameras, made it obvious. *Howard Stern, I'm not.* He diplomatically let the matter drop, turning to camera number two and said, "Wow. Talk about a sensitive subject. Let's go ahead and give it a listen. Here's Warlord with their hit single, 'Violation'."

The screen faded to the video, a standard concert scene.

At the hospital, the woman's strange behavior had been noticed. Her sister interrupted their mother's blathering, tugging on the sleeve of her blouse. "Mother!" she exclaimed in a hushed voice. "Look!"

The older woman looked up from her needlepoint. She'd seen this behavior in her eldest before, this almost lucid reaction to some outside stimuli. She knew not to dash the younger woman's hopes. They had argued for years over what triggered the response. She had long ago stopped getting excited about it. Her afflicted daughter would follow this by either returning to her catatonic state or screaming and fighting off her hallucinatory attacker until sedated.

"Yes, honey, I see," she said, returning to her project. She kept a close eye on her daughter, appearing not to pay attention.

"But what's she looking at?" the younger woman wondered. It was her theory that if they could figure out what caused these breaks, they might be able to reach inside and pull her sister out. She rose and stepped over to the wheelchair. Kneeling beside it, she took her sister's hand. "Sylvia?" She followed the nearly sane gaze.

"Wow!" Nosering exclaimed with a smile. "That's a pretty intense song!"

"Yes, it is," Hampton agreed. "That's why we decided to include it."

"We've had reports of a lot of ... negative response as well. People have been picketing your shows and the record stores that carry your CD all over the country. How do you feel about all that?"

"Personally?" Torrin asked. "I consider it fantastic. By raising hell over it, they're putting more light on the CD, and we, in turn, get more publicity." She looked into the camera and said with a triumphant gaze, "Thanks for the support!"

"Mother! Isn't that Torrin Chizu?"

Sylvia looked into the evil gray eyes of her demon, heard the honeyed voice thank her – *thank her!* – for her support. The voices screaming welled up from her wounded soul, obliterating the vision.

Sonny lugged her suitcases up the stairs to her room. She dumped the bags on her bed and looked around, hands on her hips.

It felt weird to be back home and in her room. She had, in effect, been living with Torrin for the entire tour, sleeping in the same bed every night for seven months. Returning to sleeping alone wasn't going to be easy.

It was the end of September and a typical Portland day. A light drizzle kept the air smelling clean and fresh, the cloud cover kept everything a light gray. Sonny went to her window overlooking the backyard and stared at scenery that was both familiar and not.

She saw the redhead, an unfinished cigarette dangling from her lips. Torrin clambered down the stairs from her room. She stopped at the patio long enough to take a final drag before tossing the butt into the can. Beneath her, Sonny could hear the sliding door.

Well, maybe she'll chill on the drugs now, the brunette hoped, moving back to the bed and fumbling with the fastenings on a bag. *No need for her to be up all the time anymore.* A knock on her door interrupted her thoughts and she looked up.

Torrin leaned against the doorframe, arms crossed and an easy grin on her face. "Hey, sexy."

The smile was returned, despite the mood. "Hi. Got everything unpacked?" Sonny got the bag open and peered down at the jumble of clothes.

Torrin shrugged. "You could call it that," she allowed. "All the clothes are in the same corner."

"Ah, you're a slob," Sonny laughed.

Moving into the room, the guitarist chuckled. "And you're a neat freak." She settled down on the corner of the bed and captured one of her lover's hands, pulling her close.

Sonny closed her eyes, feeling Torrin's arms around her waist and a cheek resting against her belly. She ran a hand over the older woman's shoulders and back, the other caressing red-gold tresses. A feeling of love welled up within her heart. The urge to speak it was so strong it hurt. She bit back the words.

Ask her, ask her, ask her! a voice whispered urgently. *No way, Horny Torry! It's been nice with a steady piece of ass, but face it ... You ain't the 'living with' type!* Torrin inhaled deeply, trying to draw all the comfort she could. The tiniest voice said, *Stay with me, accept me,* love *me.*

Feeling her lover stiffen, Sonny sighed imperceptibly and slid from the embrace, knowing it was going to end soon anyway. She returned to her bags as though nothing were wrong, sorting through her clothes. *God, how much longer can I do this?*

Torrin watched silently, a hidden war raging within her soul. She wanted so badly, *needed* Sonny so much. But she didn't know why she needed and wanted. The guitarist only knew that it made her weak and vulnerable. The unknowing power Sonny held over her was distressing. Voices screamed and argued and bickered until the quiet one was drowned out.

All she knew was that the loneliness of her room was intolerable. She found herself drawn to Sonny's room. *I need a distraction.* Torrin considered asking her lover along but decided against it. *We're too close already. I need some distance.*

Rising, she smiled at Sonny and walked to the door. "I'll see ya later, sexy."

A moment of panic hit Sonny. "Wait!" She thought rapidly as her lover turned back to her, curiosity on her face. "Uh, where ya going? You want some company?" she finally asked, attempting to sound nonchalant.

Despite her initial desire for the dark woman's company, Torrin shook her head with a rueful grin. "Naw. I'm not going anyplace in particular. Just out tom cattin'."

"Oh." Sonny swallowed.

Torrin stomped down the pain of her lover's crestfallen face.

Yer doing her a favor, Horny Torry! "Later." She turned away.

The phone rang on the nightstand. As the guitarist sauntered out the door, Sonny picked it up. "Hello? Oh. Yeah, hold on." She held the receiver to her chest and called, "Torrin!"

"Yeah?" came from the hallway.

"It's for you. It's White Horse."

Torrin stepped back into the room. "Thanks," and took the receiver. "Hello? Yes. Really? Why?" Puzzlement became grimness. "I see. All right. I'll be there." She hung up.

"What's up?" Sonny asked, concerned by the mood change.

The redhead glanced sharply at her, almost surprised to see her there. "Uh ..." She shrugged. "I have a meeting with some lawyers tomorrow." She moved to the door again.

"But ... *why*? Did they give you a reason?"

The mask, which was never far away, was back in place. Bored eyes looked at her. "Someone's filing a civil suit against me, and the lawyers wanna go over it before I get subpoenaed."

Dark brows furrowed. "A lawsuit? Whatever for?" She watched her lover shrug and leave the room. "Torrin?"

Sonny's Journal – September 22, 2002

Well, the tour's over and we're home. I'm too late to register for fall semester, so I'm going to go back to work at my old job until December.

It felt strange to be back. We've all changed, I think, everybody in the band and myself. It was pretty awkward with Torrin this afternoon. I think she just wanted company when she came in. Why else would she have come to my room? Then she pulled away – same ol' same ol'.

I really love her. But, I've been too scared to tell her. I know she'll run away when she finds out. She's got it in her head that she doesn't deserve love – and until she decides differently, she won't accept it from anybody. Not even me.

I can't go on much longer like this. She's destroying herself with the drugs and alcohol. I can't talk to her, not about the things that are really important to me. I feel kinda selfish for saying this, but I don't deserve this. I know that telling her my feelings will cause her to bail on me, but I have to tell her before I explode!

And when she's gone, I'll remember her and love her anyway.

I just hope that somebody somewhere will be able to reach her, get her to see she's not a bad person.

I was planning to tell her tonight, but she took off after that call from White Horse. When Tom got back from the store, I put him up to calling them and digging for some information.

When Torrin was a kid, she was apparently involved in some big incident with an adult. She had lots of charges on her – assault, battery, possession and usage of illegal substances. Even attempted murder! Then all the charges were dropped. Now that she's gotten famous and has some money, the family of this shadowy victim has come forward and slapped a civil suit down to get some cash.

So until we find out exactly what's going to be happening, I'm gonna keep my mouth shut. If this is as serious as the lawyers are making it sound, she'll need all the support she can get. And if I say anything, she just might disappear. That won't help.

Torrin came home drunk. I don't think she had any drugs. She usually goes for the uppers, and alcohol doesn't touch her when she's flying. She went right to sleep tonight, though, which is why I think she stayed away from the stuff. I'm watching her sleep as I write this.

Once this mess is cleared up with the suit, I'll tell her. I have to. Or else I'm going to go crazy from this inability to share with her.

Anger, confusion;
your eyes reflect both.
Suicide is better than this.
TORRIN C. SMITH, "PERSONAL HELL"

Part VIII: Vicious Truth

I remember the day she died,
blue eyes black.
TORRIN C. SMITH, "SLAVE CRIME"

1997

The techno-goth music was loud, the bass causing her eardrums to vibrate as she moved through the crowd towards the bar. Torrin's only concession to the gothic nature of the club was jet-black hair. Her clothes, of course, were black as befitted a heavy metal aficionado, her naturally light skin seeming to glow against the dark backdrop. She was fourteen, having had her birthday three weeks prior.

Torrin sidled up to the bar and ordered a soda, paying for it with the last of her cash. *Better pick something up, Torry, or your gonna be in some serious pain.* She took a sip before turning to size up the crowd as she lounged against the bar.

The club's interior was black, floor to ceiling and wall-to-wall. Every shiny surface was chrome and chain and mirror. Behind the bar, the mirror was etched with an intricate design of cobwebs. A few wall sconces held dim lights that looked like brushed silver, gleaming dully.

It was a standard Friday night, the mix of minors and adults about equal at the Erato Nightclub. To the right was the dance floor, a mass of people moving to the beat of a song. On the left were tables and chairs, filled to capacity. There were plenty of people who appeared attached, groups of twos and threes sprinkled throughout the establishment – runaways escaping the chill of winter, school kids trying to be risqué. A massive group of about ten laughed uproariously at a table in the back corner. However, a few others could be seen – adults sitting alone, scanning the crowds, cruising, searching. Hunting.

As was she.

Warming from the heat of the collective crowd, Torrin unzipped her thin, corduroy jacket, removing it to reveal a cropped tank and little else. She sighed in relief as the material was removed from her arm. The cloth brushing against her new tattoo was agony. Her father commissioned it – *Lucifer* – payment for a job well done. Red eyes glared at her. *Who sees who?*

"Nice tat," a voice commented from beside her.

Torrin looked into blue eyes. "Thanks," she said, allowing her vision to suggestively amble up and down the woman beside her. "Got it done last week."

The woman nodded. She appeared to flush a little at the frank gaze, tucking dark brown hair behind one ear. "Mind if I ...?" she asked, reaching towards the tattoo.

"No. Go ahead. It's a little tender, but it's healing fine." The woman slipped a long hand around her upper arm, and Torrin could feel the back of the woman's knuckles brushing the side of her breast. As the woman appeared to study the colored skin, the teenager studied her.

She was in her mid-twenties, dressed in gothic clothing. A long black skirt, slit up the side, revealed dark stockings and long legs. The white ruffled collar of her shirt was opened to her bosom, a black leather collar gleaming in the lights of the club. A leather cuff adorned her right wrist, an intricate silver bracelet on her left. There was a delicate chain connecting the bracelet to a ring on her finger.

Cuff, collar and a slave bracelet ... Looks like ya got a custy, Horny Torry! To test her theory, Torrin let her presence fill the area. Her confidence made her appear to tower over the woman.

In response, the woman seemed to shrink, but she didn't release Torrin's arm. Rather, her thumb moved in teasing circles, just on the edge of the irritated flesh. Eyes peered at her, gauging.

Bingo! Play your cards right, Torry, and Lucifer'll leave ya alone tonight. Her voice pitched low, Torrin asked, "Like what you see?"

The woman blushed again, dropping her gaze.

"Don't look away when I'm talking to you."

Eyes snapped to the youth. The woman swallowed nervously, but there was another light in her gaze. Imperceptibly, her breathing rate increased.

Torrin kept her mask on, a sovereign authority that made people think she was far older than she was. "You didn't answer my question," she said, raising an eyebrow. "I don't like to repeat myself."

Ruby lips parted and a whispered "Yes" was uttered.

Nodding thoughtfully, Torrin picked up her drink, taking a long swallow. Her eyes never left the woman. She set the glass down and reached for the woman's free hand, drawing it to her mouth. Cold lips pressed into the woman's palm, and she watched her prey's eyes flutter closed. She stepped closer, those same cold lips lightly brushing an ear. "How badly do you want it?" she asked.

The woman shivered, her hand clutching Torrin's arm, but didn't answer.

Letting it slide for now, Torrin pulled back a bit. She moved her arm from the woman's grasp and slowly slid onto her barstool. "Maybe you should tell me what you want. And then I'll tell you what I want." *Give it to me, babe.*

The woman stood still, apparently debating. Chewing her lower lip, her dark brows furrowed in thought, she drifted closer to the regal teenager, a moth to flame. She was still silent.

Torrin sighed in exasperation. *Time's a wastin', Horny Torry. Either shit or get off the pot.* "You don't do this very often, do you?" she observed. At the woman's headshake, she pursed her lips. "Here's the deal, babe. This is the negotiation phase. You tell me what you want, and we see if we can work out a ... compatible transaction."

"I understand," the woman said, her voice low and skin flushed.

"And what you want *is* ...?"

There was a long pause. "You," she eventually responded. Her following words were in a rush, as if fighting to get them out before she lost her nerve. "I want you to ... um ... be in charge, to force me." Blue eyes looked away, face crimson, voice lowered in shame. "To have your way with me."

Fingers touched the woman's chin, guiding her head to look at the teenager. *Is she a candidate?* "What are the limits?" Torrin asked.

The woman looked surprised. "No limits."

Torrin's eyes widened. *Ahhh, the night is good.* "No limits?" The eyes narrowed and wandered over the woman again. *No wonder she's so submissive.* "Public sex? Showers? Scat? Bleeding? No limits on any of it?" *She doesn't look like a kid, though.*

The dark head shook. "No limits."

Torrin inhaled deeply, trying to puzzle her out. She'd been hooking for Louis for four months. Usually, she brought him money, though he was always on the lookout for new "adventures" as he put it. Torrin had only found one other person who was willing to roll over and accept whatever another could dish out, regardless of the dangers or consequences. Those were the only kind her father would accept. Her mind shied from the memories of that encounter. "What about safe words?" she asked, already knowing the answer.

"No safe word. I can take whatever you've got."

An eyebrow rose at the subtle challenge. *Got a live one here, Torry!* a voice crowed. This had been a tough night. She hadn't made much money, and Louis was waiting at home. A whisper deep inside said, *Don't do it. She doesn't deserve it.* Torrin stomped the voice down. It'd never done her any good when she was a kid; it wouldn't help her now. She turned her gaze to the crowd, appearing aloof as she scanned the patrons. "You got a car?"

Relieved that her search appeared to be over, the woman nodded, a smile coming to her face. "Yes. It's in the parking lot." She, in turn, looked around their immediate vicinity. "Do we have to leave just yet?"

Time to play the game. Flinty eyes gazed on the woman, at odds with the seductive grin playing across Torrin's face. "No. Not yet." She pushed away from the bar. As the woman moved to join her, she pressed a hand against the white clad shoulder. "Stay."

The woman froze at the command, trembling.

Stepping behind the woman, Torrin tilted her head to one side, regarding the long form. *Very nice. Lucifer likes 'em tall.* The palm slid from the shoulder, meandering down the back, across the swell of hip and down the thigh and calf. Torrin, squatting beside the woman, felt a familiar tingle at the sight of the shapely leg peeking from the cloth.

Startled, the woman shook as she felt the hand slide up the inside of her leg, pausing to knead a firm thigh. Another jump when the girl found her garters, snapping a strap before continuing her path and brushing the moist panties.

Torrin rose, removing her hand from the damp cloth. *Oh, yeah. She's a hot one.* The smallest whisper was heard, *Stop this! This isn't right!* It was ignored. The ebony-haired teenager rose, pressing her body against the woman's back, one arm wrapped around her waist, the other hand pulling dark brown hair aside. She had to stand on tiptoe, but was able to breathe into the woman's ear. "What's your name, babe?"

The woman's belly cramped with sensations of dread and arousal. "Sylvia," she said hoarsely.

"Sylvia." The name rolled off Torrin's tongue. The beat of the music seemed to surround and invade the pair. "Lose the panties," she ordered.

"B ... but ... I *can't!*" the woman gasped, eyes rolling to look behind her. The hand on her waist slid up and harshly tweaked a nipple, and she gasped again.

"Let's not use that word. I want your underwear off." Torrin growled, knowing full well that the woman couldn't comply, not without removing the stockings and garter belt first.

Sylvia swallowed, panic fluttering her heart. "The garter belt ... It's *over* my panties," she whispered, half afraid and half hopeful there would be reprisals for her refusal.

Appearing to consider this, Torrin's hand gently caressed the breast it had just pinched. *Time to up the stakes.* "Get my jacket and come on," she said, dropping her hands and stepping away.

The woman obeyed.

Torrin led her prey into the bathroom, ignoring a couple making out in the corner. She moved down the line of stalls, all without doors, and ushered the woman into the last one. Taking her jacket from nerveless fingers, Torrin draped it over the stall wall and pushed the woman's back against the partition. She pressed against her, nibbling at her neck. "Grab the top of the wall," she murmured.

Sylvia did as told, stretching herself out, pushing her breasts forward into her new mistress. There was a soft snick as Torrin pulled away, and a stiletto was suddenly caressing Sylvia's cheek.

"Don't move." Again the woman obeyed, and Torrin idly traced a path across smooth skin. Part of her mind wondered what kind of person got a kick out of being submissive. It was a puzzle to her. *I sure as hell don't like it.* That thought brought memories of Louis and his friends, flashes of pain and blood and screaming. She shut them down. *Not now!*

The stiletto's long and torturous trail roamed over Sylvia's body. Her eyes were closed and she quaked, but her hands never left their position on the stall, and she made no moves to pull away. Her breathing quickened as the tip scratched across the material of her shirt, circling her nipples and tickling her ribs.

Torrin concentrated on the task at hand. She had to admit that this was a turn on, this absolute control wielded over another person. The effect it had on the woman before her was erotic, and she could feel her heart speed up. *But it's not for you, Horny Torry.* Focused on the task at hand, she quietly asked, "You got friends here?"

"No," Sylvia panted. The edge of the stiletto was moving down her thigh. As the blade slid beneath the dress at about knee level and drew itself upward, she shivered at the feel of her stockings catching on the tip before whisking away. Then it was past the material, pressing inexorably along her inner thigh, her muscles shaking in tension.

Using a knee to widen the stance, Torrin slowly caressed the woman's panty-clad center with the point of the sharp instrument. The resulting whispery moan brought a rush of arousal, and she unconsciously licked her lips. With her other hand, she guided the stiletto into the leg opening. "You *did* say no limits?" the teenager husked.

Sylvia swallowed, feeling warm steel against her nether parts, pressing gently against her erect clitoris. "No limits," she gasped, fighting the urge to rub against the sweet, dangerous pressure.

With a quick, precise move, Torrin twisted the blade and tugged, severing the offensive material. The woman could feel cool air against her center, the severed cloth brushing against her pubic hair.

"Problem solved." Slowly, the stiletto retreated, spreading humid warmth in its path before it was gone. "Open your eyes."

Peeling her lids back, Sylvia saw the stiletto glistening wetly before her.

"Clean it." Gray bore into blue. As the woman delicately began licking the blade, Torrin growled in appreciation. *Take her now!* a voice demanded. Another whined, *No! Lucifer'll kill ya!* She closed her eyes, wrestling with her desires. Louis' voice echoed in her head, *Either bring home money or bring home a bitch tonight, Horny Torry. Your choice. You know the consequences for failure.*

Lucifer shook her like a rag doll, ignoring her cry of pain. "A reminder is in order." Horrified, Torrin watched as her precious guitar smashed to the ground. He let go of her to concentrate on his destruction, and she vainly tried to intercept, to stop him. He snarled and shoved her away, stomping on the body until it splintered. Her heart as broken as the instrument, she slumped to the floor.

Sylvia watched the play of emotion on the pretty face, watched the eyes close, wondered if this woman could give her what she so desperately craved. She finished her chore, enjoying the salty taste of her juices mingling with the metallic tang, enjoying the fear coursing through her veins.

At the stall entrance, there was a gasp followed by a giggled, "Sorry!"

The knife disappeared in seconds and Torrin glared at the intruder. "Back off!" she snarled. "We're busy!"

The interloper rolled her eyes and grimaced. "Chill, sweetheart! I'm going!" She could be heard grumbling to a companion as she moved out of the doorway.

Torrin sighed deeply, her mood broken. *Probably just as well.* She pushed away from the woman's long form, dropping her knife into her pocket. *That was nice. Gonna have to try that again someday when I've got more time.* She could hear the music outside, recognizing the opening strains of one of her favorite songs. "C'mon, Sylvia, let's go." Torrin scooped up her jacket and handed it to the woman, turning away.

The Bloodsport song was slow and seductive. *I'm gonna meet them some day,* she mused. *No matter what Lucifer says!* Through the beginning piano strains the voice of the lead singer could be heard. Leading her prey onto the dance floor, Torrin found a relatively quiet corner. She took her jacket and tossed it to the ground, turning to face the woman with her arms crossed. "Dance for me."

Sylvia appeared surprised at the command. Her heart fluttered with nervous anticipation, and she glanced around the dance floor, watching other couples moving in time with the music, seeing the tables of spectators watching the floor, watching her. Jerkily, she began to move, her embarrassment at dancing alone causing her to lose the beat. There was sudden, sharp pain as Torrin stepped forward and twisted her arm behind her, turning her to face the tables.

"*Look* at them!" Torrin ordered.

The sharp pang in Sylvia's shoulder warred with her increased excitement as she did so. People in all manner of gothic dress and undress drank, laughed and seriously conversed. Some were watching Sylvia and her tormentor with eyes of wariness, interest, avid curiosity and lust. She felt Torrin's breath in her ear.

"Ignore them. *They* aren't important. *I am!* Dance for me. Or this ends." Torrin applied a smidge more pressure on the trapped arm to make her point, knowing that the submissive in her arms would do as she was told. Then she released her prey and stepped back.

Sylvia turned around, a slow pirouette. She licked her lips, a passion glowing in her eyes before she closed them. There was a moment of stillness as she prepared herself. She began moving, following the words of the song.

Her mouth cotton, Torrin licked dry lips. *Fuck, I wish I had money for Lucifer tonight!* she mourned, watching the woman lose herself in the deep bass and metal guitar strains.

The slow beat was erotic. Sylvia moved to the sound, hips swaying, her arms and hands moving in the air around her with alluring intent. Hands ran through her hair and she tossed her head back, revealing her collared throat as she caressed her breasts, holding them, pushing them upwards. An offering.

Smoldering eyes opened and she eased forward, wondering if she could get away with touching her mistress. Sylvia circled to one side, draping an arm over Torrin's shoulder, dragging her hand across flesh and cloth and hair as she slipped behind the still form. She pressed herself against the girl's back, sliding down, hands moving on strong thighs.

Torrin forced herself not to react, though she trembled inside at the raging passion. The dark-haired woman continued her circuit until she was standing before her, arms draped over her shoulders.

Torrin's hands found the woman's hips. Sylvia undulated against her, head thrown back in invitation. Eyes raking hotly over the offered body, Torrin felt pressure building in her loins as the woman ground against her thigh. With a feral snarl, she swiftly bent forward and took the smooth flesh above the collarbone into her teeth.

The woman gasped at the attack, startled. She pressed harder against the well-muscled thigh between her legs, groaning out over the music, no thought to the eyes that were watching them. Her hands were buried in ebony hair as her vampire, her mistress, devoured her.

Things were getting out of control. *Not now! Not yet!* Torrin pulled back as the song ended, forcing the woman away from her. The long hands in her hair tried to push her back into place, but she wouldn't have it. A flash of anger and she growled, "Back off, bitch!"

The tone and words splashed cold water onto Sylvia's desire, trepidation rushing to fill the void. Her arms dropped and she bowed her head, hands fidgeting, shaking from her thwarted desire.

Torrin resumed control, forcing down her fiery need. With a stern look, she circled Sylvia. Another song started. Dancers left and others arrived to take their places, but they were left alone in their corner. "Does your mother know you're a slut, Sylvia? That you come to a place like this and let people fuck you? *Hurt* you?" she asked, brushing the woman's ear with her lips, simultaneously pinching her ample rear with sudden viciousness.

Sylvia's eyes were shut and she shuddered, blushing. There was another pinch, this one on her upper arm, and she forced herself not to jerk away from the flaming sensations. "No. No mother." The lips moved to her other ear, she could feel a tongue lick the delicate organ, and she sighed.

"What about Daddy? Does he know you like to be brutalized? In pain? Screaming?" Torrin reached inside the slit of the skirt and pinched the tender inner thigh of one leg, knowing she was leaving marks.

The warm hand still inside her skirt moved in slow circles over sensitized flesh. "No, I don't have a father," she said. That appeared to be the correct answer, because the fingers under her clothing reached up and caressed her opening, gathering moisture.

"You're so wet, Sylvia." Torrin caressed the hood of the woman's clitoris, feeling her lean back. *I've gotta get us outta here. Lucifer's waiting.*

Sylvia almost fell as the hand moved and the body behind her stepped away. She teetered and regained her balance, opening her eyes once again. Blushing, she saw people avidly watching the drama on the dance floor, the warmth intensifying between her legs.

Torrin moved back around, licking her finger clean, trying to gain control of the voices whirling about in her head, telling her what to do. She stepped away and picked up her jacket. "Let's go."

The woman swallowed in anticipation before following her mistress out of the bar.

Sylvia parked where she was told and shut down the engine. They were in a fairly well to do neighborhood: a place of BMW's in every garage and the requisite "help" working in gardens and kitchens during the day. It was nearly midnight, however, and all was dark and quiet. Lights could be seen in a few windows, mostly on the upper levels with drapes tightly drawn.

Torrin popped her seatbelt and opened the car door. "C'mon," she said, stepping into the chill air, breath puffing into a cloud of vapor before her.

The woman nodded meekly and followed.

Her senses on alert, Torrin eyed the suburban setting where she resided. It was a pretty sure bet that the occupants were wrapped up in their own lives. No one would notice the neighborhood rebel returning home with the catch of the day. *Fuckin' sheep.*

Torrin led her prey, not to the house they had parked near, but down the tidy little alley behind it. Her back still twinged from the beating last month when she'd stupidly had her prey park in the driveway. Louis had not been happy.

Three yards down Torrin reached a high wooden fence. At the gate she yanked on a heavy cord, opening it onto a well-manicured lawn. She quickly ushered her charge in before locking the gate with a padlock hanging on a nearby peg.

She took Sylvia's arm roughly and hustled her across the yard to the back door of a Victorian style home. A light was on in the living room, shining dimly through to the kitchen window. *Good. Lucifer's still up. Wonder if he's got company.* Torrin pulled her prey up the stairs, purposely putting her off balance so she stumbled, making noise on the porch. The hand tightened on the woman's upper arm, crushing the flesh, and Torrin growled, "Be careful."

Sylvia's arm ached under the viselike grip, and her mouth was dry. She stood quietly as her mistress dug keys out of a pants pocket. Her blood was singing in anxiety, wondering what would happen to her once the door closed. Then it was unlocked and opened and she was propelled inside the yawning darkness.

Pushing the woman before her, narrowed eyes peered past and down the hall to the living room. Torrin locked the door without looking, an automatic gesture as she saw a shadow moving at the front of the house. *Make it look good.* "Take off the skirt," she ordered, eyes glittering in the dim light.

Not expecting the command, the woman hesitated.

Torrin was on her quickly, a hand pulling the dark hair, yanking Sylvia down. She bent over and hissed into her ear, "I gave you an order." With surprising strength, she grabbed the skirt's waistband and tore it from the woman's body. The sound of ripping cloth and buttons clicking on the floor echoed in the kitchen.

Tears were in Sylvia's eyes, tears of pain and embarrassment and relief. She was bent double with the tattered remains of her panties brushing against her ass. Her mistress was standing beside her, supporting her, holding her by the hair as her center glistened wetly for anyone to see. This was exactly what she needed.

Torrin ignored the dark silhouette in the doorway, silently watching the proceedings. If Louis wanted to join, he'd do so. Until then, his voyeuristic tendencies were to be indulged; he was merely a fly on the wall. *Shit. If that were the case, I'd have taken a flyswatter to him years ago!* Torrin shook off the thought. *Get to work! Before he gets to work on you!*

Sylvia jerked forward, the resounding slap of flesh on flesh ringing through the air. Her hair was pulled tightly and a stinging erupted on her rear. She was spanked again, her other buttock receiving a similar warming followed by her mistress' hand caressing the sensitive skin. Despite herself, she moaned and pushed into the touch.

"You like that, huh?" Torrin asked, dipping a finger into wetness. When there was no answer, she pushed Sylvia away, causing her to stumble and fall against the refrigerator. "Answer me, dammit!" she yelled, apparently furious.

The woman held a hand to her rib cage, a bruise developing from hitting the door handle. Her eyes were wide and she peered fearfully at the ebony-haired youth. "Yes," she whispered. "I like it." Relief flowed through her as Torrin appeared mollified.

Torrin fought down the nausea that was developing. *Quit being a wuss! Beat the bitch and get it over with!* The whisper was back, making itself a nuisance, stirring up the already boiling mess in her gut. *Stop now. Make a stand. Violence isn't the way.* Rage welled up from her constantly warring interior took over, and she stepped forward.

Even as Torrin approached, Sylvia tried to straighten. She saw the flash of fury and raised her hands in reflex protection. Her wrists were plucked out of the air and pressed against the freezer door on either side of her head. The woman felt refrigerator magnets poking into her shoulders and back, her mistress pinning her to the appliance.

The woman squirmed beneath Torrin, exciting her. "That's it, babe. Fight it," she hissed. The struggles intensified on command and her arousal increased as they wrestled, despite her disgust. *Whaddya expect from yerself, Horny Torry? Fruit doesn't fall far from the tree. Granted, he ain't your real dad, but you are what you eat.*

It stopped being a fight when a thigh pressed into slick flesh. Sylvia groaned aloud, her sex throbbing from the contact. She clutched the appendage between her legs, rubbing against the coarse cloth. Her vampire was growling, chewing hard on the tendon beneath her ear, humping her in return. "Yes," she whispered.

In the doorway, the silhouette had not moved. *Not now! Gotta get her downstairs!* Panting, Torrin pulled away, smiling at the whimpered moan of frustration. "Patience comes to those who wait, babe." With rabid fierceness, she devoured the woman's mouth, swallowing the groan as she bit down on the soft lower lip. Retreating, she released one of the woman's wrists and grasped the ring in her collar. Roughly, she pulled Sylvia toward the basement door. "We've got a long night ahead of us," she promised, stepping into the darkness and drawing the woman with her.

The silent shadow followed.

Torrin released Sylvia's other wrist, hitting the light switch as she passed at the top of the stairs. She moved swiftly down the steps, tugging the woman behind her, keeping her off kilter.

The stairs opened onto a mid-sized room. On the left wall were a washer and dryer. A utility sink on the far wall shared space with a solitary toilet and what appeared to be a makeshift shower – a showerhead hanging from the ceiling over a drain in the concrete floor. To the right was a doorway, gaping blackly, as was a door in the remaining wall next to the stairs. It was to the second door that Torrin dragged her charge.

Stepping inside, the teenager flicked on another light. She pulled Sylvia through what appeared to be a small family room. An entertainment center sat beneath the stairs, and comfortable chairs and tables were placed strategically. There was another door here, this one closed. And on either side of it were bamboo wall hangings.

Sylvia was roughly deposited on a couch, and she felt her mistress' hand leave her collar. She watched Torrin go to the stereo system, shrugging off her jacket and tossing it into an armchair. The CD selection was perused, a case chosen and pulled out, the disc put into the player.

As the strains of classical music filled the room, Torrin schooled her features to not reflect her distaste. *How Lucifer listens to this shit is beyond me.* Having heard the same music through every abusive encounter with her father and his friends only served to help her shut down further on some of her deepest emotional levels. The whispered voice was finally silenced.

Sylvia swallowed nervously as her mistress turned to her, a manic gleam in her eyes and a smile that was almost a snarl. The woman's belly was aflutter, and she could almost feel herself soaking the sofa cushion beneath her.

With slow, seductive movements, Torrin went to the closed door, pulling her keys from a pocket and unlocking it. The door swung open onto darkness, and she held out her hand to her prey. "Playtime."

The woman saw not a teenager, but a strong youthful angel of darkness with red eyes glittering from her arm. As if possessed, she rose and went to her vampire mistress, a part of her realizing that this was final. There was no going back from here. The gray and red eyes mocked her, promising her that things would never, ever be the same.

Sylvia took Torrin's hand, allowing herself to be led into the darkness.

Present

Sylvia's scream amid the harsh voices and laughter pierced her consciousness. Torrin bolted straight up in her bed, the scream echoing on the edges of her mind. Hands on her body tried to pull her down, and voices were whispering to her. Torrin scrambled away until she fell off the edge of the mattress and scuttled away to crouch on the hard floor.

Wild eyes looked around. A mattress on the floor, the smell of rain and candles, pale blue eyes watching in shock and a whispered voice trying to soothe her. *A dream! A fucking nightmare!* The relief that welled up caused a lump to form in her throat, and the guitarist felt the sting of unshed tears. *No! Don't cry! Lucifer hates that!*

Sonny slowly eased forward, continuing her litany of calming sounds. Her lover was cowering nude before her, all disheveled hair and panicked eyes. She slid off the mattress and scooted closer. Her first attempt at brushing the red-gold tresses away from Torrin's face were rebuffed, a hand reaching out to swat hers, the body flinching away. Refusing to be daunted, the dark woman forced past the feeble defenses. Soon, she was seated on the cool wooden floor, rocking her lover in her arms.

The tossing and turning originally awakened the photographer. Her usual tricks to calm Torrin down during a nightmare didn't work. A blood-curdling scream erupted and scared the daylights out of her. As Sonny held and caressed the woman in her arms, she could only wonder at the depth of pain that had to be buried inside. *What happened to you, love? What can I do to let you know it's safe to deal with it? That I'm here for you?* Knowing there would be no answers from her broken lover, she whispered calming words and rocked her, swallowing the desire to cry in sympathy and frustration.

As the terror faded, a bone deep weariness invaded her. Torrin stopped fighting her lover's assistance, too emotionally weak to put up any more of a struggle. She relaxed into the embrace and enjoyed a modicum of peace before the voices could reassert themselves.

Long minutes passed. As Torrin gained her composure and woke a bit, she began to pull away. Sensing that the nurturing moment was now over, Sonny stopped rocking and loosened her arms. "You okay?" she asked softly, brushing aside a wisp of hair.

Torrin looked away, embarrassed, struggling with her mask. "Yeah. I'm fine." She sighed deeply, noticing the foul taste in her mouth and dryness of her eyes. *That's right! You tied one on last night, Torry,* Louis's voice echoed in her head, as it had for years. "I need a drink of water," she mumbled, pulling farther out of Sonny's grasp.

"Okay." The long hands gave a final caress. "I'll get it. You get back in bed."

Nodding, the guitarist crawled to the mattress and sat on the edge. She rubbed sleep from her alcohol-puffed eyes and glanced around. Torrin couldn't remember getting home the night before. Obviously, Sonny had gotten her upstairs and undressed. The clothes she'd been wearing were sitting in a neat, folded pile nearby. *If I did that, I was drunker than I thought.* She rooted out a cigarette and lit it.

Sonny approached from the tiny bathroom and handed her lover a glass. "Here ya go, sexy." She smiled at the brief look of thanks as Torrin took it from her and had a long swallow. Climbing onto the mattress, she curled up on her side behind Torrin and propped her head on an elbow. She gently ran her palms along the available skin.

The water was cool against Torrin's parched throat. She drained the glass and set it down on the floor, sighing again at the comforting sensations on her back. Eyes closed, she enjoyed the caresses for long moments, no sound in the room except their even breathing.

Sonny had laid her head down, peering at the guitarist's profile as she smoked. *I wish it could always be this way,* she thought wistfully.

Deep in the abyss of self-disgust, Torrin mused, *I wish this was real.* But, as usual, the voices were there to torment her, deny her, tell her the reality of her world. Torrin took a deep breath, breaking out of her reverie. Turning to glance at the bedside clock, she noticed a strange look on Sonny's face. Her eyes narrowed, her mask firmly in place. *What the fuck was that?*

The brunette dissembled, shuffling the feelings of tenderness and love away. "What time's your appointment with the lawyers?"

she asked, scratching the smooth skin beneath her fingers.

Torrin studied her for long moments, suspicious. "At eleven." She looked at her clock. "I've gotta get ready. The next bus out is in half an hour."

With a startled look Sonny said, "Bus? You can't ride a *bus*, Torrin."

"Why not?" Torrin asked with irritated puzzlement. She rose and padded to her clothing.

Eyes rolled in exasperation. "You're the guitarist for Warlord, sexy. You get on a bus, you'll get mobbed." Sonny sat up, reaching for her clothes. "Remember what you told me about that little store in New York."

Torrin sniffed at the T-shirt she had worn the night before, smoke and whiskey and sweat making her nostrils twitch. She tossed the offending item into the dirty clothes corner and rummaged in another pile of material. "Well, how the hell am I supposed to get there? Call a fucking limousine?" Vague memories of the bars she'd been at plagued her, and she remembered feeling surprised at how many people wanted to buy her drinks. *Well, duh, Torry. You need a clue.*

"No, silly," Sonny said with a slight grin. "We'll call a cab."

Freezing in the process of pulling her shirt on, Torrin stared at the younger woman. "Whaddya mean *we'll* call a cab?"

Here it comes. Sonny shrugged, buttoning her jeans. "I'm coming with you."

Torrin's breath caught and her pulse quickened. *No! She'll find out!* Another voice, the one that sounded like her father, spoke in a snide tone. *Well, hell, Torry. Isn't it about time she did? Found out exactly what kind of animal she's been sleeping with for over a year? Exactly what kind of damage you do?* The guitarist shook her head and continued pulling her shirt on. "You are *not* going," she intoned.

A dark brow rose. "Yes, I am. You can bar me from the meeting, but I *will* be there when you get out."

Stomping on the panicked, babbling voice, Torrin gave her lover a stern frown. Sonny stood before her, hands on hips and reflecting the look back at her, determined. The whisperer said, *She should be told.* And for once Torrin listened to the quiet voice, agreeing. *Maybe that'll send her packing. Nothing else has.* There was a dry chuckle. *Oh, yeah, Horny Torry. If that doesn't do it, nothing will.*

Sonny raised her chin defiantly, knowing what her lover's response would be, knowing she'd have to put up one hell of a fight. Knowing she'd probably have to get a separate cab and meet the guitarist at the White Horse offices. Her mouth dropped open in surprise at the response.

"Okay."

In shock Sonny watched her lover stoop to pull her boots on. *That was too easy*, she considered, a trickle of fear mixing with the elation of winning the goal.

Sonny sat in the meeting room with Torrin, two White Horse lawyers and the vice president, Jonathan Allen. "I still think we should wait for Tamara to get here," she said to her lover.

The redhead shrugged. "What's gonna happen is gonna happen. Ain't nothing she can do about it."

Pursing her lips, Sonny refused to respond to the doom and gloom.

"I'd like to thank you for coming, Torrin. Sonny," Allen said with a smile. "We just want to go over our bases before they call you in for a court appearance."

Torrin nodded. "I understand. Have you been in contact with Mueller's lawyers?"

Lawyer Number One nodded, handing over some papers. "Yes. They're suing you for half of your income on the sales of this album and any future recording projects you might be involved with."

"Also, I believe a lump sum was asked for," Lawyer Number Two mentioned, rooting through a manila folder. "Ah ... Yes. Three hundred thousand."

Sonny looked dumbfounded. "Three hundred *thousand*? Plus half her royalties? Isn't that extreme?"

"What happens to my contract with White Horse?" Torrin asked, ignoring the young woman's outburst.

The men looked from one to the other. "Uh, well, that depends on the public relations aspect," Allen finally allowed.

The guitarist regarded him coolly. "Give me some examples here, Jon."

The VP blew out a breath, obviously uncomfortable. "Well, if the Mueller family insists on going to court and refusing a lump settlement, we can count on quite a bit of bad publicity." He fiddled with the cuff of his shirt. "Frankly, Warlord is too new to handle that kind of negativity. Granted, your first CD is going like wildfire, but until you have a successful second recording, you're considered a flash in the pan."

Sonny stared blankly at the executive, her mind refusing to wrap around what she heard. "So ... what? You'll drop the band because of this?" she questioned, her brow furrowed in growing anger.

"No," the guitarist answered for them. "They'll drop me. The band can go along just fine."

Realizing that Torrin was taking everything in stride, Allen nodded, relieved. "Yes. Each individual member signed the contract. The remaining members of Warlord will be on contract for the required four recordings." As the storm clouds gathered over Sonny, he held up his hand and smiled winsomely. "That doesn't mean we'll have to resort to that, however! We could still get a settlement out of court!"

"You can't *do* that!" Sonny insisted in a loud voice. "You can't just throw her to the wolves! She's the best thing Warlord has got!"

"Sonny ..." Torrin growled warningly.

"No!" The woman turned to her lover. "You can't let this happen without a fight, Torrin!" She lowered her voice, trying to sound calmer. "If you go to court, we'll find the best lawyer around. This has got to be a mix-up. I know the charges against you were dropped! You shouldn't have to pay guilt money to a greedy family! You didn't *do* anything!"

Gray eyes flashed and rage boiled beneath the surface. "You got a copy of the original police report?" she asked the lawyers. At their nod, she waved her hand, asking for it. A thick folder was removed from a briefcase and shoved to her.

Sonny studied her lover as she flipped through the file, concern on her face. *She's just gonna roll over. She thinks she deserves it! She doesn't!*

Looking through the file brought back a rush of memories howling through her mind. *Oh, yeah, Torry! Wasn't this fun? Oh, man! They've even got photos here!* She glanced at the lawyers, noting how quickly they looked away from her manic gaze. *Betcha it's been the talk of the company for the past week*! Deep inside, the swirling agitation of buried memories reared its ugly head.

"Torrin," Sonny began, preparing to state her case.

"Shut up," the guitarist snarled. *Irrational rage, screams of pain, blood and leather. Laughing voices, crude speech, begging whispers.*

Shocked, her lover stared at her.

Torrin laid the file open on the table in silence, spreading out the glossy eight by ten color photos. *Watching eyes, smeared crimson on white cloth, grunts of rape, pain.* "Remember how I told you I'd hurt you?" When there was no answer, she snapped, "Do you remember?"

Swallowing, scared, instinctively not wanting to go through the door that was open before her, Sonny nodded.

"Meet Sylvia Mueller," Torrin said harshly, holding up a photo. *Sound of flesh on flesh, ripping cloth, metallic taste.*

The face of a woman staring dully out of the picture was almost unrecognizable. Blue and red and mottled, one eye swollen completely closed, the nose broken and bloated. There were marks around her throat, almost black in their color, and blood trickling from her scalp and ear.

Sonny winced and looked away. A strong hand grasped her neck, pinching the nerve there and causing pain, forcing her to look at the pictures. *No no no no no ...*

"And *this* is Sylvia Mueller." Another vivid picture, a hand and forearm that was abraded from ropes and sliced up. "And *this.*" Cigarette burns on thighs. "And *this.*" Bleeding, oozing welts on thighs and buttocks. "And this. And this. And this." With each photo, Torrin held her lover's neck, forcing her to witness the destruction of another human being. *The smell of burnt flesh and fear and death and decay.*

"No!" Sonny whispered, trying to shake her head in denial.

"*Yes*!" the guitarist insisted. "*I'm* responsible for this! *I'm* the one who did the damage!" Her grin was turbulent, an insane light glowing in her eyes. "I put her in a fucking *mental* institute, Sonny! She's a fucking *vegetable*!"

Wide blue eyes rolled to catch sight of this woman, this stranger smiling at her from the depths of hell. "But ... "

"No buts, Sonny." Torrin released her and pushed forward, forcing the dark woman to lean back. "I *enjoyed* it," she hissed. "Watching her scream and bleed and beg. It was one of the *best* things that ever happened to me." *Eyes reflecting nothing, and nothing, and nothing ...*

Horrified, Sonny fought back a wave of nausea. Her head shaking numbly, a part of her refusing to believe the evidence she saw, the confession she heard. Feeling her stomach roll, she stumbled out of her chair and ran from the room, tears flowing freely down her face.

It was quiet in the emotionally charged room.

You go, Torry! I'm impressed! Chip off the ol' block! Torrin took a deep, calming breath, fighting the beast down and returning it to its cage. *It was the only way to get rid of her. She'll be safe now.* The whisper returned. *Will she? Or will* you *be safe?*

Shaking off the voices, the guitarist looked up at the men still in the room. A red-gold eyebrow rose at them. She gathered up the photos and put them back into the folder as they looked away and shuffled papers, flushing.

Allen cleared his throat cautiously. "Um, Torrin. That's not quite what the report said."

Torrin shrugged with a nonchalance she didn't feel. "It had to be done." *Now she can have a life.* Deep inside, she curled up into a little ball. *And you can come back to hell, where you belong.*

There was a knock on the door and her lawyer, Tamara Hampton, came in, looking puzzled. "What happened to Sonny? She ran out the doors and wouldn't stop when I called her."

Sonny's Journal — September 23, 2002

Oh, god! What am I gonna do? That poor woman!

Torrin sat hunched over the bar, nursing her drink. She'd been here since the meeting concluded at White Horse, not wanting to go home, not knowing if she had a home to go to. *Horny Torry, the Wonder Whore! Shoulda known better than to hook up with the kid anyway,* an oily voice stated. *She isn't your type.*

"Got *that* right," she muttered darkly, tossing the remainder of her whiskey down her throat. She rapped her knuckles on the bar, getting the attention of the bartender. Pushing the glass away, she ordered another.

The older woman studied the redhead carefully as she removed the empty glass and put it in the sink. The kid had an amazing tolerance level. She already had five doubles, and it didn't look like it was affecting her. Shrugging and shaking her head, the woman poured another and settled it on a fresh napkin.

Torrin took a swallow, enjoying the burn down her throat, and glanced around for the first time.

The Athenian was a small establishment, lesbian-owned and -operated. Being a Monday night, things were pretty quiet. The television over the bar was showing a game, though it didn't appear anyone was paying attention. Beneath it, the relief bartender was slouched on a stool playing video poker, soft bells and music at odds with the roar of a television crowd as a team scored.

Past the bar was an alcove that held a pool table. Three women were smoking cigarettes and enjoying a game, chattering and laughing. The only other occupants of the main bar were the couple behind Torrin at a small table against the wall, engrossed in conversation.

The guitarist was antsy. She needed something, something to help her forget the fiasco at the meeting, the pain and fear in Sonny's eyes, the disgust welling up. She'd left her stash at home, however, and didn't know anyone here. The alcohol wasn't touching her. *With your tolerance it'll take so much booze, you'll die from alcohol poisoning.* There was an idle thought that perhaps that wouldn't be such a bad thing, but Torrin dismissed it. *Like you deserve to 'get away from it all', Torry. Yeah, right!*

Seeing the pictures at the meeting had opened up memories, recollections she'd thought were locked up forever. *Hell! I thought the whole thing was* done *forever.* Disjointed flashbacks kept occurring, derailing her train of thought and interrupting a perfectly good pity potty session.

Heavy leather restraints around thin wrists, a flash of metal as the chain was attached, hanging the woman from the ceiling. Louis watching, directing.

"Well, hey there, sexy!" a voice insinuated itself into her thoughts.

Torrin turned and watched a woman settle down on the stool beside her. The mask fell into place, and she grinned at one of the many women she'd bedded over the years. "Hey, babe, how's it going?"

Tossing her hair back with a smile, the brunette said, "Pretty good. How's fame treating ya?" She waved the bartender over and gave her order.

Shrugging ruefully, the guitarist said, "It's been a roller coaster." *Unnatural rage overcoming her. The heavy strop rising and falling, over and over and over.* The drink was delivered, and she told the woman behind the bar, "Put it on my tab."

The groupie smiled. "Heard you're not available any more," she said, fishing for information. "Something about somebody's kid sister ...?"

"Old news," Torrin responded, taking a swallow and looking away. *Visions of Sonny's face, twisted in passion just before an orgasm. Sylvia's blue eyes fearful and needing.*

Sensing a recent rift, the groupie scooted a little closer. "I think I remember her. Dark hair, blue eyes?" At the agreeing nod, she looked into her own drink. "Didn't think she was quite your type, ya know?"

Steeling herself, Torrin muttered, "She's not." The voices in her head roared and sighed in a maelstrom. *Goddamn this noise in my head.*

A tentative hand reached out, gently caressing the musician's thigh. The hand became bolder when it wasn't rebuffed. "Want company tonight?"

Torrin considered. *It's been a long time, Horny Torry. You remember how to play the game?* She covered the woman's hand with her own and squeezed. "Yeah. That'd be nice." *You'll never forget, Torry. You were born and bred to play this game.*

The groupie was barely able to refrain from crowing delight. To bed Torrin Smith of Warlord now that she was famous? Definitely a major coup in the rock and roll world. "Ya know, I've got some stuff. Didn't you like downers?"

The night was a blur of alcohol and music and flirting and drugs. Floating on downers, drinking shots of whiskey, dirty dancing at several bars. Soft and rough, dark corners of heavy breathing and inadequate climaxes. Trying to forget. Trying to remove vivid flashes of pale blue eyes full of love. Trying to deny.

Other flashes, scenes of violence and rape. *Eyes pleading for relief from pain, retreating into themselves.* Unable to block them. Unable to drive them away. *Violation, desecration, penetration, complication. Angel bleeding from the tainted touch of her caress. Soul bleeding.*

More booze. More pills. More sex. Nothing works.

Finally, everything mercifully darkens.

Sonny's Journal — September 28, 2002

Day Five:

Torrin's still in intensive care. They plan to remove her from life support tomorrow morning. I hope her body can take it. I hope she wants to live. I'm pretty sure she was so messed up that night she just wasn't paying attention. Didn't realize exactly how much she'd been drinking when she took the pills.

God, I hope she makes it! I don't know what I'll do if she doesn't.

Lando's with her now. I'm here to relieve him. He said he was going to play her guitar and sing a while he was here this morning. She needs music in her life, even now. It was a hell of a fight letting visitors in, let alone 'round the clock surveillance. But Tamara really came through for us. She had nurses and doctors running every which way Tuesday morning!

White Horse still *hasn't recovered. The band could lose their contract or be sued, but everybody's stuck together and told the label to shove it. No Torrin, no Warlord, no albums. I'm so proud of these guys! I told Torrin long ago that Warlords stick together. Wait'll she finds out just how tight-knit we are!*

I finished reading all the paperwork that Tamara gave me. We both realize that it's an ethical no-no to give me the files, but after the scene at White Horse, she thought I really needed to read it. I feel so drained and exhausted. I've spent a lot of time crying for my brave woman — I know she's never allowed herself to.

She lied about some things to me, to us. Like, she's only a few months older than me. All this time she'd been making it appear that she was oh-so-much-older ... only to find it's been by five months! She had a fake ID when she joined Warlord. (Now I know how she knew where to get mine!)

Her last name's not Smith. Her stepfather legally adopted her when she was three. Her last name had been Chizu. When everything went down in Boston that was the name they had her under. When she ran away from her foster home, she took Smith.

I remember the night she found me walking home from that fiasco of a date. She told me then that her dad had molested her, took her virginity. She neglected to mention that it wasn't just him ... It was his friends, some members of his family, even complete strangers! Oh, I wish I could throttle the bastard! He did so much more to her than she lets on. He was heavy into sadism and trained her from the time she was little.

The case was just one big convoluted mess — people pointing fingers, name-calling. There was a lot of press over it in Boston. Chizu spent a lot of time and effort trying to get Torrin to take the rap. And she let him, refusing to testify against him. God, she was so messed up! It's a wonder she's survived this long with all that pain.

It's no wonder she doesn't want my love. She really thinks she doesn't deserve love. And it's on such a deep level I don't think she realizes. I don't think it's so much that she doesn't want it, but that she doesn't want to need. That's what scares her silly, drove her to try a last ditch effort to get rid of me, get rid of the band. Get rid of everything she loved.

She loves me. I know it now.

And the woman she was reported to be with that night! I'd like to get my hands on her, *too! Giving downers to her when she'd already been drinking. Grrrrr ... At least she had the presence of mind to call 911 before bailing from the hotel. Otherwise, Torrin would be dead now.*

And she still may be. If her body can't take over when they remove life support ... No. I can't think like that. She'll know I've given up when I talk to her if I go in like that.

All this information and confusion ... I went to the mental health wing, to find someone to talk to. I can't say that I understand what's been going on within Torrin. But I've got to try. The lifestyle she was raised in ... I can't even fathom! I've spoken with a counselor twice this week, and I have another appointment day after tomorrow. I've begun reading up on the BDSM lifestyle on the web and at the library. Some of it's not pretty, but it is consensual. The counselor suggested I look at child abuse and incest issues, too. I need to understand! To know *how she could have been involved with Sylvia Mueller's destruction, to know* why *Sylvia responded the way she did.*

I've been reading her a trashy romance novel I picked up at the bookstore. A lesbian one! Ha ha ha! If that doesn't get her out of it to demand an action adventure, nothing will!

Well, I've gotta go. I'm up next and Lisa relieves me in a few hours. Except for a few hours at night, we've been sitting with her in shifts, keeping up conversation and stuff. We're hoping we can keep her mind alive – to bring her out. It's worked for some; it'll work for her. She's too damned ornery to die.

I know it.

Suicidal dreams
mean everything.
TORRIN C. SMITH, "FUTURE FORGOTTEN"

Part IX: Awakenings

What's left for me now?
Vegetable existence,
my life's purpose.
TORRIN C. SMITH, "UNHAPPY ENDINGS"

She didn't know how long it had been. At some point, the blackness faded away, like fog burning off in the noonday sun. Leaving her ... here. *Wherever here is.*

As time passed, sensation and awareness of her surroundings increased. At first it was simply that she existed. Nothing more. Then coolness, a not-uncomfortable breeze occasionally brushed her skin. Next the feel of rough-hewn wood and she discovered she was seated, her elbows and forearms resting on a table.

This realization caused the blackness to ebb further, and she was able to see the table, its surface scarred. She saw the glass in her hand before her fingers registered the touch. A vague curiosity overcame her, and she tensed an arm, watching the muscles play beneath her skin. Another experiment and the glass rose to her lips.

The smell of apples assailed her nose, and she peered inside, seeing amber liquid. Taking a taste, she was startled by the riot of flavor on her tongue. *Apple cider never tasted like this!* She drained the contents with the air of a woman dying of thirst, using fingertips to catch the overflow at the corners of her mouth. The cool liquid coursed through her, strengthening her, bringing her further into the now.

She set the glass down and released it, splaying her hands across the table. Looking down at herself, she saw the familiar shorts, her belly bare below the sports bra. The floor beneath her combat boots was wood as well, and covered with sawdust. *A wood shop?* Odors reached her nostrils and she knew she was wrong. *It wouldn't smell like beer and chicken!* Her stomach grumbled loudly, mouth watering from the aroma of freshly roasted meat.

As if on cue, a form materialized out of the darkness. An older woman stepped toward her, long dark hair going white, laughing gray eyes holding hints of past pain. She wore a blue dress, an off-white apron, discolored from years of use, around her waist. With a warm smile, she said, "Are you ready for something to eat, sweetling?"

Staring blankly at the woman for long moments, she found something about the eyes familiar but couldn't quite place it. The woman reached toward her to brush hair away from her face. Flinching, she blocked the touch with her forearm.

The woman's eyes became sad rather than angry, and she pulled back. "I've got some nice chicken and vegetables for your supper. You just sit here and I'll get it."

As the woman turned away, she felt a vague sense of panic. She opened her mouth to speak, a croak coming from her once again dry throat.

Turning, a concerned smile crossed the woman's face. "Don't worry, sweetling. I'll get you some cider, too." She leaned closer and peered into disbelieving eyes. "You're *not* alone."

She knew it was true, her unease fading under that gaze. *They look like my eyes.* There was a wink, and the woman moved away again, toward the darkness. She concentrated on the woman, watching her move away. The darkness faded farther as the woman walked, appearing to shepherd it before her. Other sights and sounds and smells caught her attention, and she realized she really wasn't alone.

She was in a large room, a wooden construction of some sort. A fireplace crackled to one side, an iron hook held a pot of wonderful smelling stew over the flames. Several people were in the room, dressed in strange clothing and eating or drinking or talking to one another. The woman in question disappeared through a door by a bar.

She studied the other people, finding some familiar. Over in one corner, she could see Atkins with her guitar. He appeared to be singing to himself. She could barely make out the tune and realized his voice was hoarse. *He must have been singing for a long time.*

At the same table was Middlestead listening to his band mate play. Nearby, Foley and Hampton were sharing a cup of something. As she regarded them, they both turned and waved at her before going back to their discussion. Their voices tickled the edges of her mind, not quite able to catch what was being said. *Wonder where Sonny is.*

A plate with a wonderful aroma was placed in front of her. She looked up into laughing eyes.

"Here you go, sweetling. There's nutbread for dessert if you want it." The woman poured cider into her glass. Finished, she stood for a second, expectantly.

She cleared her throat. "Um ... Thank you," she finally responded.

The woman smiled. "You're welcome, sweetling." She moved away, stopping to refill the glasses of her patrons.

Her stomach growled again, aching with need. She dug into the repast with relish, almost groaning in ecstasy at the flavors assailing her senses. Working her way through steamed vegetables and tangy chicken, her hunger abated. *I've gotta be in heaven.*

Her brow furrowed. *Why the hell would I think that? I'm not dead* ... Gray eyes narrowed, flashes of whiskey and sex and drugs flickering through her mind. "Am I?" she asked aloud.

"Not yet," a low voice responded.

She looked up. And saw ... "You're ... me?"

The redhead before her grinned. "Yep. Who else would you listen to?" She settled down on the opposite bench, a glass of water in her hand.

Torrin studied the woman across from her suspiciously. A closer inspection proved that it indeed was herself sitting there. The eyes were the same, as was the face, the hair. There were subtle differences, though. Her face wasn't as hard, the eyes not quite so wary. While she was dressed the same, there was no tattoo on her arm, and her body had a rosy shine of good health.

The other Torrin allowed the inspection, her mouth quirked. She drank in silence.

Looking around the room – *tavern*, her mind supplied – once again, Torrin said, "Okay. If I'm not dead, then where the hell am I? What is this place?"

With a shrug, the Other's grin widened. "An ancient memory, a limbo of sorts. A place you created to feel safe and wish to experience again." The smile faded and she tilted her head, her eyes intensifying. "But this is only in your imagination."

Torrin's eyes narrowed. "I don't know what you're talking about," she said without thinking. *But, it* is *safe here.*

The Other smiled. "Yes, you do. You've just decided to be

stubborn about it."

Torrin let it slide, a scowl on her face. It felt *right,* and that irritated her, but her mind was occupied with other things. First and foremost, the fact that the voices that usually inhabited her head were ... missing.

"They don't belong here. They aren't a part of you. *This* place is."

"How do you know what I'm thinking?" the guitarist demanded, a trickle of anxiety in her heart.

The Other drank from her glass again, peering over the rim. She set it down. "I'm you."

Torrin snorted in derision. "*Trust* me, babe. If you were me, I'd know it." She glanced to one side and saw a peasant at a nearby table. "What's he? I've never seen him before." She scoffed.

The Other leaned back. "No. Just window dressing. Not like them," and her long arm waved toward her band mates and friends along the wall.

Instinctively, Torrin's eyes followed the arm, watched her friends as they conversed or sang. Brightness caught her attention and she noticed others who hadn't been there upon her first examination – a doctor and a couple of nurses sporting white jackets and uniforms, standing by a window. The doctor had a stethoscope around her neck and a chart, discussing something just out of earshot while one nurse nodded and the other prepared a hypodermic.

So much for feeling safe! she thought. She heard another voice in her head. *They're only trying to help you.* The whisperer was still there, the one that had been there all her life, the advisor that was consistently wrong, suggesting things that only caused more grief, more pain, more hurt.

Torrin shoved her plate to one side. "You gonna tell me what the hell is going on or what?"

"Definitely haven't learned patience, have you?" her doppelganger said with a wry grin. She shook her head and waved a finger at Torrin's apparent attempt at a response. "Sorry. Rhetorical question. Let's get on to what you want to know."

Sourly, the guitarist nodded.

"You're not dead, Torrin. But it's still a possibility at this point. You'll be removed from life support soon, and no one's sure whether or not you'll fight to remain alive."

"So this is a delusion because of the downers and booze?" she asked, feeling on firmer ground.

The Other's eyes widened in surprise. "No. I told you. This is an old memory. A place of safety. This is where you've gone to escape the world."

Torrin rolled her eyes and looked away. "It ain't like the real world is all that great, ya know," she muttered. "It's full of shit and blood and pain. Nothing more."

"And Sonny," the woman added, her expression pained.

Their eyes met for mere seconds before Torrin looked away. *Whaddya getting so worked up for? It's just a hallucination!* She heaved a sigh. *Or is it?*

"Go look out the window."

Torrin debated doing as she was told, part of her not wanting to give in to this strange woman who looked so much like ... *me,* the whisperer filled in. *That does it!* She dug in her figurative heels and shook her head.

Exasperated, the Other sighed deeply. "Damn, that stubborn streak is a mile wide." She also shook her head and added, "Fine. Then don't." She waved the older woman to them, lifting her glass as a signal.

Despite herself, the guitarist glanced at a nearby window. It moved closer with surprising speed until it was directly in front of her. There was no place to go, and she could only stare out at the scene before her.

A hospital room with sunlight entering through a window, changing of the guard as Atkins rose and Sonny hugged him. Words were exchanged, but Torrin couldn't hear them. Then her band mate was gone, leaving her guitar in the corner by the bed. Sonny looked upon her still, pale form with deep sadness. She leaned over, kissing her on the forehead.

Torrin could feel a light caress on her forehead as she watched.

Sonny pulled a book from her pack and settled down. She found her place and opened it, her mouth moving as she read aloud to the comatose woman.

Almost. Almost, she could make out the voice. Make out the words.

"Hardly shit, blood and pain," the Other's low voice said.

Torrin started and the window was suddenly where it was

supposed to be. She was still seated at the table, the woman across from her. Her glass had been filled to the rim with more apple cider. "Look, what the fuck do you want from me?" she growled.

"To admit that you love and are loved."

Gray eyes blinked in incomprehension. "*Love*?" she sneered. "Love is a myth. It doesn't exist." *But isn't that what you feel when you're with ...* "And even if it *did* exist," Torrin hurriedly added, "I don't deserve it."

"Why?"

"*Why*?" Torrin spat in disgust. "Get a clue, bitch! If you're me, you know *exactly* why!"

The Other studied her for long moments. "So, what Lucifer started, Sylvia finished?"

"No. What *I* started finished Sylvia."

Lips pursed in reluctant understanding, the woman nodded. "You talking about this?"

The window rushed back with a vengeance, making Torrin feel a bit dizzy.

A young girl with inky black hair was tying an older blindfolded woman, restraining her wrists, hanging her from a chain in the ceiling of a typical dungeon. Chains, whips, clamps, strops, rack, leather harnesses, dental chair complete with hydraulic drill. A bamboo screen was raised, revealing a small man of dark European descent, smoking a cigarette and watching the scene.

Stomach clenched in memory, Torrin's mind blithered on other topics, trying to ease the familiar feelings of panic and loathing. *Jesus. Was I ever really that young?* She tried to turn away, but couldn't move, helpless as she watched the past replay itself.

The young girl began doing things to the woman, slapping her, caressing her, applying nipple clamps, attaching restraints to her ankles, a spreader bar. Pulling a cellular phone from his pocket, the man in the window made a few phone calls, idly stroking his manhood between cigarettes.

"Stop this!" Torrin demanded, her voice echoing eerily.

He rapped on the window, calling the girl from the room, giving her money and a pack of cigarettes in reward. He ordered her to strip and she obeyed. After a fierce kiss, he handed her pills, insisted she take them, give them to the woman inside. Which she did.

The feelings from the drug she had taken all those years ago began to surface. Torrin watched her younger self go back into the room and administer the pills to her captive. Fear and anger began pulsing within her breast.

The girl continued torturing, teasing, tempting. She retrieved a leather strop and began to give the woman what she'd come for. Stinging lashes were laid on back and buttocks and thighs. The girl became paler as the drug took effect. And the woman began to look less like she enjoyed the treatment, beginning to struggle against her restraints.

The fear and anger Torrin felt exploded into fury. She shook with it, sweat running from her in rivers and teeth grinding painfully together, fists knotted.

The girl began to growl, using more force. What had begun as pink welts soon became red. The edge of the strop began slicing pale skin, blood welling up, staining the leather, further striping her back. The woman screamed in pain and terror. The man pulled his member out and began to masturbate.

Torrin's heart ached at the violent explosion from her younger self, revisiting the morass of seething emotion that had set her on her course.

Her own low voice soothed over the violation of her soul. "Do you actually believe that there wasn't something going on here? Something you had no control over?"

The man reached climax, using his stepdaughter's shirt to clean up the mess. Another man joined him, and they chatted as the girl vented her fear and rage. The men laughed before entering, the first man intercepted the girl, removing the strop and tossing it to the new arrival. As the second man continued what the girl had begun, the first strapped her to the rack.

"You don't remember much past this point, do you?" the Other asked.

Torrin sat ramrod straight, breathing heavily. The emotions seething through her had disappeared, and she was left with a vague physical detachment and exhaustion. She swallowed, mouth dry, and lifted the cup of cider with shaky hands.

"Do you remember what happens next?"

She shook her head. "No," she said in a low voice. "I woke up in my room the next day."

The Other leaned closer, peering at Torrin in concern. "You stayed away from the dungeon for quite a while, didn't you? It was days before help came?"

Needing no window to relive the memory, Torrin nodded, eyes closed.

The girl snuck into the dungeon while all were asleep. She was horrified by the amount of damage done to the once beautiful woman. With solid resolve, she retrieved the bloodied and tattered shirt, dashing out of the house with it. The girl stuffed it into the garbage can in the alley, right next to the old pizza she'd had for dinner. She went into the house and picked up the phone.

"What'd you tell them to get them there so quickly?"

Eyes stinging, the guitarist gave a watery snort. "You know. Told 'em I'd been shot and hung up."

"How many days was it?"

"Two," was the whispered response.

"For saving her life, for bringing your father to justice, for stopping the vicious group of sadists who cared for nothing but their own entertainment, you don't deserve to love or to be loved?"

"No!" Torrin pushed away from the table, rising in her denial, wanting to leave this conversation, this tavern. Long arms reached out to stop her, and she turned and swung.

With ease, the Other dodged the blow and caught her hands, pulling her into an embrace that was more a wrestling match. The redhead struggled to get away, to run from the tears that were threatening, knowing that should she cry, she'd never stop. Refusing to be daunted, the Other held on tight.

Torrin's dominant will finally broke as great sobs shook her small body for the first time in her conscious memory. She cried for her broken childhood, the torments of her father, the abandonment by her mother. All the disgust and hatred and doubts, the sympathetic looks from strangers, the knowledge that nothing would ever save her, stop the pain, stop the hurt, stop her rage and violent soul.

The arms holding Torrin eased as she stopped fighting. She was whisked up and carried like a baby back to the table. There the Other settled down on the bench, cradling the woman, rocking, caressing, singing gently in a low voice.

Hours seemed to pass before the misery finally reached its end. Sobbing quieted, and the tears tapered off. Torrin felt exhausted and drained. She sleepily listened to the woman singing, her voice surprisingly like Sonny's. Completely relaxed in the embrace, feeling wonder at the familiarity of it, Torrin asked, "Why are you here?"

The singing stopped, and the Other hugged her gently. "Because you don't think Sonny's strong enough to handle it."

Recognizing this truth, Torrin nodded.

"But, she *can* handle it," the woman continued. "She has me to fall back on." Long fingers brushed red-gold hair, tucking it behind an ear.

Gray eyes narrowed as she tried to comprehend the statement. Even as she tried to think, she realized that the woman holding her wasn't her doppelganger.

Her eyes closed. *So tired.* The memory faded. Instead, she heard the low voice of the woman – *Sonny* – holding her, speaking to her.

"Next time we'll grow up together. I want to ..."

"... be there for her from the first, to protect her from the world's evil." A few more paragraphs and Sonny closed the book, finished. She looked at the figure in the bed, trying to see past all the tubes and wires.

Gray eyes looked back at her.

Sonny's heart lurched. *Calm down, girl! It could just be an automatic reaction! You've seen it before!* She set the book down and rose.

The eyes followed her.

Swallowing, half in fear and half in hope, Sonny stood next to the bed and leaned closer. "Torrin?" she softly asked.

Under the oxygen mask there was a croaked response.

"OhmigodohshitIloveyou!" The young woman dived for the call button and mashed down on it. Within seconds, a bevy of white clad men and women burst through the door and hustled her to one side. She watched anxiously as they poked and prodded and took vital signs.

"Back off!" Torrin growled, her voice raspy from lack of use.

The sound of her irascible lover sent a shiver of happiness through her, and Sonny couldn't help but giggle at the stern-faced nurses.

Refusing to be daunted, the staff continued their ministrations until they were satisfied. The head nurse turned to her as they all filed out, a warning on her face. "Don't tire her out," she ordered. "I'm going to call the doctor."

Sonny approached the side of the hospital bed, reaching to take her lover's hand. "Hey, sexy," she murmured with a large smile on her face.

Grinning, Torrin answered, "Hey there." She weakly squeezed the hand that was warmly wrapped around her own. "How long?"

"Five days." She brushed the bangs from the guitarist's forehead. "You passed out in a motel room and someone called 911."

Torrin nodded. Her eyes closed, and she let herself float with the feelings of love that emanated from Sonny. The voices in her head were strangely silent, but she was sure they'd return with a vengeance once she acquired more strength.

The brunette continued to caress her lover's face, a slight twinge of anxiety fluttering through her heart as her eyes sagged closed. Her lover's breathing remained normal, and she sent a silent prayer asking that Torrin not return to her coma.

Now's the time, woman, before you turn chickenshit. Torrin opened her eyes and stared intently into pale blue concern. She chewed her upper lip a moment. "I love you, Sonny," she rumbled. There was a sudden increased beeping as the monitor picked up her heart rate.

Sonny blinked, stunned. *She said it?* The words echoed in her head. *She said it!*

The smile that broke out on her lover's face seemed to brighten the already sunlit room. Torrin felt tears of relief fill her eyes, and for once, she didn't fight them away. *She can handle it.*

"I love you, Torrin," Sonny said, bringing Torrin's hand up to her lips and kissing it. "For a very long time now."

"I know. I ... wasn't able to hear it." Torrin swallowed, nervous. "To say it."

"It's okay," Sonny soothed, knuckles brushing a fine cheek. "You don't have to talk now. Just rest until the doctor gets here."

"No." Her grip on Sonny's hand tightened. "There's something else ..." Torrin searched her mind for the words.

Sonny waited patiently, letting her lover work through years of self-discipline, self-hatred.

"I ... I have a problem." Hot tears leaked from her eyes.

"Several of them." The guitarist closed her eyes in misery. *I have to get through this! She can handle it!*

"I know. I know," Sonny said. "It's okay."

"No, it's *not* okay!" Torrin exclaimed. Her eyes flew open, burning with intensity. "I can't handle this alone. I'm an alcoholic and a drug addict. I need help." Pause. "I'm so sorry I hurt you." *There! I said it!*

Tears of sympathy, relief and joy flowed from the dark woman's eyes. She leaned over the bed. "I'll help you. We'll work it out together," she promised.

Sonny's Journal – October 30, 2002

Torrin gets out of the hospital today. She's completed the program with flying colors and has really been working hard to clean herself up.

It's funny, but her struggles have brought something to Lando, too – he's cleaned his act up quite a bit as well. Of course, he wasn't as heavy into the drugs as Torrin, but he's cut way back on his drinking and carousing.

I've been meeting with my counselor every week, that and attending AA and joint counseling sessions with Torrin. It's been very educational. I hope I can get through my own issues with her problems. I hope I'm able to help her get through this. She says she knows I'm strong enough now. Makes me feel both happy and sad. I'm happy that she feels she can trust me, but sad it took so long and so much pain before she figured it out.

White Horse has kept the contract. The band goes in next month to negotiate the next album. Torrin's musical output has nearly tripled while she's been in the program. The drugs were interfering with her creativity and she didn't know it! She's written at least two dozen songs in the last two weeks!

The Muellers have dropped their civil suit. With Tamara and White Horse on it, there was no way they could get money out of Torrin. The police records pretty well exonerate her of the whole mess, laying the blame on her stepfather and his cronies. Torrin still hasn't forgiven herself, though. She's been working with Tamara to start a trust fund for Sylvia Mueller to defray the costs of the hospital where she's been placed. It's probably not what the family wanted, but Torrin needs the chance to repay Sylvia for all the trouble she feels she caused.

The press, of course, has had a field day with all this. Amazingly enough, the band's album's gone double platinum! White Horse was worried about losing money, and it only served to increase the band's popularity!

I hear Tom calling. Gotta go pick up Torrin. On her first night of freedom, we're gonna take her out to dinner.

I can't wait to hold her, to wake up with her beside me.

Making amends won't be easy.
I'm so glad I have you with me
to ease my soul.
TORRIN C. SMITH, "RESTITUTION"

About the Author

D. Jordan Redhawk spent her childhood dreaming of the arts – music, sculpting, writing and painting. Her first "band" was purely speculation between a handful of third, fourth and fifth graders. (No one will ever know the musical revolution of the Mustangs.) It was with great devastation in junior high that Redhawk realized she couldn't sing.

Seeking solace, she concentrated on her art, teaching herself to draw. At the tender age of thirty, Redhawk attended college and discovered airbrush. Deciding to take the plunge, she focused on making her name in the science fiction/fantasy world.

A move forever changed the course of her life. Unable to continue painting due to lack of space for a studio, Redhawk discovered fan fiction on the web. Voraciously reading all she got her digital hands on, she was soon left bereft, not finding the story she wanted to read.

So she wrote one.

Redhawk currently resides in her beloved Portland, Oregon. Her wife and two cats care for her and do quite well, considering her cantankerous nature.

Redhawk can be reached at redhawk@djordanredhawk.net.

Also by D. Jordan Redhawk

TIOPA KI LAKOTA
Published: October 2000
ISBN: 1930928033

Anpo, a Lakota woman raised as a warrior, rescues Kathleen, the golden-haired woman of her vision. A vision that includes not only Kathleen's coming, but also the infliction of great pain. Must all dreams come true?

Now Available from Fortitude Press

THE AVERAGE OF DEVIANCE
BY K. SIMPSON

After *Several Devils*, Devlin Kerry and Cassandra Wolfe aren't just friends anymore, but they'd rather not advertise. Trouble is, they're already in advertising, where secrets are practically illegal. Word is out ... so to speak.

Worse, Dev has a demon. Cassie says it's her own fault for being celibate for years ("You can't go around not sleeping with people and *not* expect to get into trouble"). They thought they'd exorcised the demon, but Monica is back. And this time, she plans to stick around.

This sequel picks up where *Several Devils* left off, as the staff of J/J/G Advertising tries to get back to normal the morning after a wild Halloween night. But every day is Halloween at J/J/G, the way these people behave, and everyone there is a devil of some kind. The last thing Dev and Cassie need is an actual demon – a chance for mischief that Monica can't resist. Thanks to her, they have trouble coming from all directions: co-workers, clients, TV reporters, the family-values crowd and even a possum.

Worst of all, a new co-worker may not be what she seems. Dev and Cassie are about to learn the true meaning of "hell to pay."

ISBN: 0971815011

Also by K. Simpson

SEVERAL DEVILS
Published: August 2001
ISBN: 0967768799

Even though she's in advertising, Devlin Kerry doesn't believe in Hell; she thinks that would be redundant. But a demon named Monica believes in her. Between her demon and her best friend, Dev's in for a devil of a time.

Now Available from Fortitude Press

THE BLUEST EYES IN TEXAS
BY LINDA CRIST

Kennedy Nocona is an out, liberal, driven attorney, living in Austin, the heart of the Texas hill country. Once a player in the legal community, she now finds herself in the position of re-evaluating her life - a position brought on by a personal tragedy for which she blames herself. Seeking redemption for her tormented past, she loses herself in her work, strict discipline of mind and body, and the teachings of Native American roots she once shunned.

Dallasite Carson Garret is a young paralegal overcoming the loss of her parents and coming to terms with her own sexual orientation. After settling her parents' estate and examining her failed past relationships, she is desperately ready to move forward. Bored with her state of affairs, she longs for excitement and romance to make her feel alive again.

A chance encounter finds them inexplicably drawn to one another, and after a weekend together, they quickly find themselves in a long distance romance that leaves them both wanting more. Circumstances at Carson's job develop into a series of mysteries and blackmail attempts that leaves her with more excitement than she ever bargained for. Confused, afraid, and alone, she turns to Kennedy, the one person she knows can help her. As they work together to solve a puzzle, they confront growing feelings that neither woman can deny, complicated by outside forces that threaten to crush them both.

ISBN: 0971815003

Now Available from Fortitude Press

I FOUND MY HEART IN SAN FRANCISCO
BY S.X. MEAGHER

Despite the questions of her roommates and the objections of her fiancé, Jamie Evans persists in enrolling in a college course that seems an odd choice for a young woman of her background. What no one can know is that the course, The Psychology of the Lesbian Experience, will propel Jamie onto a journey of self-awareness and realization.

For the required fieldwork, Jamie is paired with the darkly beautiful Ryan O'Flaherty —a boldly "out" and sexually adventurous lesbian. This somewhat unlikely pair slowly, and sometimes painfully become aware that what they feel for each other is more than just friendship.

The temptation to live life on her own terms is great, but so are the costs, as Jamie struggles to break out of her establishment-fashioned, pre-ordained mold. If she can summon the courage, however, she might find out that love, and life, have so much more to offer than she had ever dreamed.

ISBN: 0971815038

Now Available from Fortitude Press

THE LIFE IN HER EYES
BY DEBORAH BARRY

Real love is not for the faint of heart, and the courage it takes to survive its loss, and love again, is more than the average soul can bear.

Rae Crenshaw does not lack for companionship. The tall beauty radiates charm and confidence, but this attractive combination conceals a vulnerable heart that has known far too much pain. She finds solace for her emptiness in casual trysts, maintaining a severe emotional distance, all the while seeking that which she feels can never be found again.

Evon Lagace's young life has been one of extremes - a failed dance career, a precious, beautiful relationship, and a traumatic, crippling loss. Once so full of exuberance and happiness, she must now struggle to find peace amidst the despair and loneliness.

Share the tears and the triumphs of these two remarkable women as you celebrate their journey to the realization that perhaps, for a lucky few, second chances can exist.

ISBN: 0971815046

Now Distributed by Fortitude Press

AT FIRST BLUSH
A JANE DOE PRESS ANTHOLOGY

Twenty-two stories of first glances, first blushes, first loves and first times - of all kinds. Representing a variety of voices, the stories reflect a diversity of experiences. All profits from this anthology will be donated to charity.

The table of contents from this wonderful collection of stories:

ISBN: 0971154996

Now Distributed by Fortitude Press

CONSPIRACY OF SWORDS
BY R.S. CORLISS

FBI Agent Alexia Reis is an out-lesbian determined to make it in the bureau. As a junior agent she spent time in the research department, as well as the serial crimes unit where she and her partner, David Wu, were recognized for their work. After breaking several major cases, the two are moved to the hate crimes unit, which is Alex's true area of expertise.

Following the murders of several prominent activists and politicians, Alex and David become part of a task force charged with solving the killings. Together, they are sent to protect a newly declared candidate for the U.S. Senate. For the first time in her career, Alex is named the agent-in-charge, and when the candidate is assassinated, she can't help but take it personally.

During the investigation the agents run into ex-CIA assassin Teren Mylos, who is convinced her partner's death is somehow connected to the FBI case. While wary of each other, Alex and Teren agree to share information in an attempt to find answers to the deepening mystery.

The case takes them to Europe and back, searching for pieces to the unfolding puzzle. As they dodge killers and turncoats, they come face to face with Nazis old and new, stumble upon a hoard of looted gold, and uncover a conspiracy that stretches over forty years and two continents.

And, somewhere along the line, they discover each other as well.

ISBN: 0971154902

Now Distributed by Fortitude Press

EXCHANGES
BY JOHN-DAVID SCHRAMM

Can God change gays? This question tumbles around inside the minds of both lead characters in *exChanges*.

Marcus and CJ both give up a great deal to join Crossroads, a year-long, residential program dedicated to helping gay men and lesbians find "freedom" from homosexuality through the power of Christ.

"Camping out" with five other men and a house leader, CJ and Marcus begin to confront themselves while being strangely drawn to one another.

Follow these two men as they dive into the rules and policies of this ministry program led by former drag queens and pornography kings. As each man confronts his own issues, he begins to see a path that could never have been covered in the Crossroads recruiting brochure.

ISBN: 0971154937

To Order:

Title	Quantity	Cost per Unit	Total Cost
At First Blush		$21.99	$
The Average of Deviance		$12.99	$
The Bluest Eyes in Texas		$15.99	$
Conspiracy of Swords		$19.99	$
exChanges		$13.75	$
I Found My Heart in San Francisco		$18.99	$
The Life in Her Eyes		$13.99	$
Warlord Metal		$13.99	$
Shipping and Handling	First Book	$4.50	$
	Each Add'l Book	$2.00	$
	Texas Residents Add 8.25% Sales Tax		$
		Total	$

To order by credit card, please visit our Web site at:
www.fortitudepress.com.

To order by check or money order, please mail the above form to:

Fortitude Press, Inc.
Post Office Box 41
Melbourne, FL 32902

Coming Soon from Fortitude Press

MIND GAMES
BY RYAN DALY

Rachel "Tuck" Tucker is a high-powered player in the world of investment banking. Ruthless and beautiful, she goes through bank accounts and women at lightning speed. Yet her wealth comes from insider trading, in the most literal of senses.

Since childhood, Tuck has been gifted with the ability to leave her physical body and take over other people's, imposing her considerable and decidedly devious will on their actions while leaving them none the wiser. She has used her ability for wealth and pleasure, never giving any thought to those she used along the way.

Her world changes rapidly when she becomes trapped in a body not her own. Complicating things further, she's stuck inside a man. A married man. With children.

Working against time and forces she doesn't understand, Tuck struggles to return to herself. But doing so would almost certainly mean losing her accidental life and Kate, the wife of the man she's replaced. A choice that becomes harder for Tuck with each day spent with her new family.

An intriguing novel of suspense and romance, *Mind Games* shows why it's always better to be yourself.